SECRET OR SHUTOUT

A TEAMMATE'S SISTER HOCKEY ROMANCE

D.C. EAGLES HOCKEY
BOOK 4

LEAH BRUNNER

CONTENT WARNING

Dear Readers,

First, I wanted to provide a content warning. that Secret or Shutout contains themes of divorce, PCOS, and infertility.

Secondly, I want you all to know that every PCOS journey looks different. Farrah's story doesn't reflect everyone's story. My own PCOS journey has looked different from Farrah's in many ways.

Thirdly, to avoid confusion, Ford Remington is referred to as Remy in this book. Some will read the D.C. Eagles series in order, and others will read them as stand alones. Calling him Remy makes it easier so we're not going back and forth.

Thank you for reading, and I hope you love Bruce and Farrah as much as I do!

And yes… there's a happy ending. 🤍

To my PCOS girlies, this one's for you. 🩶

PROLOGUE

BRUCE

WILL I meet the love of my life in this dive bar? No. But sitting at home watching 2000s romcoms wasn't accomplishing the task, either.

I should be on top of the world tonight. I just got back from a stint of away games on the West Coast, I'm one of the top goaltenders in the NHL, I'm young, good looking—at least that's what women tell me—and I'm single.

I try to remind myself how awesome my life is as I nurse an old fashioned and look around my favorite bar, which seems a little darker and more soulless than usual. I can't shake the feeling of melancholy as I take in the wood floor and wood-paneled walls. I love this place because it feels like a cabin, but tonight it's just dull brown.

My best friends—my D.C. Eagles' teammates—no doubt went straight home to spend the weekend with their wives. They're probably canoodling by the fire or telling them about the goals and assists they racked up the past few games. Meanwhile, I'm alone. This single and ready to mingle thing really isn't doing it for me anymore. Being at home in front of the fireplace on this cold December evening, curled up with a woman who loves me. Sounds pretty damn good right now.

I'm on my second old fashioned when movement on the barstool a few down from mine catches my attention. I glance over at a woman with long, dark hair—my kryptonite. She fills out her black leggings and light-blue sweater very nicely with a curvy body I would worship.

Wait, what was I feeling melancholy about? The light but pleasant buzz has me thinking life isn't so bad after all. I'll meet the love of my life, eventually. Hell, maybe she's sitting right next to me.

I snicker to myself, only it must've been louder than I thought because the woman a few barstools down whips her head in my direction. A cascade of dark, shiny hair falls over her shoulder with the movement.

"What so funny?" she asks, her tone more annoyed than amused.

If I were a betting man, I'd bet she had a really crappy day.

I smirk, but she doesn't smile back. "I was just thinking I could meet the love of my life any moment. Isn't that wild to think about?"

The woman studies me with her dark blue eyes. There's something vaguely familiar about her...have I hooked up with this woman before? No. I'd remember those eyes.

"The idea of love seems great, but you're probably better off alone. Trust me." She turns away from me as the bartender places a Long Island iced tea in front of her.

I whistle. "Careful there, those are dangerous."

"Who are you to tell me what to do?" her tone is snappy.

I smirk because I like a woman who can bite. "Just trying to help. I learned the hard way how powerful a Long Island iced tea can be."

"Good," she says dryly, bringing the straw to her pretty pink lips and sucking down half of the cocktail in two seconds flat. She lifts her hand, signaling the bartender for another one. "That's what I'm hoping for."

My eyebrows shoot up. "You might want to slow down a bit…"

She narrows her eyes at me. "I'm here tonight to have some fun, okay? If you're going to be the fun police, I'll move to a table." She points a finger in the direction of a corner booth across the room. I notice her glossy, pink nail polish and wonder if her toes are painted the same color.

I hold my hands up. "Sorry. I'm not interested in policing your fun. I'm here for all the fun, actually." I wink, and her shoulders relax.

"Okay, good." The bartender places another drink in front of her, and she thanks him, then sips through the straw. "These barstools are super uncomfortable." The woman arches her back and rubs a spot right on her lower back. "They are not made for people in their thirties."

"You're thirty?" I ask, genuinely surprised. I would've guessed she was a little younger than me.

She sighs. "Thirty-one."

"You look younger," I admit.

"So do you. Twenty-two?" Blue Eyes asks.

"Twenty-six." I finish my drink, and she mirrors my movement, taking a large gulp of hers as well.

The woman's eyes graze over my face. I'm wearing a black baseball cap and some blue light blocking glasses. I don't need glasses; I just find it keeps me from being recognized.

"There's something familiar about you," she finally says.

"I thought the same about you." I smile. "Maybe we met in a past life."

She hums to herself then wiggles on the barstool. "Would you want to move to a booth?"

"Absolutely." I bring my hand up, gesturing for the bar tender to come over to let him know we're moving.

The woman sighs in relief.

"George, bring us some wings to the corner booth, eh?" I yell across the bar. This woman will need some food to offset the alcohol at this rate. George nods and continues wiping off the bar.

Grabbing my old fashioned, I turn and follow her to the booth. It's one of those rounded booths with a circular table, so we both scoot in toward the center—close enough to where we can talk, but not quite touching.

Blue Eyes spins her near-empty Long Island iced tea between her hands showcasing an empty ring finger.

She sips her drink through her straw, but nothing comes up but spluttery air. She stares at her umbrellaed glass and frowns.

"You want some water?" I ask, and she pouts for a moment before she nods. I raise my hand in the air again. "George! The lady needs some water!"

George nods and wipes his hands on a towel. When I turn back to the woman, I'm met with the most breathtaking smile I've ever seen. It's enough to light up this dimly lit, rustic bar. What on earth is a woman like her doing in a grungy bar like this?

Then again, I could ask myself the same question.

"Wow."

"Wow, what?"

"You have a beautiful smile."

She blushes and toys with her straw. "I'm not here trying to pick up a man. I just want to..." She trails off, like she can't find the right word.

"Want to what?"

Her mouth pulls to the side. "Forget. Just for tonight."

I chuckle. "Perfect, I'm great at forgetting."

She looks at me in confusion, so I explain, "I've had one too many concussions."

Her dark eyebrows raise. "Really? You must have a dangerous job."

I grin. "You could say that." I mean, I do have pucks flying at my face at a hundred miles per hour on the daily.

A waitress stops in front of our table with a tray of chicken wings, a glass of water, and another old fashioned. I guess George noticed my drink was empty. I look over at him and he gives me a salute.

I thank the waitress, and she scurries off to her next table, the place is busier tonight than it is most nights.

Blue Eyes takes a wing and begins to nibble on it. She's trying so hard not to make a mess. I grab one and rip it apart, sure that there's barbecue sauce all over my face. I swallow my bite and give the woman next to me a sloppy grin.

She bursts into laugher. "You're disgusting."

I gasp. "Rude! There's no elegant way to eat a chicken wing. Just go for it. What happens at George's stays at George's."

She considers my words for a moment before grabbing another wing and devouring it unabashedly.

"Exactly. You're a quick learner."

She snorts a laugh, and I laugh with her. She's quite the sight with her messy face.

An hour later, we've finished the wings and drinks, and we're pretty much best friends. We've talked about every-thing under the sun, except for two things—our names and why she's here.

"So," I say, draping an arm across the back of the booth. The woman stares at it like it's a puma that might jump out and attack her. "What are you trying to forget?"

She blows a raspberry. "Everything. I don't want to talk about it." Blue Eyes leans in closer to me, staring at me with those gorgeous eyes. We're both tipsy enough to throw any awkwardness out the window. We just met tonight, but the alcohol has helped us get past any defenses we might've had up… except for those involving whatever it is she wants to forget.

"Okay. I'm here to distract myself," I say, leaning in the same way she just did. "And you've been a beautiful distraction."

She snorts, her head falling back as she laughs. "Wow. Does that line usually work for you?"

My surprise at her outburst quickly changes to humor. "Well, yeah. Honestly."

She purses her lips, looking me over. Her hand comes up and removes my hat; then she pulls off my glasses. She squints as she studies me without the hat and glasses hindering her view. First, she looks at my hair, then my face, then my arms and chest. The rest of me is hidden by the table. Which is unfortunate, because *the rest of me* includes all my best parts.

"I believe you. You're very handsome." She says it so matter-of-factly, it almost doesn't even seem like a compliment.

"You think so?"

She rolls her eyes. "You have the swagger of someone who knows how good looking they are. Don't play coy."

I chuckle. "I think you're attractive too. Gorgeous, actually. That was my first thought when you sat at the bar."

Her eyes widen. "Is that why you agreed to share wings with me?"

"No." I shrug. "I was hungry."

She giggles and swats my chest playfully. I have a feeling when she's not drinking, she's not this giggly. But it's a really cute giggle.

"But the company was a nice perk," I say with a wink.

She laughs again and places her elbows on the table, then rests her chin in her palms. "Why did you need a distraction tonight?"

A strand of dark hair falls into her eye, blocking my view from the pretty blue. I'm pleasantly buzzed, as is she. Cautiously, I bring a hand up, allowing her time to swat it away if she wants. But she doesn't, so I sweep the strand out of her face, then gently tuck it behind her ear.

"Because I'm all alone," I admit. I probably wouldn't have told anyone that if I hadn't had two old fashioneds…or was it three?

She brings her arms back down, folding them in her lap. "You're not alone now." She leans in just a little more, her eyes slowly fluttering closed.

I know when a woman wants to be kissed, and this is a sure sign. I'm anxious to kiss her, too. But first I take a moment to appreciate her beautiful face up close. She has slightly tanned skin, like she's bronze year-round—perhaps a Mediterranean heritage. Her eyelashes are long and thick, and I can tell she's not wearing much makeup. Her lips are pink, the same color as her cheeks when she blushed earlier, and they're plump and pouty.

I lean my mouth closer to hers, bringing my hand up to her face and then stopping myself. "Is it okay if I touch you?" I ask, my voice barely loud enough to hear.

"Please do," she whispers back. "Help me forget."

With that, my hand comes to rest on her jaw, cradling her face. I have an overwhelming sense of peace as my hand meets her skin, like my body knows on a deeper level what an honor it is to touch her.

Her lips part, and I close the distance. Blue Eyes kisses me with so much unreserved passion, I get a distinct feeling this woman is always a force of nature to those around her. Passionate, strong willed, determined. The thought turns my blood hotter and our kiss deeper. I taste her sweet cocktail on her lips, as I savor the exploration of our mouths. Our lips entangle, getting acclimated to one another. Her hands come to my chest, and she squeezes my pecs with a light touch, appreciating the muscle there. At least I hope she is.

She hums. "How'd you get so strong?" she asks, her eyes still closed.

"It's part of my job," I tell her, appreciating that she noticed.

Blue Eyes dives back into our kiss, my pecs forgotten—as well as whatever was bothering her when she walked into this bar.

———

The next morning, I grab a peppermint mocha latte—don't judge, they're amazing—at the Starbuck's drive thru. I'm nursing a headache from one too many old fashioneds last night, but even my headache can't keep me from smiling every time I think about that kiss. Wow.

I'm a good kisser. I know because I've been told that by every woman I've ever kissed. But until last night, I don't think I'd ever kissed anyone who did it as passionately and unreservedly as I do. I always give one hundred and ten percent in the kissing department—I'm a certified lip to lip over achiever. But last night made me realize that all the other women I've kissed were just half-assing it.

And I never even got her name. Or number. I'm a freaking idiot. We both called Ubers and went our separate ways, and I was too intoxicated—by the woman *and* the drinks—to ask for her name.

Tired of dwelling on my moronic mistake—possibly the biggest mistake of my life—I pull out my phone to text my team captain—Ford Remington to the D.C. Eagles fandom, and Remy to everyone else. This Starbucks is close to his house, and he has the best in-home gym I've ever seen. A good workout with my man will rid me of this hangover.

BRUCE

Hey, man. You working out today? And can I join you?

He replies quickly, like he already had his phone in his hand.

REMY

Sure, I just got out here. The side door to the garage is unlocked.

BRUCE

Great! See you in a few, Cap'n.

When I arrive, Remy greets me at the side garage door, dressed and ready to workout. He's big, almost as tall as me, but my opposite in every other way. His eyes and hair are dark, and even his personality is different than mine. Where he's calm and serious, I'm chaos on blades…ready for fun, or shenanigans. Wherever the wind might take me.

He gestures for me to follow him into the gym, and the color of his hair makes me think of the woman from last night and how dark her hair was. And soft. And shiny. So freaking shiny.

Sheesh. Even looking at my team captain makes me think of her. Get yourself together man.

We get started working out, silently doing our own thing, until he interrupts my thoughts of blue eyes as I'm doing squats. Wonder what she's doing right now? Does she have a hangover?

"So, how's it going? You still looking for a wife?" He teases.

Well, I'm never telling him anything again. Actually, that's not true. I couldn't keep my thoughts to myself even if I tried.

Instead, I laugh. It's not often Ford Remington makes a joke. "I was doing okay until I heard you all went lingerie shopping for your wives and didn't invite me."

The man blushes. Remy just got married—rather suddenly, I might add—which shocked all of us. But he seems smitten with his wife, Amber, who happens to be his childhood best friend.

He quickly changes the subject.

After an hour, we're done with our workout and I'm preparing to head back home to my cavernous penthouse suite—much too big for just myself, but I used to like it—when Remy surprises me by inviting me inside for coffee. Remy likes his alone time, and I assumed he'd be anxious to spend the rest of the day alone with just his wife. But I quickly accept because I haven't met his wife yet, and I hear she has a really cute baby. I love babies. Who doesn't?

I follow him inside and into his spacious kitchen. The smell of sugar and flour and freshly baked goodies makes me inhale long and deep. My mouth is watering, and that's before I see the very nice backside of a woman in his kitchen.

Her back is to us as she removes muffins from the oven, but I know it's not Amber because Amber has red hair, and this woman has dark hair piled high in a messy bun on her head.

Dark hair.

Impossibly shiny hair.

My breath gets caught in my lungs as I wait for her to turn around. I think Remy is speaking to me, but I can't hear anything. My senses are focused on the dark-haired woman with the gorgeous hair and a backside so amazing even her pink flannel pajama pants can't hide it.

It feels like everything is happening in slow motion when she finally turns and smiles at us. Familiar blue eyes, and a smile that's been etched into my brain.

Seeing me, she smiles kindly before the smile freezes and her eyes go round and wide.

I half notice Remy's wife, Amber, ambling into the kitchen, arms full of an adorable baby girl with the same red hair. Remy introduces me to his wife, and I manage to mutter a greeting to her, my gaze fixed on Blue Eyes.

"Bruce, I'd like you to—" I can hear Remy speaking, but everything fades to a dull roar, the only point of clarity is the dark-haired woman standing in front of me.

"Bruce? Earth to Bruce," Remy says, waving a hand in front of my face, and I shake my head.

"Sorry, what?" With an effort, I pull my attention away from Blue Eyes and turn toward my friend's wife.

I must ask to hold the cute baby, because Amber hands her to me. I glance down and the baby gives me a gummy smile. With the baby in my arms, I step closer to last night's mystery woman.

The woman smirks at me as I walk toward her, everything about her feeling familiar, and yet strange, at the same time.

"And what's your name?" I ask. "I'm Bruce. Starting goalie for the D.C. Eagles."

The pretty smirk stays firmly planted on her face. I want to kiss it off her.

"That's my very *married* sister, Farrah," Remy responds for her.

CHAPTER 1

A YEAR AND A HALF LATER

FARRAH

IT'S a chilly day for April, even here in Virginia. Albeit, not as chilly as it is in Ohio where I'm from. But it also likely seemed cooler there because of the icy way my ex-husband treated me.

Who knows, maybe Ohio springs were quite balmy, but my memory is tainted.

I rub my hands together in front of the hot stove in my brother's mansion, where I've been staying since my divorce. He and his wife have the fanciest kitchen I've ever had the pleasure of baking in, and the two of them can barely cook pancakes. What a waste.

Turning the oven light on, I check the round, vanilla cake tiers that have been baking for thirty minutes. They're slightly browned around the edges, but I'll give them two more minutes.

Setting the timer on the oven once more, I walk around the kitchen, catching a glimpse of myself in the large mirror in the dining room. All this baking has my butt looking a little rounder than it was over a year ago when I moved here to be my niece's nanny and lick my post-divorce wounds. I could be self-conscious about the added ten pounds or so, but instead I feel good about it. I'm happier now, enjoying food with family and friends. No shame in that.

The smell of vanilla cake fills the kitchen and dining room, causing my stomach to growl. I glance at the cupcakes on the counter. I have two extras I don't need for the retirement party this weekend, which means a yummy snack for me and my niece, Nella.

I quickly add some frosting to the tops, just in time for the oven timer to ding.

Rushing toward the oven, I grab some potholders and slide the cakes out and onto cooling racks...perfectly browned on top. I smile to myself, knowing they'll taste amazing for the people who booked Melarrah Events for Saturday.

The doorbell rings and my brother's large dog, Rose, runs toward it, nails clacking against the tile. I know that's the Mel in Melarrah...my friend Mel, who happens to be married to my big brother's assistant captain on the D.C. Eagles NHL team. Our company name was her brainchild, a combination of Melanie and Farrah. She's really into mixing names together—hence her and her husband's couple name, *Wesanie*.

Tossing the potholders, I rush through the dining room and large foyer to get the door, giving Rose a few pats before opening it. Melanie grins at me, her light brown hair blown out and styled as always and her giant blue eyes giving her that precious princess appearance. Mel is carrying a leather satchel that I have no doubt is perfectly organized with the retirement party plans inside. She's even wearing dark jeans and a blazer, like we're running a real business—which I suppose we are. It just hasn't taken off yet. Either way, it's making me rethink my black leggings and ice-blue long sleeve tee.

"Farrah!" Mel says, pulling me into a big hug. I hug her back tightly, appreciative of the hockey wives inviting me into their fold. Back in Ohio, I left my group of friends behind, and they let me go a little easier than I thought they would, which hurts. I still talk to my friend, Megan, occasionally, but no one else. And even Megan barely seems to have time for me anymore.

But here in D.C. I have a whole new family. The only downside is I can never, ever get away from hockey…and a certain hockey goalie who always sneaks his way into my head.

"I just took the cakes out," I tell her, ushering her inside and closing the door.

She groans. "It smells amazing."

Rose licks her hand and wags her shaggy tail until Mel looks down and pets her.

In the kitchen, Mel settles on a bar stool at the marble island. She quickly begins unpacking and arranging the papers and schedules we need to finalize.

The baby monitor lights up and I hear my niece softly calling for me. I glance at the video monitor and see her standing in her crib and grinning. She looks right at the camera and waves. Silly goose.

"Well, looks like Nella is joining our meeting."

Mel chuckles. "I was hoping I'd get to play with her."

I run up the stairs, wondering if I'll have a chance to sit down at all today. But I wouldn't give this job up for anything. Hanging out with an adorable toddler every day? Yes, please.

I open the door, and Nella claps her chubby hands together. "Auntie!"

I pick her up and snuggle her, rubbing my cheek against her soft, red curls. She leans into me and gently pats my back. "Oh, Nells. You're the sweetest thing."

"I'm hungwy," she says, her words colored with a lisp.

"It's your lucky day, because I have a cupcake for you."

"Mmm," she hums.

We head down the large staircase and back into the kitchen where Mel is already standing and holding her arms out for my niece. I squeeze her a little tighter, wanting to soak up the ten minutes of post-nap snuggles she gives. It's the only time each day she's not too busy for cuddling.

"Come on," Mel teases. "Give her over. You get the snuggles every day."

Reluctantly, I hand her to Mel.

Nella is the first child for my brother's group of close-knit teammates. West—Mel's husband—Colby, and Mitch, are all married, but no babies yet.

Bruce McBride is the only one in their friend group who's single. At least, I think he's still single. The thought of him dating someone makes my stomach twist in a knot. Which it has no right to do since he's not mine. And he never will be. No matter how hard he tries. If life has taught me anything, it's that men don't know what they want. And they definitely don't want women who can't bear them children. Although maybe it's not fair to lump all men into the same category… I mean, my brother adopted Amber's baby as his own.

Why can't more men be like that?

I glance at my niece, snuggled into Mel's arms and an overwhelming feeling of longing and loneliness passes over me, that familiar dark cloud I've learned to live with. I don't know if I'll ever have children, but I know if I do, it won't come easily. And the last thing I need is yet another impatient man in my life trying to rush me when I have no control over what my womb is willing to do.

Nella's head full of red curls pops up from Mel's shoulder when she spots the cupcakes. "Cake!"

We laugh and Mel hauls her over to her highchair in the dining room right off the kitchen. She buckles her in, and I cut the cupcake in half before handing it to her.

"Do you want one, too?" I ask Mel, knowing if she eats the extra, I won't get one.

She licks her lips. "Yes, please. You sure you have enough?"

I nod and hand her the marble cupcake with chocolate buttercream frosting. She settles back on her bar stool to eat it, and I begin looking through the schedule for Saturday.

"You're not having a cupcake?" Mel asks.

I look up at her and see her sympathetic gaze. "I'll be okay."

She screws her lips to the side. "There were only two extras?"

I nod. "It's fine; I can have one if there are any leftovers on Saturday. And I've already tasted all the frosting."

"We can split this one." Mel looks down awkwardly at her cupcake, one bite taken out of the side.

I laugh at her pout. "Please don't let me stop you from enjoying that delicious treat. Watching friends enjoy my baking brings me so much joy. Seriously."

She sighs. "Well, okay." Mel takes a delicate bite, and her eyes roll back in her head. "Oh wow. You've outdone yourself this time. This is orgasmic."

My head falls back as I laugh. "Should I tell West you said that?"

She snickers. "He probably wouldn't appreciate it."

We laugh and I continue looking at her well-organized papers while she finishes her snack.

"So, Saturday we need to be there at ten sharp?" I ask.

Mel opens her mouth to answer at the same time Nella screams unhappily, arching her back and trying to get out of her highchair.

"I want down!" she whines.

"Hold that thought," I say, wetting a cloth and using it to clean off Nella's messy hands and face before lifting her down to the floor. Rose is ready and waiting for her play-mate and licks her face as soon as she can reach it. Nella squeals then runs into the living room where she has a play kitchen filled with little wooden baked goods I got her for her first birthday. Rose follows her.

She holds one up for us to look at. "I'm making cake! Mmm."

I laugh and allow my chuckle to turn into a sigh. "We're never going to get this event planned."

"It's already planned, and everything is good to go," Mel says in a soothing tone. "You just bring the cakes and we're golden."

I smile. "Okay, that I can manage."

Fifteen minutes later, Mel has given me a quick rundown of how Saturday's retirement party will go for a local Army general who's stationed at the Pentagon.

She ushers herself out so she can make it to the venue in time to finalize details and I check on Nella. She's still happily playing in her kitchen, her oven mitts on the wrong hands.

My mind wanders to a certain blond goalie and I pull up a text thread I've read over the past year about a million times. I know I'm torturing myself, but it's the sweetest kind of torture.

. . .

December 20th

UNKNOWN NUMBER

You're married?!

FARRAH

Not anymore.

UNKNOWN NUMBER

promise me you're not married... I don't
make out with married women.

FARRAH

The night we kissed I had just signed my
divorce papers. I'm sorry for bringing you
into my drama. I had no idea who you were.

UNKNOWN NUMBER

If you're not married, then this isn't over,
Yeux bleus.

December 25th

UNKNOWN NUMBER

Merry Christmas, Yeux bleus. When can I
see you again?

January 12th

UNKNOWN NUMBER

I know you're going through a divorce, and
if you're not ready for anything I
understand. Just talk to me.

June 23rd

UNKNOWN NUMBER

You looked amazing tonight. And the cake you baked for Remy and Amber's wedding reception was incredible.

UNKNOWN NUMBER

Talk to me, Yeux bleus.

September 1st

UNKNOWN NUMBER

Do you ever think about that kiss?

UNKNOWN NUMBER

I do.

Every time I read these texts; I wonder what yeux bleus means. I'm sure it's French since he's Canadian, and I've come close to looking it up but always stop myself. I learned with my ex that nicknames that seem cute can be very disappointing. Connor's grandmother was German, and he called me *fleischpastete*. He told me it was a German sweet and I thought it was so romantic…until his grandmother informed me it meant meat pie, and he calls me that because I was, quote, 'pleasantly plump.'

Yeah, I think I'll remain blissfully oblivious this time.

CHAPTER
TWO

BRUCE

The D.C. Eagles #1 Fan Page On Hockeyisbetterthanfoot-ball.com

Craig Nottingham: Bruce McBride sucked during last night's game. The man is losing his touch!

Todd Ferguson: Oh, shut up! The people on this page are a bunch of fair-weather fans. Really pisses me off.

Craig Nottingham: *GIF of penguin slipping and falling on ice*

Harry Johnson: Bruce McBride has a ninety-eight-percent save rate this season, number two in the NHL. I think we're lucky to have him! And he's easy on the eyes, so he brings in more female fans. And we love women in hockey. #feminism #badassgoalie

SNICKERING, I log off my secret Hockeyisbetterthanfootball.com account—Harry Johnson—for the evening. Sometimes the trollers need to be trolled. I set my phone down and look up to see West Kershaw, my teammate and assistant captain, staring at me. His cute little wife, Mel, is also staring at me. We're all seated in their living room since they invited me over for dinner. My teammates and their wives take turns inviting me over probably to make sure I actually eat some vegetables once in a while. All of my teammates and their wives, they all live in the same gated community, half of them even in the same cul-de-sac, even. I'm the only one who still lives in downtown D.C.

"What's so funny?" West asks, arching a blond eyebrow.

I clear my throat. "Oh, nothing. Just a weird text from my mom," I lie.

My team captains and team management do not condone horseplay of any kind, especially not trolling grumpy fans online. This is my little outlet for stress relief, I'm not about to get myself suspended over it.

His eyebrow arches even higher. "You're lying."

Mel laughs and shoves his shoulder playfully. That's what I want. Someone to sit next to me and be mean to me... but in a hot way.

His wife—who's more than a foot shorter than me—gets up and walks into the kitchen, presumably to check on dinner, and I wonder if it's weird for her to be that close to the ground or if she's just used to it.

My teammates are big guys, tall and broad, but I'm the tallest one at six feet six inches, and the bulkiest—likely because I'm single and have more time to work out than they do. But I've always been big. Maybe it's genetic. I wouldn't know since I've never met my birth father. My birth mother is an average-sized woman, though.

"It's ready!" Mel hollers from the kitchen.

West and I race each other into the large dining room, the layout of their house is similar to the other guys' but also vastly different since Mel organizes and cleans all the time. It's like a cozy hospital in here. Not like Remy and Amber's house that's littered with baby toys, or Mitch and Andie's house that's covered in youth hockey equipment from her little brother, Noah...or even Colby and Noel's house where there are always books and papers laying around.

There's not a single item out of place at West and Mel's house.

Mel narrows her eyes at us as we bound into the dining room and come to a screeching halt in front of her. "Would you two sit down before you make a mess?"

West elbows me in the ribs as he pushes past me, and I lift my arm to grab him around the shoulders but stop when Mel gives me a stern look.

"Yes, ma'am," I mutter, taking my seat beside West.

She serves us some delicious-looking chicken pot pies and takes a seat on the opposite side of her husband.

"Mel, this looks incredible." West leans in and kisses his wife, and she swats him away.

"Thank you," she says, giving her husband an adoring look.

I'm going to puke all over the table if these two don't knock it off.

"What's the matter with you?" West asks.

I hadn't realized I was making my disgusted face out loud. I tend to do that. Oops.

I look between the two of them. "You two need to get a room, that's what."

Mel rolls her eyes. "Be nice or I won't give you any dessert."

"There's dessert?" I perk up in my seat.

West grimaces. "Sweetie, I love you. But your desserts

tend to be a little interesting." Mel likes to make everything healthy…with very little sugar.

Mel waves him off. "Don't worry, Farrah made the dessert."

My whole body comes to life at the mere mention of Farrah Remington's name. I can almost taste her lips on mine, even though it's been a year and a half. "Farrah, huh?" I feign nonchalance. "How is Remy's baby sister these days?"

West pins me with a knowing glance. He doesn't know about the kiss Farrah and I shared, but he knows about my interest in the dark-haired beauty. I confided in all my teammates about my crush after meeting her, except for Remy. I wasn't about to tell him how hot his sister is.

"She's doing great!" Mel says with a smile. "She's busy with Nella during the day, then she does all the baking for Melarrah Events. We only have a few events a month so far, but with Farrah's delicious cakes, I think word will spread quickly."

Farrah's delicious cakes. Those three words have me thinking about a cake I'd like to bite into. And it's not made with flour and sugar.

West notices my glazed expression and elbows the side of my arm while Mel isn't looking.

"Stop that," he whispers through gritted teeth.

"Sorry," I whisper back. "I just really love cake."

West glares at me, understanding my double meaning.

I dig into my pot pie, ignoring him. The pie tastes decent, but Mel definitely made the crust with almond flour.

"Oh! I almost forgot." Mel sticks her index finger in the air. "Could you help us set up tables Saturday for the General's retirement party?"

West frowns. "Sorry, babe. I can't. Remy and I have the

groundbreaking ceremony Saturday for the park that the Eagles built at the children's hospital."

"Drat." She sighs. "I forgot about that."

"You?" He smiles. "Forgot?"

She shakes her head. "My head has been so fuzzy lately; I think I need more sleep."

West looks at his wife in concern.

"I can help set up tables," I offer, always looking for an excuse to be around Farrah.

"Really?" Mel's eyes widen with relief and excitement. "That would be amazing if you don't mind."

"Just text me the time and address and I'll be there."

She nods her thanks, and we finish our meal. I eat mine quickly even though it's a bit dry and difficult to swallow. But I'm excited about dessert so I muddle through. It sounds stupid, but knowing the dessert was made with Farrah's own hands has my heart beating a little faster.

Once West and Mel finish their dinner, Mel strides into the modern kitchen and pulls something out of the fridge. It looks like a layered, creamy dessert.

"All right, here's the tiramisu Farrah made for us." She sets it gently on the table and heads back into the kitchen— likely to grab a spatula and small plates.

I get up and follow her. "Go sit down, you already made us dinner. I'll get the dessert stuff."

She smiles and hands me the plates. Knowing my way around their house pretty well by now, I grab three forks, the plates, a serving spoon, and some napkins, then head back to the table.

"Thanks for making me look bad," West mutters.

I shoot him a winning smile. "Every guy looks bad when I'm around. It's the sheer space my masculinity takes up."

West snorts. "Okay, whatever."

Mel sighs. "You two are ridiculous."

West smirks at me; we both know our teasing is good-natured. That's the weird thing about teammates, especially me, West, Remy, Mitch and Colby. We act more like brothers than anything, which is nice since I didn't grow up with brothers. My older sister is cool, though.

Mel relaxes in her seat as I dish out a scoop of tiramisu for each of us. The ladyfingers layered into the dessert are shaped funny, telling me Farrah made them herself, she didn't just go out and buy premade lady fingers. I smile, feeling like I know her a little better now despite the fact she'll barely look at me...or talk to me. I must be a glutton for punishment though, because I keep texting her every few months even though those texts always go unanswered.

Sitting back down, I scoop a large bite of the creamy dessert into my mouth and nearly moan out loud. "Is this what heaven is like?" I say around my mouthful.

"I'm fairly certain no one talks with food in their mouth in heaven," West says, taking a bite. His eyes widen comically. "Oh, wow," he mumbles.

"No talking with your mouth full," I mimic him.

He rolls his eyes.

"Farrah can bake anything, I swear," Mel says, taking a small bite and closing her eyes to savor it. "You should try her sticky buns."

I swallow, my throat suddenly feeling dry as I think of Farrah's sticky buns.

West elbows me in the side for the third time tonight. "Dude!"

"Sorry."

I return to eating my dessert, but my thoughts remain faraway wondering if I'll ever get the chance to kiss Farrah again—or try her sticky buns.

SATURDAY MORNING COMES and I'm up early to get ready for our fifth official Melarrah event. My garage-turned-studio-apartment is small, with just a bathroom, minimal kitchen, and bedroom/living room combo, but after living in a large suburban home with my ex that always felt cold and empty, I prefer the cozy space. It feels warmer and homier than my big, beautiful house in Ohio ever did.

Remy was willing to shell out the money for contractors to transform the space since it meant having more privacy with his new wife. And I love having my own space, and my own entrance, so it feels like I can get away when I want.

My queen-sized platform bed is right in front of a cute, round window covered with gauzy curtains. A white canopy hangs over the bed and flows down to the floor. The flooring is black and white tiles, and a single shiplap wall ends just before the bathroom door, where a small bathroom holds the basics: a shower, a toilet, and a pedestal sink. The opposite wall is mostly covered with sage green built-in shelves and a half kitchen takes up the wall across from my bed with cabinets the same color as the bookshelves. The kitchenette has a tiny sink, and an even smaller stove top and slim fridge. It feels like a European cottage, and Remy let me pick everything out.

I take a few steps away from my bed to my armoire and select a pair of black pleated trousers I bought last week, pairing them with a black bodysuit. Mel and I agreed an all-black look would be professional for events.

I brush my long hair and braid it back so it won't get in the way. My braid falls past my bra strap, I make a mental note to ask Amber for a haircut soon. Perks of having a hair stylist as a sister-in-law.

Walking to the bathroom, I take my time doing my makeup. It's nice to have an excuse to get ready, as going from a corporate job to nannying hasn't allowed me many opportunities to get fancy. I do a full face, complete with highlighting, contouring, and eye. "Not bad," I murmur to my reflection.

Right before I head out the door of my apartment to walk to the big house, I slip on a pair of black flats that will keep my feet comfortable all day as I set up the venue with Mel and West.

Unsurprisingly, when I enter the big house, Remy and Nella are already awake and in the living room. That girl is an early riser, much to her parents' dismay.

"Well, good morning," I singsong, causing Nella to look up from her TV show and come running into my arms. Goodness, I love this girl.

"Morning, sis." Remy runs a hand through his short hair, his eyes droopy like he just woke up.

"You look tired," I tell him, letting go of Nella and heading into the kitchen to finish the last touches on the General's cupcakes. Everything is done except for the tiny,

American flag toppers and placing the tiers of the tall cake together.

"Gee, thanks," he grumbles.

"Do you guys have plans today?" I ask, gathering the supplies I need from the cabinet.

He follows me into the kitchen, little Nella on his heels. "Daddy!"

My brother smiles and lifts Nella into his arms. "Yeah, West and I are part of the ribbon-cutting ceremony for the new park the Eagles built. Amber and Nella are coming along."

I hum as I listen and remove the cakes from Remy's side-by-side refrigerator. It takes a couple seconds for his statement to register. "Wait, West will be there too?"

"Yeah." Remy sits on a bar stool and settles Nella on his lap. "We'll be gone most of the day."

I blow out a deep breath. "I thought West was coming to help us set up the venue."

Remy thinks for a moment. "I'm sure Mel has it all planned out and has someone coming to help you two. And if she doesn't, you call me, and I'll send one of the guys on the team."

My shoulders relax. "Okay. You're right. I'm sure she has it all planned."

An hour later, Remy helps me load the cake and cupcakes into boxes and into my small car. Then I make my way from our suburb in Virginia to the urban venue in downtown D.C. It's one of those older buildings that's been stripped down to its exposed brick and open beams.

After parking in the temporary loading zone, I text Mel to let her know I'm here and get out of my car to open the trunk and get the cupcakes.

I nearly jump out of my skin when an all-too-familiar deep voice rumbles behind me.

"Hello, Yeux bleus," Bruce says in his French-Canadian accent. I don't always notice his accent, only when he speaks French. And he seems to only speak French when he's creating names for me. Because whatever he just said is definitely not French for Farrah.

I turn and look at him over my shoulder and my face heats just like it did in that bar a year and a half ago. Why does my mystery man—and the best kisser in the universe—have to be my brother's teammate and one of his best friends? Not to mention he's too young for me. Bruce still has years ahead of him to date and fall in love. I've been there and done that, only for it to go up in flames. I'm in no hurry to do that again.

But my, what a beautiful twenty-something male he is. The blond hair that's shaggy on top and shorter on the sides —allowing me to see his ear piercing—does something to me. Something tingly. I never would've considered a piercing to be attractive, but he makes it look so dashing. The small diamond stud completes the whole wild look of Bruce McBride. His skin doesn't have a single wrinkle yet—only taut, smooth flesh just like, I'm sure, the rest of an annoyingly perfect body.

"Bruce," I say finally, giving him a slight nod.

"I'm here to help for the day since West can't be here," he offers, moving closer to me and trying to make eye contact.

I cannot look into those eyes. The first time I looked into those sky-blue orbs, I invited him to join me in a corner booth...the second time, I scooted closer to him in said booth...and the third time, I allowed him to kiss me like I've never been kissed in my life. I haven't recovered since. So, who knows what would happen if I looked into Bruce's eyes for a fourth time? I swear he's some sort of Medusa with those things.

"Are you ever going to look at me again?" he asks, his voice quiet.

I carefully hand him the tall cake box, remembering the way his muscles felt beneath his shirt and knowing he has plenty of strength to carry it inside for me.

"I don't think it's a good idea."

He chuckles. "*Looking* at me?"

I look at his nose, but not his eyes. "You know what I mean."

He leans in. "I'm just a big, dumb blond. Spell it out for me."

A cool spring breeze passes us and draws Bruce's masculine scent with it. Even the wind is against me.

"Despite all those pucks to the head, I know you're smarter than people give you credit for," I say, meeting his gaze for a fraction of a second. Not long enough to throw myself into his arms or anything.

I grab the cupcakes and march quickly past him. I can hear Bruce laughing behind me as he follows me to the main room in the venue where we're setting up the desserts for the party.

Mel is already in the center of the room, kneeling and taping the cement floor where she wants the tables placed.

"Farrah! You're here!" she gets up and gives me a big hug then turns to Bruce. "You can put the cake on that round table over here." She points and he follows without argument.

Bruce transfers the cake easily, not balking at the weight of the five-tiered masterpiece, then he bounds back over like a happy puppy wanting to take orders on what to do next. Goodness, but this man will make some girl a fine husband one day. That eagerness to please will go a *long* way.

Mel tells him to set up a table anywhere he sees tape on the ground, and he gets to work quickly. I watch him for a second, noticing how his grey, athletic shorts ride up on his thighs every time he bends to pop the table legs out. And his arms... my mouth goes dry as they bulge and flex through his black tee with every motion.

Mel's voice draws me back to reality. "Hey, Farrah, do we need to move the center table, or do you think it's fine where it is?"

I blink a few times, forcing myself to look away from the very enthusiastic blond goalie. "I think it's fine as is," I answer, even though I don't know what table she's talking about. Mel is the detail person here anyway; I'm just the baker.

"Great!" she grabs the pen from behind her ear and checks something off the list she's holding under her arm. "You look cute by the way, love the pants."

"You're just not used to me wearing anything but sweats," I tease. "You look great too," I tell her, glancing down at her cute black dress that has short sleeves and hits just above her knees. She's wearing black flats with it, and I feel like a giant beside her. Mel is five-feet-two to my five-seven. She's cute and petite and I could be jealous... but instead I'm focusing on the fact that I can reach things off the top shelf of the pantry, and she can't.

We all have our strengths, you know?

"Thank you! Why don't you park your car, then we'll start decorating. Here's the ticket for the parking garage." She hands me a ticket with a barcode from the venue and I head that direction.

I don't realize Bruce is following me until I'm buckling into my seat, and he slides into the passenger side. I jump. "What are you doing? You almost gave me a heart attack."

"I didn't let Mel walk through the parking garage alone, and I'm not about to let you do it either. I'm here for a reason, so let me help." He's all long limbs and heavy bulk, dwarfing the seat of my small car. It's like watching Buddy the Elf trying to fit at an elf-sized desk.

I open my mouth to argue then snap it closed…because honestly, I hate parking garages.

"Fine," I say, putting the car in drive and pulling inside the parking garage entrance. It's dark and dreary, the way all parking garages are, and I'm grateful for Bruce being here.

"You look beautiful," he says.

Did I just say I was grateful for him being here? I changed my mind. The man is nothing but trouble.

"Aren't you going to compliment me, too?" he asks.

I whip my head over to stare at him. The audacity.

"I saw you staring at my legs earlier." He winks at me before I can look away.

I gape at him, and I can feel my cheeks burning. A horn honks behind me and I realize I've come to a stop in the middle of the parking garage. I start driving again and park in the first spot I find.

I unbuckle my seatbelt and turn to open my door, but Bruce reaches out to stop me, gently placing his hand on my forearm. "Wait," he says, and I turn to look at him. His face is serious. "It's been a year and a half, Farrah. I get that you're not into me, or whatever. But can't we be friends? I'm tired of things being weird between us. It was just one kiss."

I sigh in resignation. He's right, we have to see each other a lot. We have the same friend group. My brother is his best friend and team captain. There's no avoiding each other. But the word *friend* also leaves a heavy feeling on my shoulders. Friends implies we'll never be anything more, and that's what I wanted. Bruce clearly didn't put much weight into that kiss if he says it was *just one kiss*, so I shouldn't either, right?

Right.

"Okay," I tell him with a nod. "Let's be friends." The word *friends* tastes sour on my lips.

He sticks his massive hand out in front of me for a friendly handshake and my mind goes back to the way it felt cradling my face, how the rough calluses against my smooth skin gave me goosebumps that night over a year ago. Just the memory gives me goosebumps all over again.

But I can be friends with someone I find attractive. Just friends. I'm not ready for anything more, and I'm not sure I ever will be.

I shake his hand quickly, not wanting to linger on the way his swallows mine up.

"Friends," I say, ignoring the warm sensation of his hand in mine.

"Friends." He smiles with that familiar twinkle in his blue eyes.

Once we're back inside we make quick work of setting up for our lunch time event.

At a quarter to twelve the general and his family walk through the entrance. Mel and I watch their faces with bated breath to see if they like the décor. General Williams is serious, probably around fifty years old, with dark skin and cropped grey hair. He smiles in a stern, professional way and nods as he takes in the room. His wife is much more exuberant. She's a cute woman with black hair and a curvy figure draped in a dark red dress that matches his dress blues nicely.

Mrs. William's eyes find me and Mel, and she beams. "Oh, girls you outdid yourselves!" She rushes toward us and hugs us both. She smells sweet and comforting and reminds me of my mom. It hits me how much I miss her, that's the worst part of not living in Ohio anymore.

"I'm so happy you like it!" Mel tells her. "Just wait until you taste the desserts."

"They look delicious," General Williams tells me. "Thank you both."

Two younger women follow closely behind the general and his wife. They both appear to be in their mid-twenties with flawless dark skin. One has box braids and the other has a sleek, black bob. I notice their attention isn't on the decor or the cakes...instead, they're both focused on a certain handsome hockey goalie who's helping the D.J. put the final touches on the lights and sound equipment.

Bruce's gaze flits over to the newcomers and when he notices their attention he smiles before going back to what he was doing before.

The girls titter and whisper to each other. This shouldn't bother me. Not at all.

But the evil monster called jealousy tries to make her way into my mind, anyway. The jealousy monster tries to convince me that because I kissed Bruce, he's mine.

But he's not. In fact, we're just friends. Great friends. We shook on it.

The D.J. starts up the music and this is when Bruce is supposed to leave. But the Williams girls wave him over. He lumbers toward them, a smirk on his face, looking out of place in his athletic clothing. The girls immediately start up a conversation, but I can't hear what they're saying. However, Bruce appears to be enjoying himself. He's charismatic and engaging, just like he was the night I met him. He's magnetic. I can't blame the girls for wanting to bask in his charm. And I can't blame him for enjoying their company. They're nice, gorgeous, and young.

I feel a hand on my arm and turn to see Mel looking at me with a strange expression. It almost looks like pity. "Hey, Farrah. We need to get the serving line ready."

"Oh, sure," I tell her, thankful my only job in our company is baking. She's the eyes and ears and I'm glad I don't have to pay attention to all the nitty gritty details. Although if I did, it would probably keep me too busy for my eyes to find Bruce every ten seconds.

An hour later the guests have all arrived, been served lunch by the catering company, and are now in line for dessert. General Williams takes some photos with his patriotic retirement cake and then we cut into the masterpiece.

And has Bruce left yet? No. The older of the two Williams girls invited him to stay, despite him being severely underdressed.

He's even sitting at the family table with General Williams. Every time I glance over, he's leaning in to say something and the daughter is touching him flirtatiously.

Mel keeps giving me strange looks and asking if I'm okay, which is weird. Of course I'm okay. Everyone *loves* my cakes.

I serve a slice of cake to a party guest, smiling and nodding appropriately, and when I look back at the William's table, the girls are gone, and Bruce is striding toward us.

The dessert line has come to an end, so he comes behind the table to stand with Mel and me and grimaces as he stares at the women's restroom across the room. "I'm so sorry guys, I keep trying to get away."

Mel hums. "Sure you are."

"I'm serious!" He whisper-yells. "I'm way under-dressed."

I stare at him, amused at his admission. I've noticed his game day suits are always outlandishly flashy and unique. It probably does bother him to be underdressed when he's arguably the best dressed guy on the D.C. Eagles team any other occasion. That's something we have in common. I used to be really into fashion and dressing up, but I've gotten out of the habit since nannying. I also didn't feel like dressing up after the divorce, but I think I'd like to start fixing myself up again.

"Well, this is your chance to escape from the beautiful women." Mel winks.

He eyes me, then the cake. "I know. But I wondered if I could get a piece of cake first."

"Are you serious?" I ask.

He nods. "I came to help, but also hoped to try Farrah's baked goods. *Not* so I could find a date."

The relief I feel in my chest is foolish. If he's not going home with one of these girls, it'll be some girl, eventually. Someone younger than me, with less baggage than me, and with better ovaries than me.

I slap a piece of cake onto a plate and thrust it toward him. "Here you go. Thanks for helping out today. Now you're free to go."

"See you, Bruce!" Mel says with a sassy little wave then turns to me. "Hey, speaking of dates. My brother Harrison is coming into town next weekend. He's successful, decent looking, and a great guy. I wasn't sure if you were interested in dating yet though."

Bruce gapes at her instead of leaving.

Mel pops one fist on her hip. "Is there a problem, Bruce? I thought you were heading out?"

He blinks. "Yeah, I was. Sorry. See you guys." He doesn't smile or tease as he turns and walks away. There's something pouty about his demeanor.

General Williams gets up on the small, raised stage to give a short speech, and Mel and I start to clean up the dessert table.

"So?" Mel asks quietly.

"So…what?"

She chuckles. "My brother." Mel leans in closer. "Honestly, he lives in Philly and has no interest in relocating here to D.C. So, he might be the perfect practice date. See how dating feels, you know? Gauge if you're ready."

I consider the idea, biting my lip as I think. We live in different cities, so if the date went badly, I'd never have to see him again. "Yeah, maybe you're right. A test date. You're sure he's not looking for anything serious? Just an enjoyable evening with good company?"

She smiles. "Oh yeah. Harrison would never move here. A casual date is his style."

I nod. "Okay, set it up."

"Perfect!" she whispers with a grin.

I don't know anything about Harrison, but she's right—this will be a good test run. And he's not my brother's teammate, so even better.

"Hey, Mel?"

"Yeah?"

I worry my bottom lip. "How old is Harrison?"

She looks up at the ceiling as she thinks. "He's twenty-eight."

I sigh heavily.

"Oh, stop! You're only thirty-two. And you look twenty-five anyway with that gorgeous skin of yours."

I roll my eyes.

"I'm serious! You're a catch." She playfully bumps her shoulder against mine. "I'll text him your number."

I nod once, my stomach flipping at the thought of going on a date. And not necessarily in a good way.

CHAPTER
FOUR

BRUCE

IT'S the end of the second period during our game with the Atlanta Cyclones. Their captain, Aaron Marino, is really pissing me off. He slid into my net and knocked the whole damn thing over.

Is this a normal occurrence in hockey?

Maybe.

But everything is pissing me off tonight. And I'm sure it has nothing to do with the fact that I saw all the girls sitting together in their usual section—all the girls including Farrah—but with the addition of Mel's brother, Harrison Freaking Taylor.

Harrison is a great guy, and up until I saw him sitting beside Farrah, I was a big fan of the dude. But he's looking a little too cozy.

Add that to the fact that Farrah is wearing a Remington jersey, and I'm ruffled. It's logical for her to wear her brother's jersey, I get that. But brother or not, seeing her in any jersey but a McBride one has me ready to punch someone.

Between periods, we enter the Eagles' locker room with

its polished wood, custom flooring and fancy eagle light fixture and I cannot shake this terrible mood.

Colby grabs onto the top of my helmet and gives me a shake. "Hey Brucey, you okay in there?"

I push him away. "I'm fine."

Colby's dark eyebrows rise, and those dimples that all the ladies love disappear. Before he met and married his wife, Noel, he was the biggest ladies' man on the team. "Seriously, man, what's wrong?"

West saunters over, steady on his feet despite the skates strapped to them. Sweat drips from his hair down his face, and he keeps his voice low as he murmurs, "is your hissy fit about Harrison and Farrah?"

I jerk my helmet off. "Why are you saying their names together like that?"

West holds his hands out in front of himself defensively.

"Dude," Colby says, blowing out a deep breath. "You have no chill."

"Kind of like you were super chill when Noel came to a game with Professor Dickhead?"

His head jerks back at the reminder of Noel's date before the two of them got together. Spoiler alert: he was very *not* chill during that game.

"You're kind of an asshole tonight, not gonna lie," Colby says, crossing his arms.

Colby, West, and Mitch are the only ones who knew about my interest in Farrah…only they expected me to get over it a long time ago. But I didn't.

Mitch Anderson—affectionately known as *Mitch the Machine* for his defensive skills—sees us huddled together and walks over. Coach isn't in the locker room yet for our pep talk so we have a minute to talk.

"Did you just call Bruce an asshole?" He says, his eyebrows knitting together. "Bruce is never an asshole."

"He's pining," West says in a low voice.

Mitch's eyebrows jump up to his hairline. "Over who?"

West and Colby's eyes move with purpose toward Remy, who's retaping his stick.

Mitch looks befuddled. "Remy? He's married."

I roll my eyes.

"Capn's little sister," Colby whispers.

Mitch gives me a look that says *you're asking for trouble.* "Still?"

I give him a look back that says *I know and yes, still.*

"Wait," Mitch says. "Isn't she here with Harrison?"

Colby and West glare at him, and I hear a low growl rip through the locker room. Everyone—including Remy—turns to look and I realize the sound came from me.

Growling? Really Bruce? You kissed her one time. You've got to get over it.

Remy makes his way over to the corner of the locker room where we're huddled. "What's going on?" he asks, looking confused and a little hurt we're not including him in our little powwow. Little does he know he would never want to hear what we're talking about.

He made it *very* clear when Farrah first moved here that she's been through a lot, and we should all leave her alone—specifically me, since I'm the only single one.

And I've listened. Mostly. Except for the texts that went unanswered. That reminds me, I still owe Andie—Mitch's wife—one more favor. Those were her terms when she shared Farrah's number with me. I already completed one favor—working with her little brother, Noah, on his corner shots. It didn't even feel like a favor; that was fun as hell. And Noah is crazy talented for being only thirteen. If that kid doesn't get a hockey scholarship for college, I'll be shocked.

"Nothing," I answer finally, after a few awkward seconds. "Just frustrated I didn't block that last shot by the Cyclones." It's only a half lie. Because I *am* frustrated by that, even if it's not my main source of frustration.

Coach Young finally saunters into the locker room, and we all give him our attention. He claps his hands together and purses his lips. "All right boys, Cyclones are ahead but we still have the third period to get our bearings. Thanks to you guys, the Eagles are the number one team in the Eastern Conference. The Cyclones are playing a good game, but I know you all can make a comeback tonight. So, consider this a torch lighting a fire under your asses and get back out there and play the way I know you can." He shoots me a knowing glance. "And Bruce, my brick wall, pull your head out of your butt and block the damn shots."

He spins on his heel and heads back out to the bench, leaving me grinding my teeth and trying not to show how pissed I am. I know Coach wants a cup this year. Hell, we all do. But the goalie always gets blamed. It's the worst part of being a goaltender. Everyone directs their anger towards you. Even the fans.

Colby pats me hard on the back, hard enough to feel it through all my pads. "You got this man. Ignore *you know who* and keep your eye on the prize."

He's trying to be encouraging, but little does he know I consider Farrah Remington a much higher prize than winning this game.

But still, everyone is counting on us—on me—to bring the cup home this season.

When I skate back to my net and the puck is about to drop for the third and final period of the game, I glance one last time at Farrah in the stands. She's looking right at me, not at her brother who's at center ice getting ready to face off against Aaron Marino. I narrow my eyes, even though she can't see my face through my goalie mask.

Her gaze gives me a flurry of motivation, a spark that flames. I'm going to block every freaking shot, just to impress her. Just to keep her eyes on me and off Harrison. This is what Coach Young, and my teammates don't realize… I would do absolutely anything to bask in Farrah's attention for two seconds. Pathetic? Probably. But hell, if it helps us win this game it's all good.

The whistle blows and I'm crouching into position, but Remy gets the puck, and the Eagles move into the offensive zone. Remy passes to West, and Mitch uses his big body to press Aaron Marino into the boards. West passes to Colby who shoots it at the net, but it's blocked by their goalie. It's a great block on their goalie's part, not gonna lie.

West snags the puck and gets a rebound; it goes straight through the five hole—the goalie's legs—and just like that, the game is tied up two to two.

After another faceoff, the Cyclones take possession and head straight toward me. One of their players tries to fake me out, but I stand my ground, and the puck ricochets off my skate. Another Cyclone player snags it and takes it around the net, but I'm ready for him. I see his shot go high and have my gloved hand ready to catch the biscuit, but my best friend—the crossbar—blocks it for me.

Mitch snatches the puck away from the Cyclones and takes it away from the defensive zone. I take a deep breath and give the crossbar a good-natured pat. "Thanks man."

Ten seconds before the final buzzer goes off, Colby scores a goal, and we barely manage a three to two win.

We lineup afterward on the ice to fist bump the opposing

team the way we do after every game, and my teammates give me some extra helmet taps which is hockey code for good job.

Colby and I are the last ones on the ice. He wraps me in a bear hug and whispers, "good focus, man. I knew you could keep your mind off Remy's sister if you put your mind to it."

I withhold a laugh. The whole reason I stayed focused was to impress the girl.

CHAPTER
FIVE

FARRAH

AMBER IS SO excited to have a sitter for the game tonight, she manages to organize a dinner for all of us at a local bar and even made a reservation earlier today. I guess the bar owner is a big Eagles fan and was willing to put tables together at the last minute.

Harrison, Mel's older brother, is joining us. He's kind, handsome, and has a successful job in Philadelphia as a physical therapist…but I'm not attracted to him. At all. Maybe it's the dark hair; he reminds me too much of my ex-husband—but only in looks, not in demeanor.

I've always loved blond guys. My little sister, Felicity, was surprised when I was attracted to Connor, whose hair is dark. When I was a teenager, my bedroom boasted posters of Chad Michael Murray, Cary Elwes, and Brad Pitt. Forget tall, dark and handsome and give me muscular and blond with a chiseled jawline. My dream man is Kristoff from Frozen…a simple man. He works hard harvesting ice and looks good doing it.

But Harrison is nice enough, and it's good to get out of my comfort zone and think about possibly dating again.

I ride to the bar with Remy and Amber and when we pull into the parking lot marked by a well-lit sign that says *George's*, my heart stops inside my chest. This is the bar where I met Bruce that night long ago. The bar where we kissed, and he cradled my face in his hands. No, no, no. I do not want to be back here…it makes me feel too many things.

My brother parks and gets out of the Land Rover, walking around to the passenger side and opening the door for Amber. I don't realize I'm sitting in the back seat perfectly still until I hear Remy call my name.

"Farrah, you okay?"

I shake my head and blink. "Oh, yeah." I huff a laugh. "I just forgot about something I need to do. Maybe I should get an Uber home."

"Farrah!" Amber pouts. "We never get to hang out outside of the house. Please?"

I sigh. It's just dinner. It's not a big deal. So, what if the single most sexy thing in my life happened within these walls? "Okay, fine."

As I climb out of the luxury SUV, more cars begin pulling into the small parking lot. One of them is a beat up, old Chevy that I know just by the creaky door. Bruce's truck. Remy says he refuses to get rid of it because he thinks it's a lucky charm or something.

I cozy up beside Amber. "I didn't know *everyone* was coming."

Oblivious, my sister-in-law smiles at me. "Oh of course! This might be my only night out with adults for months. We had to invite the whole gang." She loops her arm through mine and drags me along with her and my brother.

Footsteps sound on the ground behind me, but I don't look, because I'm not sure I can keep my expression under control if I make eye contact with Bruce McBride.

When we enter the bar, it looks exactly the same as it did that fateful night a year and a half ago. Wood floors, wood-paneled walls, a polished bar, and a big stone fireplace. Last time I was here it was December and the fireplace was blazing, giving the place a romantic vibe. But tonight, the lighting is brighter and there's a different bartender. It's busy, much like last time, except for the table the owner held for us. It's the same table Bruce and I sat at as we shared wings. The same large corner booth where our knees pressed together, and we leaned in to talk to each other. The same booth where I noticed the piercing in one ear that made him seem a little dangerous. The same booth where I realized there was something familiar about him...but I thought it was just the fact that he resembled Kristoff from Frozen.

Cover the man in furs and give him a reindeer, and BAM. Kristoff.

An extra table has been pushed up against the booth table so we can all sit together. I hang back, suddenly unsure how to act or where to sit. Finally feeling brave enough to glance behind me, I find Bruce a few steps away. He gives me a knowing glance, one that tells me he feels as weird about this as I do. His spine looks stiff, and his hands are in the pockets of his pants. I believe that's a faint blush on his cheeks as well...

If walls could talk—and thankfully, they can't—they'd tell all our friends that Bruce McBride had his tongue in my mouth right in this very booth.

And my, what a talented tongue. I think it moved just as fluidly as Bruce does on the ice when he's in net. Knowing exactly where to go and what to do at precisely the right time.

I shiver, but it has nothing to do with the temperature in

this bar. It's actually quite warm in here thanks to the bodies filling the space.

Remy and Amber slide into the booth first, sitting close to each other in the center. Colby Knight and his wife, Noel seating herself by Amber. Then Mitch Anderson—who's painfully serious—slides in and sits beside Remy, and his wife Andie follows. Mel and West sit next to each other at the table that's been pushed against the booth, and Harrison sits beside his sister at the head of the small, rectangular table. That leaves two seats. Right next to each other. Bruce strides over and slumps down in the seat next to Andie, and now I'm left with one empty seat right between Harrison and Bruce.

If I'd had the time to think up a worst-case scenario…this would've been it.

Swallowing, I pull out my chair and sit down. The bar is loud, and our group is adding to the noise, everyone talking animatedly about the game and how they barely came away with a win. Much thanks to Bruce for that; the last period of the game he was on fire.

Andie leans over to look at me, her shoulder length blonde hair falling around her face as she does. "Farrah! I haven't seen you in ages. You need to come to our next WAG night." WAG is what they call wives and girlfriends of athletes.

I laugh. "It feels weird since I'm not a WAG."

Noel, across the table, shakes her head. "Then let's stop calling them WAG nights. We're all just friends hanging out," she points out, ever the logical one. Colby brings a hand up and playfully pulls one of her short, blonde curls. She bats his hand away but leans in and kisses him on the cheek. He smiles so big his dimples pop.

"Po-tay-to, po-tah-toe," Andie says with a wave of her

hand, then rests that hand on Bruce's shoulder. "But hey, if you ever want to be a WAG...I happen to know a guy on the Eagles who's still single." She gives me an exaggerated wink.

I look at Bruce and his eyes meet mine. A moment passes, neither of us knowing what to say, when he opens his mouth.

But a voice on my opposite side pipes up first. "So, Farrah. What are your hobbies?"

I close my eyes briefly, turning to look at Harrison—whom I'd completely forgotten about.

Turning all my attention to the man I'm going on a date with tomorrow evening, I smile politely. "I love baking. Especially cakes and cupcakes."

Harrison smiles, he has a handsome smile with straight white teeth. The corners of his eyes crinkle telling me he's not *that* much younger than I am. "That's amazing. What's your favorite fla—"

"And they taste incredible," Bruce says from my other side. "Her favorite flavor is blueberry with lemon frosting. If that's what you were about to ask."

I turn and gawk at Bruce. Behind him, Andie covers her mouth so I can't see her laughing. Too late, though. I narrow my eyes at my friend then look at Bruce. "How do you even know that?"

He shrugs one of those big, sexy shoulders. "I notice things."

"Well, that's only my favorite flavor of cake. You don't know my favorite cupcake flavor."

He tilts his head the way a happy dog would and smirks. "Wrong."

I cross my arms. "What is it then?"

"You like your cupcakes simple. Classic. Vanilla cake with vanilla buttercream frosting."

I gape at the man.

Harrison clears his throat. "Wow. You two must spend a lot of time baking together." He huffs an awkward laugh.

I answer his statement with a "no" at the same time Bruce says, "I've tasted her cakes. Many times."

Briefly, I close my eyes to refrain from slapping my hand against Bruce's big mouth. Everyone is watching our strange trio, even my big brother, whose gaze bounces between me and Harrison and then Bruce and then repeating the pattern. Watching him watch us is making me dizzy.

Bruce manspreads beneath the table and I feel his knee fall against mine. I scoot over but bump Harrison's leg in the process, then scoot back. Bruce doesn't move his leg, and it stays firmly pressed against mine. Better Bruce's than Harrison's, though. Wait, no… I have that backwards.

Bruce leans an elbow on the back of my chair as he turns and faces Harrison. "I can't remember, do you eat cake?"

I don't remember much of what Mel has told me about her brother, but one thing I know for certain is that he's really into healthy eating, much like his sister.

Harrison shifts, visibly uncomfortable, as he answers, "Not really. I eat a pretty clean diet," Harrison's leg bounces up and down beneath the table in irritation…or maybe it's anxiety. His eyes widen and he turns to me. "I mean, not that there's anything wrong with indulging once in a while. I just feel better when I don't consume a lot of sugar." The man is nearly sweating as he waits for my reaction.

I place a hand on Harrison's shoulder. It's not a flirtatious move; I just want to reassure him that I'm not upset. "No, I get it. There's nothing wrong with healthy eating. Tasting cake flavors is part of my job, though. Possibly my favorite part." I smile.

Mel leans in. "And they're always delicious!" She bumps her brother's arm with her elbow. "You should ask Farrah what she's making for our first wedding event next weekend."

Harrison smiles and turns his attention back to me. "Well?"

I laugh. "I'm making a three-layered wedding cake and get this." I pause for effect. "It's S'mores flavored. It has marshmallow cream on the inside with chocolate chips. Then there are graham cracker crumbs layered between each cake."

His eyebrows raise. "Wow, now that sounds amazing."

"Is this your first S'mores cake?" Bruce asks. "I didn't know you made S'mores cakes."

I turn to look at him, my gaze lingering on his pout. "I guess you don't know everything, huh?"

He purses his lips.

"But this is my first one, yes," I admit. "The couple loves camping so S'mores are kind of their thing."

"Oh, I love camping too. Do you?" Harrison asks.

I turn back to face him. I hate camping, but I don't want to say that. A crick in my neck makes me bring a hand up to rub it. *Wow, I'm really getting a cramp in my neck from all this back and forth.*

"I have to admit, I'm not a big camper." I laugh and a larger, warmer hand moves mine aside and begins to gently rub the sore spot there. It's a great massage, top notch. Bruce is as good with his hands as he is with his mouth. Realizing where my thoughts are headed, I brush his hand aside, even though it feels really good. Too good.

"But I'd try glamping," I add.

Harrison wrinkles his nose slightly, forgetting himself. He carefully morphs his face back into a congenial expression. "Yeah, glamping might be fun."

An awkward silence passes between us, and I wonder what Harrison and I will talk about during our date tomorrow. It will hopefully be much less awkward without an audience.

"Mitch took me camping once," Andie says. I look over at her and see her glaring at her brute of a husband. He shrugs and then wraps an arm around her waist and pulls her closer against him.

Andie settles her hand over Mitch's and smiles at Bruce. "Brucey, do you like camping?"

Bruce snorts a laugh. "I'm more of a five-star resort kind of guy."

"Really?" I ask, genuinely surprised. "But you drive that beat up truck. I took you for a real outdoorsy type."

Harrison snorts a laugh from behind me. "During West's bachelor party a few years ago, Bruce took the master suite for himself and used the giant bathtub every night. He's *indoorsy* for sure."

Bruce scoffs in mock outrage. "That's not true. I enjoy drinking my old fashioneds on my balcony. As long as the mosquitos aren't too bad...and my outdoor lighting is hooked up."

An old fashioned. That's the drink he ordered last time we were here together.

Not wanting to encourage his possessive behavior tonight, I don't tell the man I agree with him and would much rather be only a few steps away from modern conveniences such as heating and air conditioning.

The waiter finally comes and quickly takes our orders. The guys all get water because they have another game tomorrow night, but their wives partake in fruity cocktails. I stick with a Coke Zero tonight since alcohol causes my joints to ache and makes my insomnia worse—two annoying PCOS symptoms.

Our food and drinks come out quickly. I got wings again and so did Bruce. He smirks at me as he takes in my order, and I quickly look away. If I look at him any longer, I might remember how the sweet wing sauce tasted on his lips. *Whoops, too late, already thinking about it.*

Harrison excuses himself to the bathroom and the couples are all immersed in conversation in between eating their wings and nachos. Unable to abate my curiosity, I nudge Bruce's knee with mine under the table.

"How do you know all my favorite cake flavors?"

He leans in close, and I sneak an inhale of him. He showered after the game, and he smells like fresh man soap. It's a spicy smell with a hint of nutmeg. It's different than whatever my ex used. Better.

"Yeux bleus, I collect facts about you like a sodding idiot."

Another chill runs down my spine, my stomach doing a flip. Nervously, I swallow. "Are you ever going to tell me what yeux bleus means?"

He considers this. "Next time you kiss me, I'll tell you."

"Next time?" I arch a brow.

"Next time."

CHAPTER
SIX
BRUCE

The D.C. Eagles #1 Fan Page On Hockeyisbetterthanfoot-ball.com

Craig Nottingham: This goalie has more holes than my underwear!

Todd Ferguson: Oh, leave McBride alone! I doubt you could do any better CRAIG. By your profile pic it looks like you haven't exercised in a minute.

Craig Nottingham: I have GERD! And when I played in college, I was a FORCE. I could've gone pro…but my passion was in accounting. Jerk.

Todd Ferguson: *gif of Judge Judy rolling her eyes*

Laura Miller: Would you two shut up? I'm just trying to figure out how the defense allowed sixty shots on goal. Any goal tender would've struggled. #mcbrideismy-futurehusband #bestgoalieinthenhl

Harry Johnson: I'm with Laura here (minus the wanting to marry McBride thing) when one team is outshooting another by that much, shots are gonna get through. I still think McBride is a damn good goalie. And the Eagles secured their spot in the playoffs tonight as number 1 in the Eastern conference, so let's give them a break.

Laura Miller: Yeah! And handsome to boot. SO HANDSOME.

Harry Johnson: Agreed. Super handsome.

I LOG off my hockeyisbetterthanfootball.com profile and groan. Tonight's game was brutal, and it was against our rivals, the Raleigh Renegades.

We barely came away with a win. But that's not the only thing that has me on edge. Right now, Farrah and freaking Harrison are on their date.

I glance at the time on my phone…okay, it's past eleven. So, she's probably home by now.

My stomach drops. What if she didn't go home…what if the date went well and she went back to his hotel? Is he staying in a hotel, or with West and Mel? I can't remember. I drag a hand through my hair, pulling at the strands. My heart is racing, and my thoughts begin to spiral, first imagining them kissing, then getting married, then having a brood of kids.

I open up my text thread with Farrah….the one she never responds to. I type out a text, knowing she won't reply, but texting her is oddly cathartic. For all I know she has my number blocked.

BRUCE

So, how was the date with Harrison?

BRUCE

He's a good guy. Totally wrong for you…but a good guy.

I snort a humorless laugh and throw my phone to the other side of my grey, tweed couch. It's one of those rectangular, modern, bachelor couches. The kind that looks cool but isn't comfortable at all. It feels like an Ikea couch even though it was ten grand. I remind myself to find a new designer.

Pushing myself up, I pad barefoot across the cold tile in my penthouse. It's all glossy and pristine and clean from my housekeeper, but it doesn't feel like home. Nowhere does.

Instead of texting a woman who's forbidden, I should've called my parents. But they seem awfully busy with my older sister. She and her husband live close to them in Quebec and just had a baby.

I adore my sister, but it's hard when I also feel like she has outperformed me in every way. I didn't inherit the McBride smarts, which isn't that weird considering we don't have the same genetics. But hopefully I've made up for it with my athleticism.

Once I'm in my stupid, shiny kitchen that I never use, I pull a cupcake from the fridge. I snuck this one from the event last weekend, and I've been saving it for a rainy day. It's cold and starting to get dried out, but still better than any cupcake I could purchase in a store.

I could go buy the fanciest cupcake in the city, but nothing compares to Farrah Remington's baking. And I'm not just saying that because she's gorgeous, and nice, and funny, and smells great…wait, where was I going with that?

My phone pings from the sofa across the penthouse right as I'm about to take a bite out of the confectionary master-piece. I drop the cake back on the countertop and sprint across the room.

My heart leaps like a long jumper at the Olympics when I see Farrah's name on my screen. She hasn't responded to a

text since that day after our kiss. I've lost track of how long
ago that even was.

FARRAH

Why's he all wrong for me?

A grin slowly spreads across my face.
She. Texted. Back.
I knew she still liked me.

BRUCE

1. He's not blond. Amber and Remy told me
once you're obsessed with Frozen because
of Kristoff.

BRUCE

2. He's too serious. You need a man who
can make you laugh.

BRUCE

And 3. He doesn't live in D.C. And long-
distance relationships never work.

FARRAH

Hmmm 😏 interesting points. But I'm
obsessed with Frozen because of the
music.

BRUCE

Right. Like women are obsessed with
hockey because of the sport.

FARRAH

Umm. Some of them are. Not everyone is
there to ogle you, Bruce.

BRUCE

So, you admit to ogling me?

FARRAH

You're putting words in my mouth.

BRUCE

Why are you texting me when you're on a date?

FARRAH

It's 11pm. The date is over.

BRUCE

ahhh, so it didn't go well?

There's a pause for what feels like several minutes and then finally the typing bubble pops up.

FARRAH

It went fine. But there was no chemistry.

BRUCE

It's because he's not blond…isn't it?

FARRAH

FARRAH

Goodnight, Bruce.

BRUCE

Sweet dream, Yeux bleus.

With a grin on my face, I waltz back into the kitchen and devour my cupcake. I think about our conversation and wonder if she's lying about Frozen. I mean, the music is amazing. But come on…Kristoff *is* a stud.

———

The following afternoon we're all suited up and on the ice for practice. I feel energized and ready to work, my pads in place, the cool air hitting my face, and in my home away from home—my net.

West skates toward me, grinning. I spread my legs as far apart as they'll go and yell, "free five hole!"

West laughs and shoots a puck right between my skates and into the net. Remy, Colby and Mitch follow suit, everyone taking their free shot before we start taking things seriously.

"Hey, McBride!" Coach Young yells from center ice. "You're supposed to *block* the shots."

I face palm my goalie helmet with my padded hand. "What?! No one told me. I've been doing this all wrong for years!"

He rolls his eyes and skates off to the other end of the ice to talk to our power play coach.

The guys snicker—even Mitch, the serious one in our group.

West turns his attention to Remy. "Hey, Harrison came home all smiles last night. He said he and Farrah had a great time."

Remy's eyebrows scrunch together so slightly it's barely noticeable. "Oh yeah?" he looks away, focusing on the plexiglass behind my net. "Farrah went straight to bed, so I didn't get a chance to hear about it." His eye twitches.

Wow. Remy—our honest-to-a-fault team captain—just blatantly lied. Never, to my knowledge has he lied. And he's terrible at it to boot. West doesn't seem to notice and skates off smiling.

"Why'd you lie?" Mitch asks, his head tilted in curiosity.

"What? I didn't." Remy lies again, not making eye contact with any of us.

Colby snorts a laugh. "You're full of it, Cap'n. She wasn't into Harrison, was she?"

Remy blows out a breath, knowing he's caught. He looks over his shoulder where West is talking to Coach Young. "She said they had nothing to talk about, and he wasn't her type."

Mitch's eyebrows raise. "Really? I don't pretend to understand women—not even the one I'm married to—but it seems like Harrison would be every girl's type. Decent looking, successful, respectable."

Colby leans in. "Harrison is great, but the way you just described him sounds a little boring. Sometimes women want to be *dis*respected." He winks. "If you know what I mean."

Remy's jaw drops. "That's my sister."

Colby grimaces. "Right. Sorry."

"Was her ex the serious and responsible type?" Mitch asks.

Remy considers this. "Actually, yes. The guy had first-born son syndrome like nobody's business." He scoffs. "And being a firstborn son myself, I'm allowed to say that. He had a five-year plan, and a ten-year plan...and Farrah didn't comply with all those concrete plans."

Mitch nods. "So, maybe she's looking for someone the opposite of that. Someone more flexible."

I'm flexible. Really flexible. Not just my body, but in every way. I prefer to fly by the seat of my pants. Why stress about things you have no control over?

I would make sure my plans shaped around Farrah, and

not the other way around. Not for the first time, I'm over-whelmed with hatred for her ex-husband and how poorly he treated her. I've only heard bits and pieces, but it's enough for me to understand the guy was a complete idiot.

No one in their right mind would let go of Farrah Remington once they were lucky enough to have her.

IT'S FRIDAY AFTERNOON, the day of our first wedding event, arrives. Nella is taking her afternoon nap, and I'm taking advantage of the quiet time to pipe the finishing touches onto the gorgeous tiered cake that's nearly as tall as Mel. Once it's finished to perfection, I place it in the fridge. The S'mores flavor turned out incredible. I made a mini cake a few days ago for me and Amber to taste—and Nella…she had to have a taste, too.

The formal wedding is taking place at a large Catholic church in the historic district of Alexandria, one with old brick and stained-glass windows that will look so pretty in pictures. I had a grand wedding once, and if I ever get remarried, I'll do it all differently. I'd only invite a small amount of people, only the ones who mean the most to me. I wouldn't care so much about how I looked, or how the photos turned out. Instead I'd focus on the groom. I'd pay attention to how he acted and whether he cared about those around him. I'd watch to see how he treated the people helping plan everything, looking for signs of him brushing them off or brushing *me* off. I don't think I'd care about any of the details—except maybe the cake—because I'd want to be so enamored with the man I was marrying that everything else faded. Nothing else mattered. If I wouldn't marry the man wearing a paper bag in a grungy back alley as the venue...then he's not the one, babe.

I think of the couple getting married today and how in love they were, constantly looking at each other and touching the whole time we discussed cake options. I wonder if the groom is as nice as he seems, or if their marriage is doomed like so many others. But I don't think so. He seemed so eager to do whatever it took to make his bride happy. I hope the best for them, I really do. I don't want to be one of those women who turns cynical about romance and marriage—I've watched my parents love and support each other over my entire thirty-two years of life. I know real love exists.

The memory of my own wedding makes me think of my friend Megan, one of my bridesmaids and my closest friend in Ohio. Once she got married, Connor and I would go on double dates with her and her husband, and then over the years we added a few other couples to our group, as well.

I pull up my phone and shoot her a text.

FARRAH

Hey Megan! We haven't talked in ages. How are you?

To my surprise she responds right away. She's been hard to get a hold of lately.

MEGAN

Good! Just been super busy.

That's it. There's no *how are you?* No kind of leading question or statement to keep the conversation going.

Feeling strange about it, I pull up her Instagram page to see if she's posted anything. At first, I see nothing new on her page, so maybe she really has been busy. But then I click to see photos she's been tagged in. Her familiar smile, the same one from my old wedding photos, appears in a group photo. I smile at the photo until I see who else is in it…it's from last weekend and it's our old group, including Connor. Connor has his arm wrapped around a very young looking blonde, and she's nestled against his side. It's not Connor with another woman that sends a chill down my spine, but that everyone looks so comfortable together, like they've hung out a million times. Like they couldn't care less that I'm no longer there…that I'm easily replaceable.

The woman on Connor's arm is the one who posted the photo. I tap on her profile and it's private, but all my friends —former friends, I guess—are following her.

Exiting the app, I lock my phone screen and lay it on the counter. I can't shake the feeling that my friends chose Connor over me. I don't know if it's simply because he stayed in Ohio and I didn't, or if they always cared more about him than they did me. Either way, my heart is beating unsteadily, and I have to sit down to calm the ache in my heart. These couples were my friends for years. Megan was my bridesmaid…my confidant.

Soon the monitor on the counter comes to life, alerting me to Nella standing in her crib and smiling at the camera. "Auntie, I'm hungwy!"

Her smiling face is just what I needed to erase that Instagram photo from my mind.

I rush upstairs and lift her from her crib, then change her and we walk back downstairs to have a snack. I grab some grapes from the fridge and slice them up for Nella. The utility room door that connects to the garage swings open, and my brother walks into the room, his hair damp from his post-practice shower and wearing comfortable athletic wear.

"Hey, Farrah." He smiles, then spots Nella and truly lights up. "Hey, Nells. How's my girl?" Nella claps her hands together for her favorite person in the world. "Daddy's home!"

Watching these two makes my heart feel warm and full. Proof that you can love a child who's not your blood just as much as you would a birth child. It fills me with hope and promise and joy that momentarily erases the photo of my old friends from my head.

As Remy draws another giggle from Nella, I laugh.

If I met the right guy, maybe I could fall in love again? And if that happened, I'd love to experience pregnancy and nursing and all the mom things. But experience tells me it will take a while for me to get pregnant with PCOS. I'm already in my thirties, and there's no man in my life. But either way, even if I could get pregnant, I'd really like to adopt too. There's something precious about bringing a new person into the world with someone you love. It's a new life that's equal parts of you both. But to give a child who's waited their whole life to experience being someone's entire world… to be surrounded by love and comfort? That seems so poignant to me.

"How was today?" Remy asks, drawing me from my thoughts.

"Good," I say. "Nella and I went for a walk, and we saw lots of birds today. You know how she loves birds."

Remy chuckles and nods.

"Then she napped while I finished the cake. And now I need to go make myself presentable." I use one hand to gesture at my dog-hair covered leggings and oversized tee.

My brother smirks. "I hear ya; get out of here. Nella and I are taking Amber on a surprise date tonight."

I grab my phone off the countertop. "Really? What are you guys doing?"

"Well, it's kind of a date for Amber *and* Nella," he admits. "We're going to see Disney on Ice."

"Oh my gosh, they'll both love that."

He smiles. "I hope so, I got VIP tickets so we can meet the characters after the show. I'll say hi to Kristoff for you."

I laugh. "Thanks, bro. Will you get his number for me?"

Remy wrinkles his nose. "Absolutely not."

"Rude. I'll see you later…you guys have fun." Kissing Nella on the top of her head, I say goodbye and head out the front door and follow the path to the side of the garage where a set of white stairs leads up to my apartment. Once inside, I turn on the Frozen soundtrack, just because the conversation with Remy made me want to listen. I *do* listen to other music…sometimes.

While I do my makeup my mind wanders to my text conversation with Bruce last weekend. A rush of pleasure shoots through me, just as it did last weekend when he texted asking how my date was. I shouldn't like the attention, and I shouldn't be encouraging it by texting him back. It's madness, and irresponsible. But I'd be lying if I didn't admit it's nice to have the attention of a handsome and talented man. A man who commands the attention of an entire bar without knowing it, a man whose charisma and charm makes everyone want to be around him. And to have it all directed at me? Heat rushes to my cheeks.

He acted *jealous*. Bruce McBride, who can have any woman he wants.

Connor never acted jealous. Ever. I always thought it was a good thing, that it meant he trusted me. But I think he just didn't worry because he didn't believe I could ever attract the attention of another man.

I chose to ignore so many signs of his lack of kindness I chose not to see. Like how it bothered him that I gained weight while we were trying for a baby. Every month we didn't conceive, I got a little sadder and little curvier. Not only did he give me the German meat pie nickname, but he once bought me exercise equipment for my birthday…and I told myself he simply cared about my health. Any treats I bought would magically disappear—I thought he just finished them himself. And our last Valentine's Day together, the man gave me a size four dress and said he couldn't wait for me to wear it. And I stupidly convinced myself he must not have known my actual dress size.

With a sigh, I push thoughts of my ex out of my head. He doesn't deserve any space in there any longer. I slip into my new black skirt, it's a stretchy pencil skirt number that hugs my curves perfectly. I pair it with a collared, black button-down shirt, tucked in and secured with a black, leather belt around my waist. I look in the mirror and like the final result. I'm finally enjoying dressing up the way I used to and feeling good in my own skin. I'm not an itty-bitty teenager anymore, and that's okay.

Sliding on my black flats, I head back to the bathroom for a hair clip, so my long hair won't get in my way while serving cake tonight.

Finally ready for my night, I head back to the big house to load up the wedding cake.

———

"What do you mean you can't make it?" I ask, pressing my

phone to my ear so I can hear Mel more clearly over the crowd of weddinggoers.

"I'm so sorry, Farrah," Mel says, her voice small and weak. "I was setting up everything for the wedding all day and started getting tired. I thought I just needed a quick rest, but I must have a stomach bug because I can't stop throwing up."

I soften at her words, knowing Mel wouldn't leave me to run an event by myself if she could help it. "Hey, it's okay. Is West home to take care of you?"

"Yeah, but I'm sending him over to help with the wedding."

"No, he should be there with you. What if you need something?"

She whimpers like she's about to be sick. "I'll be fine."

I sigh. "Mel, stop. It's okay. I'll call Andie and Noel; I'm sure one of them can help."

"Are you sure?" Mel asks.

"Yes, I'm sure."

"Call me back if anything changes!"

"I will," I tell her. "I promise. Don't worry, everything will be okay."

We hang up, and my hands shake with nerves. Our first wedding event and I'm all alone. Everything is *not* going to be okay.

EIGHT

BRUCE

MY PHONE RINGS from its place on the couch beside me, it's Andie's name flashing across the screen. Smiling, I pause *When Harry Met Sally* and answer. "Well, well, well. How's my favorite blonde doing?"

"I'm telling Noel you said that."

"Don't you dare," I gasp in mock outage.

Andie tsks. "Okay, mister. I'm calling in the final favor you owe me, and you're actually going to like this one."

I groan. "Sorry, babes, I'm actually really busy right now."

She tuts. "Sure, you are. Which romcom are you watching?"

I swallow. Andie knows me too well, apparently. "*When Harry Met Sally.*"

"Oh! That's a good one!" I hear Mitch whispering something to her and she shushes him. "Listen, here's what I need. Mel is sick and can't help Farrah with their wedding event tonight. Farrah is busy with the cake table and Mel needs me to fill in running the rest of the event. The problem is, Mel does the work of a dozen people, and I need someone else there helping me orchestrate everything."

I perk up, sitting forward on the couch. "Did you say Farrah will be there?"

She laughs. "Told you you'd like this favor."

"Text me the address and I'll be on my way."

"Okay. Oh!" She says the word like she just remembered something. "You need to wear all black. Business casual. Don't get too fancy, Bruce. I mean it! You can't upstage the bride."

I give her a haughty laugh, the laugh I think a finance bro would make. "Me? Upstage the bride? Please."

"Don't. Get. Too. Fancy," she repeats, enunciating every word.

"Fine, I won't. See you soon."

As soon as I hang up, Andie texts me the address of a Catholic cathedral about forty minutes away with traffic. I hope Farrah will be okay until we get there, poor thing.

I rush to get dressed in the least fancy black ensemble I own and am on my way within minutes of Andie's call.

Forty-five minutes later, I arrive at the church and walk inside in search of Farrah and Andie. I walk through the broad, wooden doors to the church and come face to face with a black-haired bride. Her eyes widen when she sees me.

The man beside her, presumably her father, gasps. "You invited Bruce McBride to your wedding?" the older gentleman asks the bride.

"No, I didn't," she answers, then turns back to me. "But you're more than welcome!"

Just then, the cathedral doors open to a room filled with people. Each pew is full of smiling guests.

The bride and her father smile at each other and begin making their way slowly down the aisle.

I'm watching them, touched by the whole scene and the beautiful flowers lining the aisle, when I hear an angry *psp*. I turn to find Andie at the top of a set of stairs and her expression is annoyed. "Bruce! Get downstairs now! You're not a guest; you're staff."

I tut, making my way over to her. "I'm too pretty to be staff."

She rolls her eyes, but she's fighting a smile. "Get that pretty face downstairs."

I follow her to find a terrified-looking Farrah behind the cake table in the reception area. The basement of the church isn't your typical dark and depressing underground space; instead it seems to only be half underground and has windows lining its walls. The large space boasts the same floral arrangements as the cathedral, and round tables are set with fine place settings. My jaw drops as I realize Mel must have done this all on her own today. At practice West said she was here setting up while Farrah was watching Nella.

That tiny woman is a powerhouse.

Farrah's blue eyes widen when she sees me, then she turns to Andie. "What is he doing here?"

"We needed more help!" Andie says, resting her hands on her hips.

Farrah comes out from behind the table, and I have to work really hard not to let my jaw drop again. Is she wearing the pencil skirt, or is the pencil skirt wearing her?

It fits her body in an unfair way. It contours to her hips and butt and makes me want to be wrapped around her too. *I'm jealous of a skirt.*

"We could've managed," Farrah says pointedly. "Mel already set everything up; we just have to make sure the line goes smoothly and tear everything down, and—"

"Wow, that sounds like a lot," I muse. "Good thing there's a big, strapping man here to help." I wink at her, and she blushes.

Good, she's not immune to me.

Andie sighs heavily. "It is a lot, and Bruce was more than willing to help. Plus, Noah is at a sleepover tonight and I want to get home before Mitch falls asleep. We never have the house to ourselves."

I wrinkle my nose. "Gross. You needed me to help tonight so you can get home for hanky panky with your grouchy husband?"

Andie smirks. "If he gets hanky panky, he's not grouchy. So, yes."

A laugh bubbles out of Farrah and the sound fills my chest in a way that makes me light, like a balloon that might fly away.

Andie's gaze lasers in on me. "I told you not to get fancy."

I look down at my outfit, high-waisted pleated black trousers and a 1950's style black sweater tucked in. Paired with some black leather oxfords, I look like I'm ready to light my pipe and read a newspaper. It's an older style, but with my haircut and ear piercing I think I give it a modernized vibe.

"This was the least fancy outfit in my closet."

"You're such a diva, Bruce," Andie teases. "Now, I need you to stand here at the beginning of the cake line and make sure everyone's staying single file to make the process seamless."

Farrah eyes me with those stunning blues of hers. "I really don't need help over here, Andie. He can do something else."

"Everything is taken care of," Andie says. "Now accept the help and thank me later."

Farrah shakes her head.

Andie strides away from us and starts up a conversation with the caterer across the room.

I take my place exactly where Andie told me to stand and Farrah begins cutting into large sheet cakes, but not the big wedding cake.

"I cannot wait to taste your cake," I say, not realizing it sounds dirty at first.

Farrah's cheeks turn a violent shade of red. Like she's half embarrassed and half angry with me for saying something so salacious. "Bruce."

"Sorry." I grimace. "I meant *the* cake. But I know your lips taste amazing. I definitely remember that."

Still red, she holds up a palm to stop me. "Just stop talking."

"Good idea," I admit. "So, what exactly do you need me to do?"

"Just stand there and look pretty," she says dryly, turning away and continuing to cut the sheet cakes in neat rows. "You'll probably get snatched up by some young ladies and be sitting at their table within a few minutes anyway."

I'm taken aback for a second, wondering what the hell she's talking about. Then I remember the general's daughters from a few weeks back and how they latched onto me the moment they spotted me. They were fun to talk to, for sure. But I wasn't trying to draw attention to myself. And I kept trying to get away.

I prop a hip against the cake table and look down at Farrah. "Ah, I see. You're jealous."

Her eyes dart up to meet mine and her mouth pops open. "I am not."

"You are. But you don't need to be. I've been trying to get you to pay attention to me for over a year. I keep trying to tell you how good we could be together, but you won't have it. You always push me away. So, stop being jealous and go out with me already."

Her chest rises and falls rapidly, her mouth popping open then snapping shut. The woman doesn't know what to say or what to do at my honest admission. It was a bold move, I understand that. But I'm sick of dancing around this. Tired of having an elephant in the room.

"Bruce, we can't. You know that."

I turn and rest my palms on the surface of the table, leaning in so our faces are close. "Why not?"

She backs away. "It was one kiss. That's all. You barely even know me."

"Really? Are all your kisses like that one? Because it didn't feel like just a kiss to me. It felt like *the* kiss."

"You're too young for me," she blurts.

I scoff. "Is that the reason you tell yourself? I'm not too young, I'm only five years younger than you."

She frowns, her eyes moving away from my face and down to the cake in front of her. "You need to move on. There are too many things I can't give you."

"Like what?"

She ignores me.

"At least give me a real reason. Just one." I blow out a breath. "Then I'll leave you alone."

She slowly looks up at me, her eyes meeting mine. Her expression tells me we're on the verge of finally getting somewhere, like she's teetering on the edge of something. Of giving in, or finally telling me the reason she won't even give me a chance. I wait with bated breath, and her mouth finally opens to say something.

"Okay, guys!" Andie interrupts, clapping her hands together. "The bride and groom just kissed, so get in position and be ready for the crowd."

CHAPTER
NINE

FARRAH

I'M SERVING cake after the guests have eaten their main course and Bruce is keeping the buffet-style line running seamlessly. He ignores the gaping mouths of the men—and the bedroom eyes of the women—as they pass him. Probably wondering why D.C.'s star goalie is a glorified wedding attendant tonight.

My brother has always shied away from the spotlight, and I've always been very aware how uncomfortable the attention made him. I'm a sponge for people's feelings and struggle not to internalize them. But where watching Remy always made me edgy and nervous, watching Bruce puts me at ease, and I keep finding myself smiling. He's working the room like a pro, and it's refreshing not to soak up another person's nerves on top of my own.

I'm having more fun at tonight's event than I have at any of our others, and I'm desperately clinging to that feeling instead of focusing on the words Bruce said out loud before the chaos began.

"Really? Are all your kisses like that one? Because it didn't feel like just a kiss to me. It felt like the *kiss."*

I didn't even have time to give him a good reason why we can't be together. I realize all my excuses seem silly to a person who hasn't had his heart completely shattered by the one person they trusted to protect them forever. And I don't trust my instincts anymore because of it.

My heart tells me Bruce is a great guy, and that he'd never intentionally hurt anyone, not even a creepy spider scurrying across his bathroom floor. I could picture him being like *oh, hey Mr. Spider, how ya doing tonight?*

But I also thought that about Connor. Except the spider part…Connor always hated spiders.

"How's it going over here?" Andie's voice makes me jump and she chuckles. "Sorry, didn't mean to scare you. You looked deep in thought." Her eyes flit to Bruce. "I wonder what you were thinking about?"

"I was not thinking about Bruce, if that's what you're hinting at," I say quickly, my voice defensive and negating what I just said.

She hums. "Okay. But he looks pretty good tonight. Not as hot as Mitch, obviously." Andie smirks. "But he's a catch, ya know?"

I smile at the next person in the line and hand them a slice of wedding cake.

I respond to my annoying friend through the side of my mouth, trying not to draw attention to our conversation. "I'm sure he'll make someone a fine husband someday."

Just then, Bruce turns and spots us talking and shoots us a brilliant smile. Pearly white teeth—courtesy of dental implants, I'm guessing. But still gorgeous no matter how they got there.

The earring in his left ear twinkles in the dim, romantic lighting and why is that little diamond stud so attractive? He's wearing the hell out of those pleated high-waisted pants as well. They cling to a butt so fantastic it could only belong to a professional hockey player. It takes a lot of leg and glute strength to do what he does on the ice, and it's hard not to stare.

I find myself wondering if he has any tattoos.

Beside me, Andie clears her throat. "You seem a little distracted, Farrah."

I whip my head to look at her. "I'm sorry, did you need something? Because I think I have it covered over here." I give her a polite smile and she laughs and holds her hands up in front of her.

"Okay, okay. I'll stop teasing. I just adore you both and think you'd be a cute couple. But I promise I won't mention it again."

I love Andie, but I don't believe for a second that she'll never mention it again. There's one friend in every group with no filter, and Andie is ours.

At around ten, the party is barely winding down. The wedding party is still on the dance floor, and the bride and groom don't look tired.

I'm sitting behind the cake table, relieved to finally rest, when Andie marches over once more. She glances down at the watch on her wrist. "All right, I'm heading home. Bruce agreed to tear down and clean up."

I arch an eyebrow. "Why would he agree to that?"

Andie grimaces. "Actually, we made a bargain a while ago and he owed me two favors. I used my last one tonight."

"Bruce McBride owed you favors, and you used one on *this*?" I would've saved those favors up forever, waiting for the perfect time to cash them in.

She grins. "Like I said earlier, I never get a night with Mitch without my brother around. I plan on staying up all night and enjoying it." Andie winks. "I'm not wasting any energy tearing down tables and chairs."

I snort an undignified laugh. "Fair enough." I somber quickly realizing with absolute terror that this will leave me and Bruce alone in this building for hours tonight.

Andie's expression turns sympathetic. "If you don't feel safe with Bruce, I can stay. I'd never want you to be uncomfortable just so I can go have a night of unbridled passion."

I laugh. "Who even says unbridled passion?"

Andie leans in. "That's lingo they use in romance novels. Do you read?"

"I haven't read a book in ages," I admit.

"Oh, girl. I'll send you a list of my favorites."

"Okay." I nod. "I'd enjoy relaxing with a good book."

She rubs her hands together conspiratorially.

"Also, don't worry about me, I know Bruce is harmless." I pause, thinking of the right words. "It's just that he flirts so much, and it…well, it makes me kind of nervous."

Andie tilts her head and gives me another sympathetic gaze. "I get it. When a hot man flirts with us, it's hard not to revert back to a sixteen-year-old."

I breathe a sigh of relief. "Yes! I'm glad you get it."

Andie leans in and gives me a hug. "All right, text me if you need anything, okay? I'll keep my phone on."

Bruce walks over from where he was conversing with a few of the groomsmen who are clearly big fans of his. "You heading home to Mitch The Machine?"

"Yes, I am," she answers with a waggle of her eyebrows.

Bruce shakes his head. "You kids have fun. I'll make sure everything is squared away here."

"Perfect," she says. "Just tear everything down and the rental company will pick it up in the morning. Easy peasy."

With a wave, she's off, and I'm left alone with Bruce

McBride. He sits beside me in an empty, white folding chair and we watch as the bride and groom dance together.

"That's the dream," he says with a sigh. "Finding your person."

I turn to look at him. "You're a pro athlete, Bruce. I'd think it would be easy for you to find that."

He shrugs. "It might be easy to find someone who wants to sleep with you, but it's not easy to find *that*."

I glance back at the bride and groom who are staring lovingly into each other's eyes as a tender love song plays from the speakers. They're locked in a sweet embrace for a slow dance and clearly blocking out the rest of the world. It looks like they would literally die for each other. It's written all over their faces. And I realize Bruce is totally right, because Connor *never* looked at me like that.

Half an hour later, the bride and groom leave for their honeymoon, and the wedding guests quickly follow their lead and head home for the night.

I sigh in relief when everyone's gone. Except the custodian who's upstairs somewhere and, of course, myself and the giant hockey goalie.

Starting on the cake table, I place leftover cake back inside the boxes. I then follow Bruce around the room folding the black tablecloths he's removing from each table he breaks down. His sinewy arms are made for this job, he quickly has half the tables stored on their racks.

I'm folding another tablecloth when he yells a word in French, something that sounds like *merde*. I rush over to him and see his finger is bleeding. Without thinking, I cup his hand in mine to get a better look. "Are you okay?"

He grimaces. "Yeah, sorry. I just pinched my finger in the table leg joint."

"Ouch," I say. "We have a first aid kit. I'll grab a band

aid." I rush back to the cake table where I left the first aid kit with my purse. Mel insists on bringing this thing to every event, and I never understood why until now. It's a minor injury, but we can't have blood trickling onto the rental tables and chairs. Grabbing Neosporin and a bandage, I head back over to Bruce. He's seated in a wooden chair that looks too small for him, and holding his finger up so it doesn't bleed on anything.

I take his hand again, enjoying the warmth of his skin more than I should. It only takes a minute to bandage the finger, but I can feel Bruce's eyes watching me closely. It's hard to work under his scrutiny…er, appreciation, perhaps.

When I'm done, I move to draw my hand away, but he closes his hand around it. I look up at him and meet his gaze.

"Thank you," he says, then slowly releases my hand, his fingers trailing along my wrist in the process.

The feel of his skin and the heat of his gaze are mesmerizing, making it hard to look away, but I force myself to. Swallowing, I step back and put some distance between us. He stands and finishes breaking down the round table that pinched the skin on his index finger.

We were working in amicable silence before, but now the air feels thick and uncomfortable. Too hot—or too something.

"So," I say, breaking the eerie quiet in the formerly busy hall. "I've heard goalies are superstitious. Is that true?"

He huffs a laugh. "Oh, yeah. Afraid so."

My eyebrows raise. "Really? What are your superstitions?"

He twists his lips to the side. "Can I trust you not to tell anyone?"

I roll my eyes. "You should know by now I can go a long time without telling secrets."

His eyes twinkle. "True." He sighs and stands a table up on its side. "First, my truck. My parents gave it to me right before a big game my senior year of high school. It was the best game I'd ever played. I still drive her to every game."

"Her?"

"Porte-bonheur." Bruce smiles, clearly still in love with his truck. "It means lucky charm."

I laugh. "You think you'll ever replace her?"

He shakes his head. "I know she'll quit running eventually. But I'll keep driving Porte as long as I can."

"Where are you from again?"

"Quebec City."

"Do you still have family there?" I ask, wondering if he misses them as much as I miss my parents. Even though they're only a six-hour drive from here.

"I do. My parents live there, and so does my older sister and her husband and new baby." He smiles fondly, but there's something in his eyes that hints at more. Behind those charming blues, there's a depth I'd never noticed before.

"That must be hard, being so far away."

He nods and begins rolling the table toward the rack. "It is, but they come to a few games a year, and I try to get out there every summer." Bruce lifts the large table onto the rack like it weighs nothing then strides toward the next table. "Besides, I have plenty here to keep me busy."

"You mean your friends?"

"Yeah, but I also have a little brother here." He sees my look of shock and laughs. "No, not like that. I'm his sponsor in the Big Brothers Big Sisters program. I also got certified to do respite care...which is just really short-term care whenever his foster parents need a break. Sometimes he stays with me for a night or two."

I melt instantly. I'm a puddle. Even my eyes are a mess, instantly feeling a little watery. "Really? When did you start sponsoring him?"

He wrinkles his nose. "Well, actually…I signed up soon after Amber and Remy got married."

I study him, searching for clues as to why that would've spurred this man to volunteer and spend his spare time with a kiddo in need.

Bruce must notice my concentration, because he blows out a breath. "These guys are my family, ya know? And it sort of felt like everyone had a new family. Except for me. So, I figured why not help a kid who needs someone?"

Is this man literally perfect? No, of course he's not. But if I thought managing my attraction to Bruce McBride after kissing him was hard…it's ten times harder now.

"I completely understand that, actually," I admit.

I understand more than he might realize. Especially after seeing that photo of all my friends back in Ohio. I feel like I've lost a piece of my heart and I'm starting over in every aspect of my life. I find myself wondering if Megan and I will ever talk again. Like *really* talk…not just exchange a few texts.

Even here in D.C., my new friends are amazing, but they're all married and will likely have kids soon and be busy, while I remain a childless divorcee. I realize there's more to life than marriage and kids… It's just that that's all I ever wanted. But I'm finding joy in discovering other things in life I'm passionate about, like baking and running this business with Mel. I'm finding peace in leaving behind old friendships and relishing in new ones. I'm finding content-ment in being an aunt instead of a mom. This new life has grown me in ways I never thought possible, and I never would've expected it a few years ago, but I find that I'm grateful for the changes that were forced on me.

Bruce studies me. "Do you miss Ohio?"

I roll my lips, thinking of my answer. "It's complicated. I miss my parents and my sister. But I don't miss my ex." I pause, thinking of Megan. "I miss some of my friends… I thought we'd stay in contact, but we haven't. I'm starting to realize I wasn't as important to my old friends as I thought."

His blond eyebrows raise slightly. "You don't talk to your old friends anymore?"

I sigh, allowing air to fill my lungs before blowing it out and steadying myself. "Do you ever feel like you're the only one who'd actually leave your phone on all night in case a friend needed you? Right after my divorce, my friends used to tell me to call them if I needed to talk. But they never picked up when I called." I swallow with difficulty, emotion beginning to well up in my throat. "I want people in my life who will be there for me. Day or night. The same way I would be there for them."

His expression softens. "I'm sorry." Bruce meets my gaze. "I know we're not exactly best friends. But I'd leave my phone on all night for you, Farrah."

CHAPTER
TEN

BRUCE

The D.C. Eagles #1 Fan Page On Hockeyisbetterthanfoot-ball.com

Todd Ferguson: BRUCE MCBRIDE! BEST GOALIE IN THE LEAGUE!

Craig Nottingham: Well, at least tonight he was. Finally earning that F&#* 10 mil contract.

Mandie Banderson: Wow Craig. Do you kiss your mama with that mouth?

Craig Nottingham: No, I don't. kissing my mother as an adult would be weird. I guess we're not all weirdos like you, Mandie.

Mandie Banderson: It was a joke!

Craig Nottingham: Also, my mother passed last year, so you're an asshole.

Todd Ferguson: Can we get back to appreciating our incredible goalie?

Harry Johnson: I'm with you, Todd! McBride played amazing tonight. Dude deserves a raise.

I LAUGH and stick my phone back in my jeans pocket as I wait for the ice cream cones from the food stand near the Washington Monument. The fans aren't too sassy this time, since we won our first game in round one of Stanley Cup Playoffs last night.

"You're weird," Jackson says, staring at me with his big, brown eyes.

I'm with my little brother today, I haven't seen him all month with all the away games and then helping Farrah last weekend.

I ruffle his brown hair with my hand, and he pushes it away. "You can't call me weird when I'm getting you ice cream."

Jackson snorts a laugh. "Yes, I can."

The preteen energy is strong in this ten-year-old. I bet he'd get along with Noah, Andie's little brother, if they ever met.

The older man behind the food cart smiles at us. "Two chocolate cones with marshmallow ice cream?"

"Yes, sir," I tell him, taking both and handing one to Jackson.

It's a pretty spring day in D.C. and we're on the water in front of the Washington monument surrounded by cherry blossoms. April in the Capitol is my favorite. And not only because the playoffs are upon us. It's the crisp air and the flowers, like everything starts new...fresh.

Jackson and I find a bench in front of the water and start on our ice cream. The marshmallow paired with the chocolate cone reminds me of the S'mores wedding cake Farrah made...except her cake was way better.

"Why are you smiling?" Jackson asks. I didn't realize he was watching me

"Well, Jackson. Someday, when you're older, you'll meet a girl who randomly makes you smile like an idiot."

He scoffs. "Girls are disgusting."

I give him a wry look. "I'll give it two years before you change your mind about that."

Jackson looks away, staring at his melting ice cream. "Mom says girls are nothing but drama."

I shoot him what I hope is a sympathetic smile. "Sometimes boys are the dramatic ones. Not all girls are dramatic. The one I'm thinking about isn't. She's kind and thoughtful."

He nods. "I think my mom could be like that." His voice is so sad, I wish I could hug him, but Jackson is very anti-hug, and I respect that.

"How is your mom?" I ask.

He shrugs and licks his ice cream to keep it from dripping. "She's good; she said she's working hard and hoping to be released early. She calls me every week." He smiles. "She's supposed to get released in a year."

Leaning forward, I rest my elbows on my knees so I can look at him. "That's great, man. Are you excited?"

"Yeah. But I worry she'll make bad friends again and go back to prison."

His mom has been in and out of prison the past couple of years. Which means he's been in and out of foster care. I feel for him.

I don't know much about my birth parents, but my birth mom contacted me once when I was around Jackson's age. I think she wanted to see me just once out of curiosity and obviously didn't want a relationship past that. But that was fine with me. I've been with my adoptive parents since I was an infant. I was one of the lucky ones, getting placed with kind, wonderful people from the start.

"How's school going?" I ask, getting the impression he'd like to change the subject.

He perks up at my question, his eyes growing round with excitement. "Good!" he opens his mouth to say more, then his shoulders droop. "Hey, do you think chess is nerdy?"

I make a *pshhh* sound. "Hell no. The only people who think chess is nerdy are the people who can't play."

He grins at that. "You think so?"

"I know so. Chess is a cool game. I'm terrible at it, though. Could you teach me?"

He nods. "Yeah, I just joined the chess team at school."

I clap him on the back. "That's awesome, man."

"Yeah," he smiles, then looks down. "I'm really good at it, but some of my old friends told me only losers play chess."

The instant protective instincts I feel toward this kid are intense and hard to push down. I want to find these kids' parents and tell them they're raising a bunch of jerk-wads.

"You should do what you love, and it's even better if you're great at what you love."

He elbows me in the side. "Like you with hockey?"

I huff air onto my nails and rub them on my shirt, throwing him a cocky grin. "Exactly. Did you catch my game last night?"

He laughs. "No, sorry. You know I'm a baseball guy."

"I'll convert you to hockey one of these days."

He squints as he thinks. "I'll make a deal with you. You beat me at chess, and I'll watch a hockey game."

"Deal."

I hold my hand out and he shakes it with a firm grip.

———

After my afternoon with Jackson, I head over to Remy's house for a barbeque. I'm the last one to arrive since I'm the only guy who doesn't live in suburbia.

I park off to the side of his house, where I can see the stairs that lead up to Farrah's apartment and hope to catch a glimpse of her. Sometimes she joins these team get-togethers, and other times she doesn't. I haven't seen her or talked to her since the wedding a week ago. We connected that evening more than ever before, really getting to know each other. It felt more like a date than it should have. But I cling to every moment I can steal, every fact I can learn.

Opening and closing the squeaky door of my old pickup, I don't bother to lock it. No one will want to steal this thing in a ritzy neighborhood filled with Porsches and Land Rovers. Doing a quick review of the outfit I've been wearing all day, I decide the green tee, fashionably distressed jeans, and leather sneakers aren't too bad. And I didn't spill any ice cream on myself earlier, so, in the event I do see Farrah, at least I'll look good.

I stride toward the front door and let myself in. Country music is playing through the speakers of Remy's home, but chatter and laughter can be heard over the music. Something smells amazing, probably marinated meat… but also something sweeter.

Andie sees me first. "Brucey!"

"Hey, babes," I say, walking over and pulling her into a side-hug. Mitch glares at me.

Noel stands and holds her hand up for a high-five. Colby is beside her and does the same.

Remy and Amber walk into the living room from the kitchen where they must've been preparing the food.

"Hey, man," Remy says.

Amber dances over, grooving to the country music.

"Glad you're finally here, Bruce. The party can finally start." She hugs me.

"Where's my bestie?" I ask, looking from her to Remy.

Amber looks over her shoulder, into the kitchen. "Farrah, do you have Nella?"

"Yeah, she's with me!" Farrah's voice yells back, making my heart skip a beat. *She's here.*

Farrah strolls into the living room with a floral apron fastened around her neck and waist, and little Nella—aka my bestie—settled on her hip.

Nella's little face lights up when she sees me and she grunts and wriggles, trying to get down. Farrah's gaze meets mine, her eyes widen, and her cheeks turn pink. Does her reaction inflate my ego? Absolutely.

When Farrah release her, Nella dashes across the room. I catch the little redheaded spitfire in my arms and lift her in the air above my head. Nella shrieks and laughs. Amber and Remy shake their heads.

"Glad you finally have someone around who likes to play as much as you do," Remy says dryly.

I place Nella back on the ground, but her tiny hand stays latched onto one of mine and she leads me over to her play kitchen. "Bwuce," she says. "Let's bake." Nella thrusts a toy cookie pan full of wooden chocolate chip cookies into my hands.

"Yes, ma'am." I get busy right away, pretending to shape the cookies and placing them onto the correct Velcro slots. "These are my favorite."

She grins up at me as I finish the cookie tray and slide it into the play oven. I glance over at her to find her staring at me. She reaches up and places her small, sticky hand on my cheek. "Bwuce is my fwiend."

Is my chin quivering? No, I'm a big, tough manly man. Of course my chin isn't quivering.

CHAPTER
ELEVEN
FARRAH

LEANING my back against the oven, I take a deep breath and savor a moment of quiet after seeing Bruce again. All week long I've been thinking that maybe I was wrong about me and Bruce. After talking while tearing down after the wedding and the conversation that came so easily, I thought maybe I should give this thing a chance.

But watching him with Nella makes me realize I was completely wrong about that. This man is a natural with children. He was meant to be a dad. Bruce will probably have a dozen kids and play with all of them and read stories to them and jump on the trampoline with them.

I have no place in that. What am I going to offer him? That we could date and have fun and then if things went well maybe we could have kids. Someday, probably years from now. If I can even get pregnant. Connor and I tried for *years*. And he got tested, confirming the fertility issue lies solely with me. A heavy weight for a person to have on their shoulders.

No. I won't take years away from him and his hypothetical children. He needs someone younger and healthier than me.

It's good for me to be reminded of this, actually. Before I let my heart get away from me...again.

The last thing I would ever do to myself is set myself up for disappointment again. And that's exactly what would happen with me and Bruce. He thinks he wants me because he's never had to chase someone before, but once he catches me, he would soon realize we would never work.

I startle when Mel sidles up next to me and slings her arm around my shoulder. "Are you okay?" she asks.

I blink. "Yes, I'm fine. I was just thinking I need to go check on the angel food cake."

By her expression, we both know I'm lying. "How are you? Been feeling better?" I study her face; she looks a little pale. I hope she's all right.

She quickly looks away from me and down at her shoes. "Uh, yeah. I'm great. Feeling good."

With sudden clarity that I realize why she was sick and why she's acting strange. She mentioned she's been tired lately; she was sick last weekend, and her skin is pale. When Connor and I were trying to get pregnant, I googled pregnancy symptoms every month, and I can't believe I just now put it together.

"Oh, my gosh. Mel...are you?"

Her eyes widen dramatically. I take her hands and drag her—gently—but further into the kitchen where no one can see us.

Mel's eyes fill with tears. "I'm sorry, Farrah. I wanted to tell you last weekend, but I just didn't know if it would make you sad. I know you tried for so long, and—"

I hold up a hand, cutting her off. "Mel, people get pregnant. You and West will be amazing parents. And I'm so happy for you."

I pull her into a hug, but my eyes are stinging as I try not to cry. Because it does hurt a little, but not as much as it would have when Connor and I were still trying. I'm glad now I didn't have children with him; that would've just made things more difficult. Some higher power obviously knew it wasn't the right time. I think I'm more hurt she felt like she couldn't tell me, that she thought I'd be sad about her pregnancy.

I don't want my friends tiptoeing around me.

When I pull back, I see her eyes are red, the same way mine probably are. "I've been so sick," she admits. "And we have five events in the next two months."

"We'll figure it out."

"West can help when he's home," she offers, her expression eager to please. "I have everything organized and laid out. How'd it go with Bruce, by the way?"

The corner of my mouth lifts. "He did great. He definitely draws attention, though."

She grimaces then laughs. "Well, he's bigger than everyone in most rooms, so."

We both laugh.

I step away from Mel to remove my apron and hang it on a hook next to the refrigerator as all the girls file into the kitchen. I find my sister-in-law's gaze and smile. "I think I'm going to head upstairs and have some me time."

"What?! No! I barely get to see you anymore," Noel says.

Amber smiles softly. "I know you've been watching Nella all day, so I understand if you want to go relax. But we would love to have you stay if you want to!"

"Please stay!" Andie and Noel beg. Both are tugging on my arms like toddlers.

The truth is I *do* want to stay, but Bruce is so distracting. And I don't want to think about Bruce.

Andie gets right up in my face, her twinkly eyes bright and mischievous. "You can't leave. We're playing NHL on the Xbox, and the guys aren't allowed to help."

A slow grin spreads across my face. "Okay, fine. I can't resist watching that unfold."

Andie claps and jumps up and down and Noel pulls me into a hug. "Oh, the guys are going to hate it, it's going to be amazing!"

A moment later, the guys come sniffing around to see if the food's ready and we make a buffet across the massive island in the kitchen. Remy smoked meat, Amber roasted potatoes, and everyone else brought various sides. I made an angel food cake with homemade whipped topping.

Once we've all eaten, we head back into the living room where Amber, Noel, Andie and Mel quickly take up residence on the large couch and get the Xbox going. The husbands, and Bruce—who's holding a very content Nella—stagger toward them, all of them looking like they're dreading what's about to unfold.

There are four controllers connected, and Mel, Andie, Amber, and Noel sit on the rug in front of the TV and pick them up. Noel holds hers upside down like she's never seen a controller before, and Colby covers his eyes with his hands.

Andie starts the game up, and it pulls up the guys' teams. She and Amber are on one team and Mel and Noel are on the other.

Andie bites her bottom lip as she looks at the players then selects a few and switches them out with other players. Mitch groans loudly. "You switched Miller for Rumpke? You've gotta be kidding me. Miller is a ninety-nine!"

She ignores him, then Mel takes over and switches the goalie for her and Noel's team. I hear Bruce gasp from behind me and turn to look at him. "McNulty has a terrible save percentage. Isn't his OVR like fifty-one?"

I have no idea what OVR is, but fifty-one must be bad?

Soon, the game takes off, and the girls are truly terrible at it. No one has scored, and so far, their players just keep running into each other and the boards. The best part is watching the guys come apart on the couch behind where their wives are sitting. West's hands are in his hair as he grits his teeth and mumbles, "They're ruining our top scores."

Remy whispers back, "I know."

Noel gives up with a sigh. "Farrah, take over for me?" her eyes are pleading so I take the controller and move closer to the TV.

I played video games when I was a kid, but it's been a while, and the buttons are different. I manage to take my player toward the defensive zone and shoot the puck toward the goalie. It almost goes in, but the goalie knocks it away.

"Farrah, not bad!" Mel encourages.

Andie rams her player into me from behind. "Take that, Farrah!"

I snort a laugh. "I see you play just like your husband."

"Harsh," Mitch says from the couch.

I worry my bottom lip and wiggle the knobs on my controller, unable to get my player to do what I want. It doesn't help that Andie keeps running me over with her player.

I'm pressing the same button over and over when a warm hand covers mine. I look over my shoulder to find Bruce sitting on the floor right behind me. He brings both arms around me and places a hand over each of mine, his thumbs showing mine where to sit on the controller and how to move the little wands. My whole body feels fuzzy with him so close; I can't hear a word he's saying.

"Like this," he says, repeating himself. His voice low and smooth as butter. "See?" His breath warms my neck, but everyone is watching, so I act like this is totally normal and remind myself to breathe. Just a friend helping a friend.

I try to do what he showed me, and my player is finally moving back in the direction I wanted. Bruce casually moves away from me, taking his warmth with him.

I exhale for the first time since his hands covered mine.

As much as I want to melt and think about the way his hands felt, I straighten my spine instead. Pretending I'm unaffected.

I move my player down the ice, and he scores a goal. Andie groans.

"There you go," Bruce says from where he's now sitting on the couch beside my brother. "Good work."

TWELVE
BRUCE

I'M in net this evening for game two of round one of playoffs, but it's extra special because it's my birthday. I'm officially twenty-eight now. It might seem childish to love your birthday, but I *love* my birthday. A whole day to do nothing but celebrate yourself? Who wouldn't want that?

And even better, I know we'll go out and celebrate after the game.

We're all in the tunnel waiting to be announced. I usually lead the group and Remy, our captain, is announced last since he gets the most hype. But right before I'm about to skate onto the ice, our general manager, Tom Parker, grabs the back of my jersey to stop me.

"Change of order tonight, birthday boy." He pats me hard on my shoulder.

I grin, hoping they have something fun planned. Sure enough, Mitch, Colby, West, Remy, and a few others are announced on the Jumbotron. Stevie Wonders' *Happy Birthday to You* begins blaring through the arena speakers.

Tom smiles at me. "All right, now it's your turn. Have fun tonight."

"Will do." I bound onto the ice, feeling excited to have my moment. The crowd goes wild and West and Remy skate toward me with a giant birthday hat made to fit over my helmet. I let them place it on my head then start dancing to the music and trying to do the electric slide. The fans love it.

I look at the opposing team sitting on their bench—the New York Patriots—and they all look bored and like they're ready for the game to start. I wink at them then make my way toward my net, but Remy smiles and points to the plexiglass between our bench and my net. I'm shocked to see not only my parents, but also my sister and her baby—who's wearing tiny headphones—and I immediately skate over toward them. They're all wearing red jerseys with my number, and my niece is swaddled in a D.C. Eagles blanket.

My dad's short, brown hair is neatly combed to the side as always, his hazel eyes shining with pride as he looks at me. I know it was hard for my dad to don an Eagles jersey when he grew up rooting for the Quebec Wolverines, so the sentiment means that much more. My mom's tiny form is swallowed up in her jersey. Her almond shaped, dark eyes sparkle the same way my dad's are. My mother has had the same hairstyle for as long as I can remember…sleek, black and styled in a short bob. My sister inherited my mom's black hair and dark eyes but has my father's face shape. And they're all under five feet eight inches. I feel even bigger than them than usual with all my gear and skates on.

I'm not sure why but seeing them here for this game makes my throat feel tight. I thought my parents had been so busy with my sister and their new grandbaby that they'd forgotten about me. But knowing they flew all the way down here to surprise me for my birthday means more to me than they'll ever know. I rip my helmet off and try to talk to them through the glass and the noise of the crowd. We can't hear each other, but I can read lips well enough to know they're saying *happy birthday*.

Remy gets my attention and moves his hand in a circle, telling me to wrap it up and I do, blowing my family kisses before moving to the goal.

The puck drops and the first period goes by in a blur. I'm feeling it tonight, obviously on a high from my big day and knowing my family is here. Wanting to win and make my birthday even better propels me to be more aggressive. If the second and third periods go anything like this one, it'll be an easy shutout—which means the other team doesn't score a single goal.

A shutout on my birthday? I couldn't think of a better present. Well, I could. But it involves Farrah Remington and a dark, corner booth.

The second period begins, and a few minutes in, one of the Patriots' players gets a breakaway and comes flying toward me. I'm ready with my legs bent and my hand up. He tries to fake me out, wanting me to expect a shot around my legs, but my instincts tell me to watch the upper, left corner, and it pays off. He picks the puck up with his stick and flicks it toward the corner, but it flies right into my waiting glove.

The center loses his footing and flies into my net, knocking me down. His stick is tangled between my skates and the refs skate over and untangle us. Mitch eyes the poor kid furiously, I can tell he's itching for a fight but holds back.

I breathe a sigh of relief when the game continues without a fight, because the last thing we need is a penalty and to give the other team a power play—which is when one of our guys is in the penalty box for two minutes.

The game comes to an end, and I get my birthday shutout—only my third shutout this season.

When I get to the locker room, Coach Young takes a moment to praise me for my shutout, then I strip down quickly to shower. I'm usually the last one out of the locker room, not just because it takes forever to get out of my goalie gear, but because there's no one out there waiting for me. Today, I'm anxious to get out to my family. I haven't seen them since we played Quebec a few months ago.

"You were on fire out there, Brucey," Colby says as he walks through the locker room naked as the day he was born. He's wearing just a smile and his shower shoes.

"Thanks, man. My birthday present to myself."

Mitch comes around the corner from the showers with a towel secured around his waist. When he spies Colby, he rolls his eyes. "Geez, Knight. Put some clothes on."

West hears Mitch from his cubby, grabs his damp towel, and rushes over to snap Colby's bare butt with it. Colby rubs his butt and screeches. "What the hell! I'm getting dressed! Mind your own business if you don't want to see this heavenly bod. That's what Noel calls it, by the way." He winks.

We all roll our eyes. I can't even remotely imagine the ever-serious Noel saying something like that. But who knows.

Remy, whose cubby is across the room next to West's, shakes his head at our antics as he ties his dress shoes then stands and strides toward us. His eyes are shifty, and I can't help but wonder if he's hiding something.

"I'm sure you're excited your family is here," he says, still not looking at me. "I guess we'll see you early Sunday morning for our flight to New York." He clears his throat.

"You're a terrible liar." I snort a laugh. "I'll see you at my surprise party in an hour."

Remy's eyes finally meet mine, and they're comically wide. "How did you know?"

All the guys groan in unison, but I just grin. "Because you just told me, Cap'n."

Remy's palm comes up to his forehead. The guy couldn't lie to save his own life.

THIRTEEN

FARRAH

"SURPRISE!" everyone yells to a grinning Bruce.

We're huddled in his incredible penthouse apartment, and I'm feeling very uncomfortable that I'm here. I was only supposed to stop by to drop off the cake then leave. But Bruce and his family got here sooner than expected, and I couldn't leave, or I would've run into them on the private elevator.

That's right. Bruce McBride has his own freaking elevator. It even has white marble floors like the rest of the penthouse and brushed gold fixtures. Bruce's home is sleek, modern, and everything you'd imagine of a rich bachelor. I torture myself by wondering how many women he's brought back here and charmed the pants off. Literally.

I shudder at the thought.

Bruce is dressed in his game day suit, a rich purple with a black shirt and tie. The way his pants cling to his muscled quads should be illegal. His blond hair is tousled from the shower he likely took after the game, and his face looks excited at the gathered crowd, but oddly unsurprised. If I was a betting woman, I'd bet my brother somehow spoiled the surprise. He can keep a secret fine unless he's asked a direct question, and then he's the worst liar.

He claps his hands together. "Wow, thanks guys!"

His parents step forward, standing on either side of him and beaming proudly up at their son. Like...really far up. Bruce looks nothing like his parents. It's shocking at first. I study them, trying to find similarities and coming up short. His dad is maybe a smidge taller than me with brown hair, and his mother is even shorter than Mel. His sister strides further into the room, a sleeping baby fastened to her front via a baby carrier. She has black hair like her mom and is as short as her mother. Then there's Bruce. All two-hundred and sixty pounds of him. Not only is he the only blond one, but he's also more than a head taller than the lot of them.

Mel is beside me, and I lean in to speak into her ear. "Am I crazy, or does Bruce look nothing like his family?"

Mel turns to me and snorts a laugh. "Didn't you know he's adopted?"

My eyes widen. I feel stupid now, that's obviously the only explanation.

"I wish you could see your face," she says through her laughter. "Can you imagine little tiny Mrs. McBride giving birth to that giant of a man?"

I shake my head, but I'm stunned by this fact about the man I keep trying to ignore. *Adopted.* Looking at him with this knowledge, it's like I'm seeing him for the first time. How he adapted to his hockey teammates being his family, how he felt out of place when they all got married except for him. And how he volunteers with Big Brother Big Sister. Bruce just wants to feel like he's part of a family, like he belongs. And he wants to help others do the same. My heart swells, bigger and bigger the longer I look at him.

I wonder if he wants to adopt someday.

I shake my head, willing the thought out of my brain. That's a dangerous and nosey place for my mind to venture. Bruce's future plans are none of my business, and they never will be. Also, Bruce is only turning twenty-eight today, so he's only had a few years of a fully developed frontal cortex. He's probably still learning how to use it.

Yes, yes. Good reminder. Bruce is not for you, Farrah.

"Well, the cake is in the fridge, so I'm heading home," I whisper to Mel.

"Are you sure? I'm sure Bruce wouldn't mind if you stayed."

"I know, but I need to clean my apartment," I lie.

I hug Mel and then move to make a quick escape before Andie and Noel notice and try to convince me to stay.

"Farrah!" I hear Bruce's booming, deep voice ricochets across the high ceilings of the penthouse. He moves quickly toward me, stopping right in front of where I stand. "Hey," he says. "I'm glad you're here."

Awkwardly, I shuffle on my feet. "I was just dropping off the cake—"

He waves his family forward. "Hey, come here. I want you guys to meet Farrah."

They rush over, eyeing me curiously. I feel like I'm under a microscope. Their expressions aren't judgmental at all, but they're hopeful. And they should not be looking between me and their son hopefully.

"Farrah is Remy's little sister," he explains. "She's the best baker in the country. Or maybe even in North America."

I roll my eyes, but a smile sneaks across my lips.

"Better than Petit Gâteau?" his father asks.

"Ten times better," Bruce answers. "And apparently she made my birthday cake."

Bruce's mother and sister smile at me. "Oh, I can't wait to

try it! Bruce is a sucker for baked goods. That must be why he's so big," his mother teases, reaching up and patting his shoulder.

His sister bounces up and down to keep the baby sleeping. "Or maybe his birth parents were Viking giants," she teases with a wink.

I glance at Bruce to see how he reacts to the mention of his adoption. He brings a massive hand to his chest and gasps. "Are you telling me I'm adopted?"

His father steps forward, his eyebrows forming a vee. "I'm sorry we didn't tell you sooner. I know you thought your hair would eventually be black and shiny like Mom's."

Bruce sniffs. "I did. It's so pretty."

Bruce's mother laughs and playfully shoves her husband. "Would you all behave?"

"Fine," Bruce says. "Farrah, this is my mother, father, and older sister, Avery." He peeks into the baby carrier. "And of course, my niece, Piper." He looks meaningfully at his sister. "If you feed her lots of protein, maybe she'll be as tall as me."

His sister ignores him, reaching forward and shaking my hand, still studying me like there's something to see here, when there's clearly not. "Nice to meet you, Farrah. My husband wishes he was here too, but he had a big meeting."

I nod and shake her hand and try not to think the worst of her husband. Big meetings were always Connor's excuse for not making it to things. But I don't want to be cynical. Some guys actually do like spending time with their wives and extended family and legitimately *do* have big meetings.

"Great meeting you all," I say. "I'm heading home now that I dropped the cake off." I turn to Bruce who's looking at me a little too appreciatively. "Happy birthday. What are you now, twenty-five?" I ask, even though I know his age. But it's a good reminder to him that he's too young for me.

He puffs out his chest. "Twenty-eight. I'll be thirty soon." He winks.

Winking at me right in front of his family? Has he no shame? I feel my face heat.

"Right, well, I'll see you later."

"Oh, please stay!" Bruce's mother says. "We ordered so much food. It should be here any minute."

I hold in a groan. How does this always happen? I've got to come up with better escape plans. Especially since deep down I don't even want to leave and go back to my quiet apartment. I want to stay and watch Bruce enjoy his birthday and see what he thinks of the cake I made. But that's how someone with a crush would act. And I *can't* have a crush on Bruce McBride.

It's one thing to be attracted to him—who wouldn't be—but to become emotionally attached? That's where I'd get myself into trouble.

I don't want trouble. I've had enough trouble to last a lifetime.

Avery rests a hand on my shoulder. "Please stay, Mom won't take no for an answer."

Not knowing how to get out of this, I nod my head. "Okay."

"Now let's see this cake!" Bruce's dad says, raising a hand in the air.

I walk toward Bruce's kitchen, a gorgeous space with a large, La Cornue stove in a dark blue color with polished brass features. I have drooled over this exact stove on the William-Sonoma website too many times to count.

I don't realize I whimper out loud until I hear Bruce's

voice. "Does my stove turn you on that much? This whole time…all I had to do was show you my oven?"

His mouth is so close to my ear that I can feel his warm, minty breath. I hold back another whimper, this one having nothing to do with his kitchen appliances. "It's gorgeous," I say, stepping away from him. "My dream stove."

He shrugs. "The only time I've used it is to heat up frozen pizza. You're welcome to come over any time and use it."

The fact that that's the only thing he uses his La Cornue oven for makes me want to sob.

My brother walks over. "Hey, quit trying to steal my baker. My oven works just fine." Remy looks at me in way I've never seen before…sort of like a bear protecting his bear cub. Which is ridiculous.

"Your oven is fine, but it's no La Cornue." I push my way past him to get to the commercial sized fridge that's empty except for the large, raspberry chocolate birthday cake and some pre-prepared meals Bruce must've ordered for the week.

I reach inside the fridge to grab the cake, but strong arms gently push me aside. "I'll get that," Bruce rumbles from behind me. *Way* too close behind me. I can feel the heat of his body through my clothing.

I quickly scoot out of the way, trying not to touch him, but my back brushes against his front. Bruce seems unaffected, even though I can barely breathe, and carefully brings the cake out and sets it on the massive countertop that looks like black onyx or some equally expensive mineral. He tries to lift the lid of the box, but his hands are so big he has to try a few times. When he finally opens it his face lights up, which makes my insides light up, too. Which is exactly why I wanted to go home.

I know exactly what he's looking at from his point of view hovering over the large, rectangular cake. I spent all morning frosting his birthday cake. The background is frosted in a light blue, with white for the ice. Then I piped on a hockey goal and a goalie wearing D.C. Eagles colors and with Bruce's jersey number…thirty-nine. It's really cute, and my hands are still sore from holding those piping bags for so long.

"Farrah, you outdid yourself," he says, smiling at me. It's not his big, beaming smile he uses when he wants attention…it's a soft smile, a smile just for me. "This is the best cake I've ever had."

Everyone gathers around to see the cake, oohing and ahhing. Bruce wiggles his way out of the crowd and strides toward me. He stops in front of me briefly before pulling me into a hug.

What is it about hugging a man in a crisp, tailored suit that just beats all other hugs? Plus, he smells incredible, like expensive cologne.

"Thank you," his whispers against the top of my head. "All I wanted for my birthday was a shutout…and a Farrah cake."

BRUCE

So, my parents think I have a crush on you.

THREE DOTS APPEAR. And disappear. And appear again.

FARRAH

Little do they know you only like me for my cakes.

BRUCE

GIF of SpongeBob waggling his eyebrows

FARRAH

Get your mind out of the gutter; that's not what I meant.

BRUCE

Riiiiiiight. I do like your cakes.

FARRAH

Knock it off, Bruce.

BRUCE

I meant the ones you bake. Wow. Not sure why you had to go and make it dirty.

FARRAH

BRUCE

For real though, best cake I've ever had.

I chuckle, knowing she likely can't tell if I'm trying to sound inappropriate or not. I've never come on this strong with a girl I like before, but then again, none of them have ever made it this challenging. I remember Colby going through this with Noel. She really put him through the ringer despite him being—arguably—the best-looking guy in the NHL.

If I genuinely didn't think Farrah welcomed the attention, I'd leave her alone. I'm not trying to be a creep. But I can see the way her eyes take me in and the appreciative glint there. She can push me away, but she's got to see how amazing we could be. Our chemistry alone is off the charts… I mean, when our hands brush, it's more palpable than anything I've ever experienced. It's like our fingers have a taste of what full skin-on-skin could be like and the cells are telling us to go all the way. Just from hands brushing.

Plus, she's a baker, and I have to eat a ridiculous amount of carbs to keep up my energy. A man gets tired of pasta. Sometimes he needs something sweet.

My father clears his throat, drawing me back to reality and making me realize I've been standing in my kitchen for five minutes thinking about Farrah and staring blankly into the room with a stupid smile on my face.

"What are you smiling at?" He asks, his hazel eyes alight.

I roll my lips. "Ah, just thinking about that shutout last night."

Dad scoffs. "I wasn't born yesterday, son."

Son. I've always loved it when he called me that. I know I'm his son, of course. But when he says the word, it's like he's choosing me all over again. A prickle of guilt hits me that I thought they were too busy with their new grandbaby to remember me. I was jealous of an infant.

"I'm so glad you guys came down," I tell him, draping an arm around his shoulders.

He groans under the weight of my body. "Merde, tu es un géant," he grumbles, the words are a French expletive paired with the word *giant*.

My mother appears at the top of the spiral metal staircase that leads to the second level and all four bedrooms. She's wearing a clean, white tunic and black leggings and she's barefoot. Her short, black bob is tucked behind her ears, and she's smiling so wide, I can barely see her irises.

"Ahh, I love having everyone together. Little Piper is asleep, and Avery is lying down too. What should we make for dinner while they're sleeping?" She doesn't wait for us to answer before she makes it to the bottom of the stairs and jabs her index finger into the air. "Miso soup and pork!"

"I think I have all the supplies for that, actually," I say, opening my walk-in butler's pantry and showing off the bare, empty shelves.

"Always a smart mouth, this one," she replies with a heavy sigh and a hand on her hip.

My phone pings, and I grab it out of my jogger's pocket. I'm hoping it's Farrah, but I'm not disappointed when I see it's Jackson.

JACKSON

> Hey Bruce, my foster mom cut her finger
> making dinner and needs to go in for
> stitches. She's freaking out, and her
> husband has to drive her. Just giving you a
> heads up that my social worker is likely
> about to call you for respite.

Wow, this is by far the longest text he's ever sent me. I usually get random memes I don't understand, or two-word responses. I appreciate the heads up, but I hate that he feels the need to be responsible for himself like this. I wish he could just enjoy being a kid without wondering where he'll be each month, or even each day.

I glance up from my phone where my parents are watching me. "Hey, is it okay if Jackson—my little brother—spends the night? They need someone for respite."

Mom's eyes soften. "Of course, the more the merrier."

"All right, I'll grab dinner supplies after I pick him up."

I quickly text Jackson back and just like he said, the social worker calls about respite. I tell her I can pick him up immediately, and forty minutes later I have Jackson in tow and we're pulling into Whole Foods. He does a low whistle as I'm pull into a parking spot.

"Damn, I knew you were boujee…but I didn't realize you had Whole Foods rizz."

My head snaps over to look at him, I try to plaster a stern expression on my face for the first time in my life. "First off, no swearing. And secondly, I have rizz for days."

He snorts. "Ohio rizz, maybe."

I gasp. "I do not have Ohio rizz." I'm not sure what that is, but I'm assuming it's not good.

Jackson crosses his arms over his blue tee. "Then why don't you have a girlfriend?"

I open the door of my pickup. "Because I'm waiting for the right woman to come along." I step out and close the door behind me. Jackson unbuckles and joins me in front of my baby-blue truck.

He looks at me with a smirk. "That's what everyone says when they don't have a girl."

I roll my eyes. What does he know? He's ten.

We walk inside and I pull up the supply list Mom texted me. We find everything quickly and are making our way to the checkout when I see familiar long, dark hair in front of me.

"Farrah?"

She turns, causing her hair to whirl dramatically. I'm mesmerized by it for a few seconds. "Bruce? You shop at Whole Foods?" Her eyebrows draw together in surprise.

I hold my arms out defensively. "Yes! I have Whole Foods rizz, not Ohio rizz."

Her eyebrows scrunch ever tighter. "I have no idea what you're talking about."

Jackson, who's pushing the cart, glances between the two of us. His little mind is working; I can see it in his eyes. He's definitely going to drill me about Farrah later. Just what I need—him *and* my family teasing me about the girl who *thinks* she wants nothing to do with me.

"Hi." Farrah does a cute little wave and smiles at Jackson. "I'm Farrah."

"Jackson," he replies with a tilt of his chin. This kid, I swear he's ten going on sixteen.

"Jackson is my little brother," I explain. "We're having a sleepover tonight. There will be nail polish, face masks, and of course…a fashion show."

Farrah snickers and Jackson looks aghast. "There will be

none of that. I'm too old for sleepovers. It's just respite," he says, correcting me.

"Respite?" Farrah asks, staring at me for answers. I like this, her paying attention to me and asking me questions.

"I'm approved for respite so if Jackson's foster parents need any help, I can step in, and he can hang with me for a few nights."

She smiles at Jackson. "That's pretty cool." Her eyes widen like she just remembered something. "Oh, hey, I was going to text you. But I left my favorite cake knife at your place and wondered if you could bring it by in the next couple of days? If you're not busy." She glances back at Jackson.

It sounds made up, but I know it's not. Farrah likes using the best quality and I have no doubt she invested in the best cake knife available and needs it for her next event. I look down at her cart for the first time and see it's mostly full of flour and sugar...but also tampons and one bar of dark chocolate. My eyes move back up to find her blushing and embarrassed.

Quickly, I think of something to say so she's not embarrassed. Not that there's any reason to be embarrassed about periods. I mean, all girls have them. Once when Avery and I were in high school she made me run out to the store and buy tampons. It wasn't that big of a deal.

"I'm actually pretty busy," I say, going back to her question. "Why don't you come get it now? And you can stay for miso soup and pork."

"I've heard Mrs. McBride is a really good cook," Jackson adds.

Well, well, well. I give him an appreciative nod. Who would've thought Jackson would make such a great wingman.

She shakes her head, making her shiny, brown hair do something intoxicating… it's like a dance of hair. I want to reach up and thread my fingers through it.

"Oh, no. I won't interrupt your evening."

"You'll be watching Nella all week, and I'm leaving Sunday for four days in New York. It's now or never. And you have to eat."

She considers this. I can tell she really wants that cake knife.

"I have a whole stash of chocolate in my pantry," I whisper.

Farrah purses her lips. "Fine. But just because I want it for our wedding event next Friday." She pauses, glancing down at her cheap bar of chocolate—at least, it's the cheapest one you can get at Whole Foods. I'd know because I try to only buy fair trade cocoa products. "What kind of chocolate do you have?"

I pump my eyebrows once. "Tony's."

Farrah makes a tiny squeak. "You might be my hero, Bruce. Whole Foods is out of Tony's chocolate."

I grin. "I have every flavor."

"Even raspberry?"

Jackson sighs. "He has raspberry. Can we go, already? I'm starving."

I DRIVE ALL the way across town just for a taste of Bruce's stash of Tony's chocolate. Freaking Whole Foods. I checked three different grocery stores, and no one had it. I crave chocolate like crazy during my period. And since my cycles are annoyingly irregular, I wasn't prepared with my favorite treats.

And, of course, I also need my expensive cake knife. The one that cuts cleanly through the cake without dragging clumps all over.

This week I'll order a backup.

My cheeks heat as I remember Bruce spying my period products in my cart. How mortifying. I'm in my thirties and embarrassed by a hot guy seeing my pads and tampons. Ridiculous.

I force the embarrassment from my mind. He seemed unaffected by it anyway. When I arrive at Bruce's penthouse, I park in one of his guest parking spots where I parked yesterday and go up the private elevator. It's handy that I already knew the code from when I brought the cake over.

When I make it to the top of the building, the door dings

and opens slowly, and I'm greeted not by Bruce and Jackson, but by Mr. and Mrs. McBride. I hadn't considered—until just this second—how it might look that I'm coming over for dinner.

I'm here two days in a row, and they're going to think there's something going on between Bruce and me.

My blood freezes in my veins…what if they know about our kiss? Is Bruce one of those people who tells his family everything? He seems like the type.

I enter the large penthouse, suddenly feeling very aware of my dog-hair covered black leggings and old Niagara Falls tee from a trip Connor and I took. I really need to throw out all clothing purchased with my ex, but I love this shirt. It's all soft and worn in.

At least I took the time in the car just now to braid my long hair, so it's not unkempt. The further I get inside the room, the more awkward I feel. And what's worse is that I beat Bruce here.

"Hi," I say, stepping closer to his father who's wearing a kind smile, and his wiry, Asian mother who has those keen eyes that seem to see and know all—kind of like Andie, but less feral.

"Hello, Farrah. Nice to see you again," she says. "Are you joining us for dinner?"

I scratch the back of my head, needing something to do with my hands. "Um, yeah. I hope that's okay. I left my cake knife here, then saw Bruce at the store, and one thing led to another."

His parents smirk at me.

"One thing led to another," his dad says slowly, with that same twinkle in his eyes as his son. Some things are genetic, but not Bruce's sense of humor. He definitely inherited this man's mischievous streak.

Bruce's parents seem like the type that dress nicely even for a simple day at home, so that must be where he got his fashion sense too. His mother is wearing a stylish tunic and black tights—free of dog hair—and his father has a Ralph Lauren button-down paired with dark, tailored pants.

"I think I know the knife you're speaking of," his mom says, waving me into the kitchen. "I washed it last night. That cake was delectable, by the way. When the Eagles win the cup this year, we'll have you make the celebratory cake." She winks.

I laugh. "Deal. I'd love to see them win."

Mr. McBride's mouth falls into a hard line. "The Quebec Wolverine's don't stand a chance." He rolls his eyes. "But the Eagles do, for sure."

I cross my arms. "Ahhhh, a Wolverines fan, huh?"

"Everyone born in Quebec is a Wolverines fan," he says. "But Bruce's team will always take precedence." His chest puffs out with pride.

His expression is one that reminds me of my parents and how they feel about Remy's teams. Being from Ohio, we were all raised as Cincinnati Cougars fans. My dad still watches all their games and fumes when they lose—he just doesn't mention that to Remy.

I glance over my shoulder; the elevator shows no indication of Bruce's arrival yet. "So, do you think Bruce will ever get rid of his pickup?"

His parents laugh heartily, giving each other knowing glances. "He'd keep that thing forever if he could. But I think it'll die in the next year, for sure."

My heart unexpectedly aches for him and his truck. "Does he have any other superstitions?"

His mother eyes his father, and they express something

wordlessly. "Our Bruce watches romantic movies before each game."

I laugh, thinking she's joking, but she doesn't crack a smile. "You're kidding."

Mr. McBride shakes his head. "Nope. He prefers the older romcoms, but if it has romance, he says it's good luck."

I look between the two of them, expecting them to let me in on the joke any moment. But they don't. Instead, Bruce's sister, Avery, appears at the bottom of the stairs. Her willowy figure is just like her mother's, but her dark eyes are sleepy like she just woke up. "Are we talking about Bruce's romcom obsession?"

His parents nod.

"That's my fault, I'm afraid," she admits as she walks further into the main living area. "I always had a romcom on, and he'd watch them with me. He somehow put together that every time he watched a romance on game day, his save percentage went up." She huffs a laugh. "I think he's full of it, and he just doesn't want to admit how much he loves romantic movies."

We all laugh at her comment just as the door of the private elevator opens, and Bruce and Jackson walk through.

"What's so funny?" Bruce asks, eyeing us with a worried expression.

"We were just telling Farrah that you're a romance queen," his sister teases.

He blushes so slightly; I almost wonder if I'm imagining it. "Name a better movie than *When Harry Met Sally*, I dare you."

I don't argue, since that's one of my favorite movies. Connor always hated watching it with me and would shut himself in our room to watch something on his laptop instead. I wonder what it would be like to curl up and watch a movie with Bruce. I bet he's snuggly. A cuddly giant with rough hands…the warmth in my face heats tells me I'm blushing.

Bruce and Jackson's arms are full of paper grocery bags, and they bring them into the kitchen. Mr. McBride high-fives Jackson. "Hey, Jackson, glad you're joining us tonight. I hear you started playing chess?"

Jackson looks down at his feet. "Oh, yeah. I sort of did."

"Well, Bruce has a chess board, so we'll have to play."

His head snaps up to look at Bruce. "You got a chess board?"

"Yeah, man," Bruce says, his lips twitching. "I have to learn so I can kick your butt."

Jackson scoffs. "Yeah, right. Stick with hockey, old man."

Wow, if he thinks Bruce is old, he must think I'm ancient.

Bruce and his mother unload the groceries, then the guys and girls separate. The guys head into the living room to play with Bruce's new chess board, and we girls stay in the kitchen. I enjoy watching Mrs. McBride's nimble fingers as she slices tofu and then mixes miso paste into the soup. She patiently explains the recipe as she adds each ingredient. At some point, I stop thinking about how weird it is that I'm here, and relax, enjoying myself immensely.

It's familiar and easy the same way it is with my own family, in a way I always hoped I'd feel with Connor's family. But I never felt accepted by them. Like how their son treated me, I suppose. It's funny the things you block from your mind until after the fact…and then you can see it with absolute clarity.

One year at Christmas, Connor's father got him a special knife with an engraved handle, and I received nothing. His father explained I'm not his child; therefore he didn't need to buy me a gift.

Something tells me the McBride's would treat their kids' spouses and treat them like their own children—which reminds me that Avery is married. I turn to her. "Avery, what does your husband do?"

She smiles. "He's a pediatric surgeon."

Ahh, so her husband's meeting was *actually* an important meeting. Suddenly, I feel bad for thinking the worst of him. *Not all men are snakes, Farrah.*

I glance into the living room where Bruce is sitting across from Jackson with a big grin on his handsome face. Jackson looks equally happy.

Some men are pretty wonderful, apparently.

So why does that make me feel so sad?

The D.C. Eagles #1 Fan page on hockeyisbetterthanfoot-ball.com

Sheryl Adams: *meme of Bruce McBride in net but his pads are replaced with images of Swiss cheese*

Todd Ferguson: 😂 they should've used the backup goalie last night!

Craig Nottingham: How come when Sheryl makes fun of McBride it's funny, but when I do it, I'm a "fair weather fan"??

Todd Ferguson: Because you're always negative about everything, Craig.

Craig Nottingham: I'm a realist.

Todd Ferguson: You misspelled pessimist.

Harry Johnson: How come you guys always blame the goalie after a loss? Why's it never the defense, or the amount of power plays we gave the other team?

Craig Nottingham: A real goalie would make up for all that.

Todd Ferguson: I'm with Harry here. Anderson and Rasmussen kept giving the other team power plays last night. It's hard for a goalie to defend when the opposing team has an extra player on ice.

Craig Nottingham: Harry, do you have a crush on Bruce McBride or something? You're 😤 annoying.

WITH A FRUSTRATED SIGH, I force myself to log off the fan group for the night. I'm just torturing myself at this point.

I'm in a mood this morning, anyway. We lost game three against New York last night and still have two days left here. I feel antsy and ready to get back home. West told us all Mel is pregnant, which is why she's been so sick over the last month. And now I'm worried Farrah won't have help during the events they have scheduled.

I want to be there helping her, but I should be more focused on helping my team. I hate the panic that seeps in when I'm not part of something…when I'm not helping in every way I can.

I wish she would've left more of her stuff at my penthouse so I could bring it to her the moment I get back. I even find myself wishing Mel's morning sickness would stay put —like a total asshole—just so I can step in and help Farrah during events.

Would somebody give me a task that involves seeing Farrah? Please. For the love.

My phone pings, and I roll my eyes, expecting a notification from hockeyisbetterthanfootball.com, but I lean forward with my heart pounding in my chest when Farrah's name pops up, instead.

Until this moment, she has never initiated any of our

conversations. It's always been me chasing her—and what a thrill the chase is—but it's nice to know she doesn't totally hate me.

FARRAH

Rough game last night. The guys were really piling up the penalties.

Finally. Someone gets it. I'm always working on my focus, and on catching pucks from every angle. It's all I work on all week during practices. But it helps if my teammates are keeping the puck out of the defensive end.

BRUCE

Yeah, not our best work last night. You were watching, eh?

FARRAH

I watch every game. I try to stay home with Nella so Amber can go to home games though.

My shoulders slump. I can't be mad at my girl, Nella. Even if she's keeping me from seeing her beautiful aunt.

BRUCE

I've missed seeing you in the crowd.

It takes a full minute for her to finally respond, and when she does, she changes the subject. I invited her to flirt...and she did not accept.

FARRAH

Question...did you watch a romance before the game yesterday?

BRUCE

You think I skipped my movie time and that's why we lost?

FARRAH

just helping you troubleshoot.

BRUCE

Actually, I watched Thumbelina. I don't usually watch cartoons…maybe they're not as lucky.

FARRAH

Maybe not. I have a recommendation for the next game.

I bite my bottom lip, enjoying this immensely. That she's been thinking about this…thinking about me.

BRUCE

Okay, shoot.

FARRAH

Footloose.

I hum. I haven't seen that one.

BRUCE

Done. But if we lose the next game, it's on you.

FARRAH

No pressure?

BRUCE

But if we win, I'll be looking for more of your recs. If we win, you're obviously a good luck charm.

Farrah shocks me with her next response. It's the closest she's ever come to flirting back.

FARRAH

Are you saying I could replace your pickup?

BRUCE

Yeux bleus, you'd be better than any good luck charm I could ever dream up.

CHAPTER
SEVENTEEN

FARRAH

IT'S FRIDAY NIGHT, and I'm sitting in the bathroom after a military promotion party—a job the general recommended us for. The venue is a local officer's club, and the bathroom is simple and clean. There's one chair in here, where I'm taking up residence because of a stomachache. The chair is stiff and uncomfortable, and making my stomachache worse. I tighten my arms around my waist but flinch under the pressure.

The party went surprisingly late; these military guys sure know how to party. Thankfully, the service members are tearing everything down, so I only have to carry the dessert plates to my car. Mel started feeling awful and left early with West. I urged her to go, knowing I didn't have much to do, and the guys just got back from New York last night.

But now I'm regretting that decision. I have a twisting, aching pain all around my belly button. My period is over, so it's not cramps. I don't know if it's something I ate, or if I'm just stressed about the events we have coming up and the fact that Mel is either exhausted, or sick, lately. She's been feeling better, well enough to help with events. But she's not the powerhouse she was before. Understandably so, but still, I'm left scrambling.

I'm not the planner and organizer at Melarrah Events—that's Mel. I'm simply here to bake.

An hour ago, when Mel and West left, I felt a tiny ache and thought nothing of it. But it's growing more and more intense the longer I sit in this bathroom. I'm wondering if I can even stand back up from the chair I'm in.

The pain intensifies and I can no longer get comfortable, even though I'm seated. I try to think of who to call…there are no scheduled games this weekend as the guys prepare for the final three games in round one next week. So, all my friends are busy. My mother is in town for a long weekend, but she's with Nella while Remy and Amber are on an overnight date. Noel and Colby whisked themselves away to visit his dad and little sister, and Mitch and Andie are out of town for her brother's youth hockey tournament.

Bruce pops into my mind, he's the only other person I know in D.C. But it feels strange to call him for a favor. I was already at his penthouse twice last weekend and sent him that flirty text that I've been fretting over all week.

What was I thinking? Hinting at being his good luck charm? So stupid.

I'm not lucky at all. I can't even be my own good luck charm!

I can hear chatter and banging around outside the women's restroom, it sounds like they're tearing down the party.

Trying not to overthink it, I pull my phone out of the pocket of my black pants, wincing with the movement. My eyes widen with the pain. Oh no, what if it's my appendix? Didn't Mel have appendicitis when she was younger? If only she was still here.

I shoot a text to Bruce, a tear streaming down my cheek as I suffer through the ache deep in my belly.

Hey, I'm sorry to bother you on a weekend, but I'm at an event, and I think I might need to go to the ER. Everyone is out of town and Mel went home not feeling well, and I don't know what to do.

My phone lights up a second later with an incoming call from Bruce. My face crumples in relief, deep down I know he'll help me—rescue me. It's nice to have someone who's willing to do that.

"Hey," I croak out.

"Where are you?"

"If you're busy, it's okay—"

He cuts me off. "Where. Are. You." His voice is calm but demanding.

Tears roll down my face. "The Gold Club right outside of Andrews Air Force Base."

He's silent for a moment, maybe he's looking up the directions. "I'll be there in thirty minutes."

"Okay." We hang up and I lower myself to the bathroom floor. I ignore how disgusting it is to lie on the floor of a public bathroom, because I can't make it another moment without lying down to relieve some pressure from my stomach.

I lie there on my side, crying, for what feels like hours. I begin to worry that everyone has left and locked up, and there will be no way for Bruce to get inside.

My heart sags with relief when I hear his booming voice outside the door. "Farrah? Farrah?"

"In here!" I say as loud as I can without jostling myself.

He bursts into the room, dressed like he was out. Oh my, what if he was on a date?

"Farrah," he whispers, kneeling down right next to me. "What's wrong?"

"I think it's my appendix," I sob. "I'm so sorry."

He shushes me, sweeping a strand of now sweaty hair away from my face. "Can you get up? Should I call an ambulance?"

"I think I can get up," I say. I try to move my legs, but it disturbs the ache in my stomach too much. Instead, I groan and lay my legs down on the floor. "It hurts, Bruce. It hurts so bad."

"I'm going to pick you up, okay? I've gotta get you into the pickup."

I nod, gritting my teeth and knowing the movement will cause more of the shooting pain.

He picks me up in one quick swoop and although it hurts, it feels good to be in his arms. Knowing someone who cares about me is here and taking care of me.

I feel faint and covered in a cold sweat. This is not my proudest moment. Bruce gets me to his pickup and somehow opens his passenger side door while holding me. It's like bearing my full weight is nothing to him. Like I'm a tiny little fairy. Which I'm not.

There's just one long seat in his old truck, he lays me onto the seat on my side, buckles a seatbelt over me, and heads toward the driver's side.

Once he's inside, he takes up most of the bench seat. I have to bend my neck down to allow him more room. Bruce surprises me by gently lifting my head and resting it on his thigh. I'm much more comfortable that way, and in too much pain to overthink it.

He starts driving and once we're well on our way, he

brings one hand to rest on top of my arm. His skin is warm against mine and I close my eyes at how comforting the contact is.

The truck is quiet as he drives. I glance up at him and notice his jaw is tense with worry. He looks wound up and ready to fight someone. Like my ailment has personally offended him. Probably because I ruined his date tonight.

We hit a bump in the road, and I groan in pain. Bruce's worried gaze flashes down to me and his arm comes to rest on my arm. "We're almost to the hospital, hang in there."

Moments later bright lights illuminate the cab of the truck, and I squint against the sudden brightness. Bruce pulls over and puts his truck in park and rushes out of the vehicle. Soon, people are opening the passenger door and making me move out of my comfortable spot on Bruce's leather seat. I'm beginning to think this old thing *is* lucky. I cry as the ER nurses lift me onto a hospital bed and wheel me through several large doorways and long, sterile hallways. Bruce runs to keep up with them, but when we get to a final door, the male nurse turns and looks at him. "Sir, are you family?"

Bruce locks eyes with me. I don't want to be alone, and he must see that fact written across my face. "I'm a friend."

"Sorry, sir. Only family is allowed back," the male nurse says, then leaves Bruce behind us as they wheel me back into a dimly lit curtained off area.

"Alright, first we need to get some information on you," the other nurse says. Her badge reads Shona. She gets behind a computer and starts asking me numerous questions. Height, weight, medications, illnesses, insurance. The whole bit. Then my vitals are taken, and the male nurse, who introduces himself as Brad, administrates an I.V.

"This will help the pain," he says. I usually hate needles,

but the needle is nothing compared to the pain in my stomach. I barely even notice it.

Finally, the two nurses tell me a doctor will be in shortly, then usher out of the room. The pain meds work their magic quickly, and the pain eases enough that it no longer hurts to breathe.

An hour later the doctor has spoken to me and ordered a CT scan. I fall asleep waiting for the radiologist to come get me and take me back, but the CT scan doesn't take long.

After another half hour, the doctor sweeps into my room again. He's a thin, balding man who looks like he hasn't slept in weeks, and I'm pretty sure he hates his job.

"The CT scan showed you had a ruptured ovarian cyst." He eyes me warily. "The cyst was about five centimeters in diameter, but they're usually not painful." Dr. Grumpy-Face purses his lips. "You're sure your pain level was a ten?"

I swallow back a snarky retort. "It was the worst pain I've ever felt."

He shrugs. "Well, luckily they're not life threatening." The infuriating man sighs. "You'll be on your way as soon as I finish your paperwork. Do you have a ride? You can't drive with the medication we gave you."

"I can find a ride," I say. I'll have to call my mom to come get me. I'm sure Bruce went home; it's been two hours since we arrived here.

The doctor nods and exits the room. I grab my phone off my lap and pull up my mother's contact information, I'm about to press call when the male nurse, Brad, steps into the room with a stapled stack of discharge paperwork.

"I'm assuming the gentleman in the waiting area is your ride?"

My eyes widen. "Oh, didn't he go home?"

He shakes his head from side to side.

"Yeah, he's my ride," my words are muddled since I can't believe he waited this whole time.

Glancing down at the time on my phone, I breathe a sigh of relief that I don't have to call Mom. It's already nearly midnight, and she would've had to wake Nella and bring her all the way across town to get me.

I sign the papers, and Brad helps me into a wheelchair, wheeling me quickly out to the waiting room where Bruce is alert and waiting in an uncomfortable-looking chair. His hair is a mess, and I wonder if he's been running his hands through it. It's sticking up in every direction and somehow this adds to his boy-next-door vibe.

Brad looks at Bruce. "You'll want to monitor her tonight and bring her back in if her pain increases."

Bruce nods, obviously taking this very seriously, and then Brad wheels me out to Bruce's truck.

Brad eyes the old pickup with a disapproving scowl while Bruce helps me into the truck. The nurse leaves quickly, taking the wheelchair with him, and Bruce and I are left alone in the quiet, dark cab.

"Are you okay? What was wrong?"

He's being awfully nosy, but if I can call him on a Friday night when he was likely on a date, can't I tell him what was wrong with me?

Is it weird to talk about my feminine health? Or lack thereof.

I bite the insides of my cheeks, wondering how much to tell him. "I'm okay, it was an ovarian cyst."

He studies me, his eyes moving over my face. "I don't know a lot about that…are they usually painful?"

He's not being condescending like the doctor, he's just curious.

"If a cyst is large, it can be painful. I knew the cysts were there, but I've never had one explode before."

He snorts a humorless laugh. "So, you're kind of a ticking time bomb, eh?"

It's oddly refreshing to joke about this. I'm so used to the pity when people find out about my medical history and how it will be difficult to conceive…but he's right. I'm like a living, breathing landmine.

I burst out laughing, which causes a dull ache around my belly button. I groan and wrap my arms around myself.

"Do we need to go back in?" he asks, his expression laced with concern.

"No, I'm fine, really. Would you be able to take me home? Or do you have to get back to your date?" The question is out of my mouth before I can stop it.

He starts the truck with a rumble from the engine then turns to stare at me. "You thought I was on a date?"

I shrug, trying to act like I don't care either way.

"I wasn't on a date. I haven't been on a date in about a year and a half," he says this sheepishly, then shifts the truck into reverse and backs out of the parking spot. "I was at a bookstore, actually."

A year and a half. Surely, he's exaggerating. "Were you looking for a specific book?" I ask, trying not to dwell on the year and a half comment.

He runs his tongue along his front teeth. "I got a book about chess. Jackson beats me every damn time, and I'm determined to best him one of these days."

I shake my head. "A little competitive, are we?"

"You don't make it to the NHL without being competitive."

"True," I say, looking away from the handsome man and

at the road for the first time since we started driving. "Wait, where are you going?"

"My penthouse."

"Bruce, I'm not sleeping at your place. Take me home, I'll be fine."

He glances at me then back to the road. "Your brother mentioned whisking Amber away this weekend, so there's no one there to help you if you need it."

"My mother is staying this weekend. She's there now with Nella."

"Okay, well this will keep you from waking them up. I have nothing going on; I can help. Plus, my place is much closer, and you look exhausted."

I sigh. His place *is* closer. It would probably take an extra hour for him to take me home… then he'd have to drive all the way back.

Sitting back against the leather bench seat, I wonder how I keep ending up at Bruce McBride's penthouse.

CHAPTER
EIGHTEEN

BRUCE

FARRAH REMINGTON IS asleep in my guestroom. My team captain's little sister. What if he was in town and stopped by? What if he somehow found out about this?

Remy has never been someone who scared me... until now.

It's eight in the morning and I'm wide awake, sitting up in my California king bed. I haven't heard a peep from Farrah, and I kept my door cracked all night in case she needed me. I want to go check on her and make sure she's okay, but I can't just waltz into the guestroom, and knocking might wake her up. So obviously, the only other option is sitting here torturing myself.

I force myself out of bed, throw on some athletic shorts, a white sleeveless tank, and my moccasin slippers, then pad down the steps and into my kitchen.

Glancing in the fridge, I'm unsurprised to find nothing in there but my pre-prepared macro nutrient meals. I don't even have eggs.

I grab my phone and pull up the DoorDash app. Scrolling through the options, I select two everything breakfasts from a local diner called Pancake Palace and pay the extra fee to get it here as fast as possible…just in case Farrah wakes up soon. The guys and I agreed to eat as clean as possible once round one is over. I'm going to take full advantage of the next few days, in that case.

When the DoorDasher arrives, I meet them in the lobby and when I come back up on the elevator, Farrah is sitting on the sofa looking apprehensive.

I smile, hoping to make her feel comfortable, and lift the bag of food. "Breakfast?"

She stands on wobbly legs, probably still sore from her uterus abruption…or whatever she called it. Poor girl. It was awful to see her in pain like that. I've never felt so helpless and miserable in my life. I'm sure my own misery was nothing compared to hers though. As she straightens and begins to walk toward me, I intake a sharp breath. She's wearing the navy Eagle's tee with the number thirty-nine on each shoulder, and baggy grey sweats that I laid out for her last night. *My* Eagle's tee and sweats.

Seeing her in my things has an intoxicating, primal effect on me…something I've only imagined before this moment. All I understand is that I never want her to wear Remy's number again. I don't care if that's her brother. *My* number belongs on this woman, or no one's number.

These clothes are way too big for her, and yet, it's the sexiest thing I've ever seen.

I close my eyes briefly to calm myself. I can't go all caveman on her—not until she wants me to.

First, we have to establish trust. Which I'm sure is hard after everything with her ex-husband. But as a goal tender, I'm nothing if not patient…I can wait for my moment. And I'll do the work it takes to show her I'm nothing like that bozo.

I hope that helping her last night was a step in that direction, but either way, I would've come to her rescue.

"Thank you," she says as she stops right in front of me. "For coming last night, and for letting me stay," she tugs at the shirt, blushing. "And for the clean clothes...and breakfast—"

My hand comes up as I gently press my index finger against her soft, luscious lips so she'll stop thanking me. The same lips I remember kissing like it was yesterday. Lips I'm aching to kiss again.

"You don't have to thank me. I promised you I'd be someone who was always there for you. And I don't break my promises."

Her dark blue eyes meet mine. The blue of her eyes is deep and dark, like the ocean. And just like the sea, she's full of mystery and promise that I want to discover. But there's always a risk when you dive into the deep, blue sea. The risk of finding things you might not like...the risk of meeting predators, of drowning...but there's also a chance to find something amazing you've never discovered before. And I'm betting on the latter. And even if I find the other things too, I can handle them. I'm willing to handle them. For her.

She swallows, but her eyes don't leave me. "I think I'm going to have to get used to that." Her gaze grows deeper, like she's searching for something in mine. "To people who keep their promises."

I nod. "I've always been told I'm a patient man."

Her blush deepens, but she doesn't look away. Neither of us say anything for a long moment. I don't want to ruin this ephemeral dance we're doing, and I don't believe she does either. But my stomach goes and ruins it, growling loudly. I grimace, and she covers her mouth so I can't see her laughing.

"Sorry. I usually eat my pre-prepped meal at seven."

She lets a laugh break free, and I soak up the sound of it. "Let's eat then. I can't be responsible for your lack of stamina during Tuesday's game."

Just this once, I let the innuendo go. Because right now Farrah Remington likes me, and I'm not about to mess that up.

Farrah's phone begins to vibrate from the couch where she left it, and she moves across the room to grab it. "Hey, Mom," she answers. I hear her mother's voice from where I stand, she sounds worried and frantic, talking fast. "Mom, I'm fine." She eyes me, then lowers her voice. "Mel took me to the ER; then I slept at their place. No biggie. I feel fine now."

I'm unsure how to feel about Farrah's unwillingness to tell her mother that I'm the one who helped and that she stayed in my guest room last night. But it's also kind of hot to be her dirty little secret...even though nothing dirty happened. I understand why she's keeping it to herself... maybe she doesn't know how much her mom adores me. I've always been her favorite on the team—besides her son.

"I'm not sure when I'll be back," Farrah hedges, glancing at me and widening her eyes.

I look down at my wristwatch. "I can take you back to your car after breakfast," I whisper.

Farrah nods. "I'll be home after breakfast; don't worry about me." She rolls her eyes, annoyed by something her mom said. "That was West talking."

I withhold a snort.

"I can drive; I'm feeling much better now. Just a little sore."

Farrah blows out an exasperated breath. "Okay, Mom. See you later. I love you, too."

She ends the call and throws her phone on the sofa. "Wow, it's like I'm seventeen all over again."

I laugh and walk the bag of food over to the coffee table, arranging our Styrofoam containers. Farrah sits beside me and opens her takeout box with a smile. "This looks amazing, thank you." She digs right into her pancakes.

"I wasn't sure if you liked pancakes," I muse. "They're simple compared to your baking."

She closes her eyes as she chews, obviously loving the food. She swallows and looks over at me, her dark hair falling over her shoulder in the process. "I've never met a sugary carbohydrate I didn't like."

I chuckle. "Same. How are you feeling?"

"Better," she says, dabbing her face with a napkin. "I have PCOS…polycystic ovarian syndrome." She wrinkles her nose. "It sounds scary, but it's common, unfortunately. I knew it was possible for a cyst to rupture; I just had no idea it would be so awful."

"Being a woman sounds really hard," I admit. I'd never really considered it before, how much women carry, how much our existence is dependent upon them and their health.

Farrah laughs, it's husky and unrestrained, filling my expansive penthouse like a symphony. The best music I've ever heard.

"It really is, you're right." She piles another big bite of pancakes on her fork then nods her head toward my big flat screen TV on the wall in front of the couch. "So, what romcom are we going to watch while we eat?"

I smirk, hoping that means she's staying long enough to watch a movie. "It's not a game day."

Her eyes sparkle. "Are you really such a rule follower? Didn't take you for a stick in the mud, McBride."

I gape at her. "How dare you. I'm the life of the party."

"Then let's watch Footloose."

I nod and grab the remote, finding the movie quickly and starting it up. I'm immersed instantly in the music and Kevin Bacon's dance moves.

Farrah and I eat together, sitting closely beside each other on the couch. It feels a lot like a date. I wish it was a date.

Once we finish eating, the movie comes to a locker room scene where the guys are walking around, and their naked butts are visible. I slowly turn my head toward Farrah. "Wow. Now I see why you wanted to watch this movie so badly."

She rolls her eyes. "Oh, please. All man butts look the same. I'm here for Kevin Bacon's dancing."

"All man butts do *not* look the same. Some of us are well-honed athletes, Yeux bleus."

Her eyes quickly move down my body, and she turns away just as fast, her face growing red again like it did this morning.

Well, well, well. I'm pretty sure Farrah Remington just silently agreed that my butt is, indeed, better than just *any* man butt.

CHAPTER
NINETEEN

FARRAH

THE DAY after my ER visit, I'm finally feeling mostly normal again. I can stand up completely straight without any soreness in my belly. The incredible pancakes probably healed me more than the hospital visit.

After finishing *Footloose* this morning, Bruce drove me back to the promotion party venue and helped me pack up everything I had left on the cake table before leaving for his afternoon practice. He left before I changed back into my black trousers and top, so I drove home with his navy long sleeve tee and sweats tucked into my large purse. They smell like him, musky and manly, and I'm seriously contemplating if he'll even remember I have them. He probably has a million of the same shirt. I'm tempted to keep them and wear them since it's the most comfortable clothing I've ever had on my body, but that would technically be stealing.

Plus, Bruce's butt likely looks better than mine does in these pants. He was right...not all man butts are created equal, and his is the best I've ever seen. High and tight and round with muscle.

Is my car AC not working? It seems warm in here.

When I finally arrive back at Remy and Amber's that afternoon, I head straight into the big house instead of my apartment, knowing my mother has been worried about me.

I walk in and she pounces immediately, looking me over like she's searching for a gunshot wound. She's still in pajama pants and a loose top, her short bob is perfectly coiffed like she just ran a curling iron through it. Her hair used to be blonder, but it's faded to grey, softening her features.

Finally, she stops her search and pulls me into a hug. "Oh, Farrah. Are you feeling better?"

"I'm okay, I promise." I walk further inside the house and Nella spots me and runs toward me; I crouch down on my knees, so the impact won't hurt my stomach and give my niece a tight squeeze. "I have a follow up with my OBGYN next week. I guess my ovaries are covered in cysts, more than when I had my last scan a few years ago. The doctor said this might happen repeatedly," I tell my mom.

Mom's mouth falls into a worried line. "I'm sorry, sweetheart. Will they have to do surgery?"

I blow out a breath, standing slowly. "I hope not."

My eyes fill with tears, and I hate how scared I feel at the idea of any kind of surgery, but especially a hysterectomy, or anything that might keep me from even the hope of having children someday.

Mom hugs me again, her slender arms going around me and her familiar scent enveloping me like a cozy, warm blanket. Mom and my little sister are just alike, both are gentle and nurturing. Suddenly, I miss my sister and wish she was here, too.

"Everything will be okay," she assures me, even though we both know there's a chance everything will not be okay.

But I do need to stop expecting the worst-case scenario

about every situation. It's weird how trauma can turn you into a cynical beast if you're not careful.

I laugh through my tears, and it sounds as forced as it feels. "Wow, I'm a mess. I'm going to go get some rest. Do you and Nella need anything?"

Nella raises her arms up, wanting me to hold her. I caress her chubby cheek instead; not sure I can handle her weight just yet.

"No, we're doing just fine; you go get some sleep. Amber and Remy will be back in a few hours, anyway." She smiles. "Will you come back for dinner, though? I have to leave early in the morning."

"Of course. I'll be back down by then."

We say our goodbyes, and I head out the front door and up to my apartment. Once I'm inside, I remove the clothes I changed back into and take a long, hot shower. The hot water eases the tension and soreness in my body. A bath would be even better, and I could've used the one in the big house. But really, the idea of a long nap and some quiet time is even more appealing.

When I get out of the shower my skin is pink and warm, and I don't bother stopping myself from grabbing Bruce's clothes and slipping into them again. The fabric of the sweats is soft, and the oversized fit is just what I need today. The shirt fits me like a dress, coming to rest against my thighs. I trace a hand over Bruce's number on the shoulder and sigh dreamily like a schoolgirl.

Groaning, I slip into my bed and snuggle against the down comforter. Bruce's shirt slides up against my face and I inhale a deep, long breath. It smells just like him and his home and makes me long to be back there, curled up on the couch while a movie plays in the background. In my fantasy my feet are in his lap, and he's massaging them and doting over me.

I fall asleep swiftly, dreaming of the giant goaltender and how well he cared for me the night before.

————

When I awake, I'm surprised to see it's already five in the evening. I promised Mom I'd come to dinner tonight, and I want to hang out with her before she heads back to Ohio.

I change into some stretchy and soft skinny jeans, a pink wrap top, and some fuzzy socks. It's not cold outside, but I'm in the mood to be warm and comfortable. Seeing that it's raining, I opt to go through the garage door at the bottom of my stairs instead of around the front of the house.

When I open the door that leads into an immaculate laundry and utility room, the sound of voices stops me in my tracks. Not my mom's voice, or my brother's and his wife's...but Bruce's. His deep, husky laugh sends a shiver down my spine. Suddenly, the fluffy socks don't seem like the best choice. I'm about to turn and rush back to my apartment when Rose trots into the room, tail wagging. She yips happily when she sees me and my brother rounds the corner.

"Farrah! There you are. We've been waiting for you."

I huff out a nervous laugh. "Sorry, my nap went a little long."

Remy leans in, quieting his voice, "Are you okay? Mom filled us in; I hope that's okay."

"Of course." I give him a soft smile. "I'm better now."

He nods as Rose and I follow him through the utility room and into the kitchen. I blush furiously when my gaze lands on Bruce's large form. I don't know why, it's not like we slept in the same bed last night. We didn't even kiss. We didn't do anything. But just the knowledge that I slept in his penthouse and just took a nap in his clothing, makes my body heat up like a furnace.

Bruce always seems to take up more space than everyone else, and not just because he's huge… It's his aura and his personality, as well. Everything about him is just…big. I blink, forcing thoughts of him out of my head before they go too far.

As I walk further into the room, I realize everyone is here. Mel and West, Noel and Colby, Andie and Mitch, and Andie's little brother, Noah. Noah is busy playing with Nella —it appears he brought over a small hockey set and is attempting to show her the ropes. I smile as I watch her try to flog him with the short hockey stick. Noah quickly catches it and shakes his head *no*.

"I wasn't expecting a party for dinner," I say in a hope-fully light-hearted tone.

My eyes move to Bruce, who's smiling softly at me. He must stop that. Those are the kind of looks that are going to cause speculation.

"I knew everyone got back today since we have practice tomorrow, and I texted your brother about dinner," West explains. "He said he had hamburgers, and I already had buns…so a plan was quickly made."

Colby drapes an arm around West's shoulders. "I missed your buns while I was gone, baby." He pretends like he's going to kiss his cheek, and West shoves him away.

"Get off of me, Knight," West rolls his eyes.

My mother walks down the stairs and joins us in the kitchen. She's changed into jeans and a simple black top. She smiles at the group that has gathered. "I just love that my Remy and Farrah have you all! It's like a home away from home. Such special friendships." She sighs happily then turns to Mel and West. "Oh! And thank you for taking good care of Farrah last night. I don't know what I would've done without you guys taking her to the hospital and letting her stay with you."

Mel turns wide eyes in my direction. "What? You went to the hospital?" Her hands come up to her face. "Farrah, I'm so sorry for leaving you by yourself! What happened?"

I don't know much about the human body—my expertise is baking—but if it's possible for your blood to freeze in your veins and for your heart to momentarily stop…that's what happens to me in this moment.

"Uhhh," I mumble, trying to remember how to form words. "I had a ruptured cyst, it's fine. I promise. I finished tearing down the cake tables this morning. Everything is fine."

Literally every single person in this house is staring at me —except Nella, who's still trying to hit Noah with a hockey stick.

I continue to stutter and search my brain for a feasible way to explain this.

"So, she wasn't with you last night?" Mom asks Mel, slack jawed. She turns and focuses all that motherly attention on me.

Mel looks awkwardly between me and my mom. I can see in her eyes that she knows she's missing something, and that she was supposed to have played along. She grimaces. "I'm sorry," she whispers in my direction.

I gulp.

Remy steps forward, looking frantic with worry. "Farrah, who took you to the hospital? You didn't call an Uber, did you? Have you seen that documentary on Netflix? They're not safe."

The deep clearing of a throat barely registers in my brain before Bruce starts talking. "I took her to the hospital. Everyone was out of town but me, and your mom was watching Nella. It just made sense for me to help. Then Farrah stayed in my guest room last night, since my penthouse was much closer to the hospital, and it was late."

I glance down at my feet and close my eyes. This is not happening. I'm having a walk of shame without getting any of the sexual benefits. How is this happening to me?

"You took my sister to your penthouse for the night?" Remy's voice echoes through the room, and I'm not sure I've ever heard him speak in such an icy tone.

Bruce scoffs. "It wasn't like that. Farrah's my friend, and I'll always help my friends if they need me. Wouldn't you?"

I look up to see Bruce crossing his massive arms over his broad chest as he awaits Remy's answer.

"Well, yeah. Of course I would. But why did you guys hide it?"

My brain finally starts to work again, and I throw my hands up in the air. "Because of this entire conversation." I groan. "I stayed the night at his place, but it was totally innocent. And even if it wasn't, that wouldn't be any of your business."

The room grows so quiet you can almost hear the silence. It rings in my ears…a warning to shut up.

I make the mistake of looking at Andie, who's smirking at me like she knows something. She thinks something happened between Bruce and I last night. As I gaze around the room, everyone is looking between Bruce and me. My speech had the opposite effect that I wanted. Now everyone thinks we hooked up.

If only these idiots knew more about ruptured cysts and PCOS, they'd know I wouldn't have had sex last night if my own survival depended on it. Not even with the biggest, sexiest, most muscular man I've ever seen.

I drag my hand over my face. "Bruce and I are just friends. Nothing happened. Oh, my gosh. I cannot believe I'm having to explain myself to you all."

"You don't have to explain anything," Bruce says, his tone serious and his eyebrows knitting together. He looks hurt, and I'm not sure if it's something I said, or simply the fact his teammates think he's lying. "She was in intense pain, and all you can worry about is me putting the moves on her? Come on, man."

Remy's jaw ticks at the reprimand. He's usually the one doing the lecturing.

"I agree," Mitch speaks up, surprising all of us. "She needed help, and he helped her. End of story." He turns his focus on Remy. "Remy, your sister is a grown ass adult. Cool it."

Remy glares at Mitch and opens his mouth but my mother raises her hand to her mouth and whistles loudly, the way she used to do when we were children. "All right. Everyone take a breath, and let's refocus. The important thing here is that Farrah needed help and had someone she trusted that she could call." Mom turns to look at Bruce. "Bruce, thank you for taking care of her."

He tilts his chin in a nod. Slowly, the group of teammates and their wives begin assembling dinner again and quiet chatter pops up around the room. Except Remy. Amber places a hand on his shoulder and rubs the spot, obviously hoping to comfort him. But my brother looks deeply troubled by this whole situation, and I'm not sure why.

What's his deal?

Mom grabs onto my elbow and practically marches me

out of the room and up the stairs to the guest room she's staying in, closing the door behind us.

"What were you thinking? Spending the night with a professional athlete? Farrah." My mother shakes her head and slumps down on her bed. "You're finally doing so well after everything with Connor. You look happy…you're making a new life for yourself. Don't go messing that up by getting involved with the goalie."

My jaw drops. "I thought you loved Bruce. Don't you bring him treats every time you come visit?"

She waves a hand. "Well, yes. He's a wonderful boy, Farrah. But he's an athlete who's surrounded by women, and he's very young and goofy. Which is highly entertaining and makes him fun to be around. I can see why you'd be drawn to him, but you and Bruce are a recipe for disaster."

I cross my arms, my ears and face feeling hot with repressed anger. "I just want to reiterate again that nothing happened at Bruce's place. Why is everyone forgetting that I was in so much pain I could hardly breathe?" I blow out a breath. "I'm a grown woman, and I refuse to hear anymore."

My mom's cheeks hollow out, like she's biting the insides of them, trying to keep her mouth shut.

"And one more thing!" I start again, unable to stop now that I'm on a roll. "You and dad *loved* Connor. You thought he was the epitome of husband material. As did I. So maybe we can't assume things about people's character." I pause for effect. "And Bruce is *more* than an immature goofball, Mom." The words surprise me as I say them out loud, but they're true. He's younger than me, sure. But he's the one in the group of teammates who's always available to lift a helping hand. And helping others seems to bring him joy. "He's a rascal, but he's also kind and considerate. Did you know he provides respite care for a boy in foster care?"

Mom's eyebrows raise slightly. "Really? I didn't know that." She studies me for a moment. "You're awfully quick coming to his defense if you two are just friends."

"Wouldn't you defend a friend if their character was in question?"

Mom rolls her lips. "Yes, I suppose so." She still looks unconvinced. "Maybe you should come visit your dad and me in Ohio for a long weekend, honey," she says, changing the subject abruptly. I know she only wants me in Ohio so there's distance between me and Bruce. "Wouldn't it be nice to see your old friends?" Mom smiles. "How's Megan?"

The picture from Instagram I'd forgotten about throbs through my head like an old wound that's still festering.

"I'm not sure; we haven't talked in a while." I breathe evenly, trying to make the tightness in my chest ease. "But I can't leave. Remy and Amber need me to watch Nella." I know Amber would take off work in a heartbeat if I wanted to take some time off, but the last thing I want to do is see the friends who so easily forgot about me.

"Okay." Mom sighs. She's still holding my hand, and she squeezes it. "Maybe when hockey season ends," she says before looking away. "Please guard your heart, sweetie, okay? I hated seeing you so down after everything with Connor. I don't want that to happen again." She gestures toward my outfit. "Look, you're even dressing up again. I love to see you doing so well."

I offer her a hesitant smile, unsure why she's judging Bruce so harshly. "I *am* doing well, Mom. And I'll be fine."

REFERRING to Farrah as my *friend* feels like referring to hockey as *just a game*.

I'm sitting on the sofa in Remy's living room, Nella is making herself comfortable on my lap, and all my friends' wives are surrounding me. The men are whispering in the kitchen as they prep the burgers, and Farrah and her mother disappeared upstairs.

And every time Remy makes eye contact with me through the open concept space, his eyes are slightly narrowed. My captain's eyes have *never* been narrowed on me.

Andie looks up at me from where she's seated on the floor. "Come on, Bruce," she whispers. "Just tell us what really happened. Did Farrah really need to go to the hospital? We won't tell the guys."

"*I'm* one of the guys, Andie. I'm not sure how I got lumped in as one of the girls."

She waves a hand in the air. "Oh, stop, you're one of the girls and you love it."

I shrug, because she's not totally wrong. I do love chilling with the girls. My teammates fell in love with some pretty great ones.

"Well, I hate to disappoint." I raise my eyebrows pointedly, because she's the one that knows just how disappointed I really am. "But I honestly just took her to the hospital and then home to sleep. She was in so much pain." I grimace remembering how I found her on the bathroom floor. "She was miserable. It scared me to see her like that."

Amber, Noel, Mel, and Andie collectively sigh, and their eyes go all soft and shiny.

"Aw, Bruce," Amber whispers. "You're falling for her, aren't you?"

I blow out a breath, which causes Nella's wispy curls to flutter. She turns to glare at me, much like her dad is all the way from the kitchen. Birth dad or not, these two have similar mannerisms. Just like me and my dad.

I swallow. "I'm not falling, Ambs. I'm crashing and burning, and I don't know how to stop."

All the girls scoot a little closer, wanting to hear more.

"But it can't happen," I say through gritted teeth, my eyes moving to the grumpy man in the kitchen—and for once, I'm not talking about Mitch. "I can't mess up my relationship with Remy or my teammates. And Farrah has been pushing me away from the start. I'm pretty sure she wants nothing to do with me." Even as the words exit my mouth, I know they're not true. If she wasn't attracted to me, she wouldn't have stayed for a movie this morning, and her eyes wouldn't find me in every room and linger on me. She wants me as badly as I want her, but the difference is, she's scared to admit it and I'm not.

Andie rolls her eyes. "Are you kidding? The constant tension between you two is palpable. I don't know how the guys didn't notice it before."

Noel slowly nods her head.

Amber pats my knee. "Remy will get over it, if you guys really wanted to make a go of it."

"I agree," Mel says. "Remy has always been the level-headed one in the group. He's protective of his sister, especially after what she went through. But if he saw you being good to her, how could he still be worried? I mean, you literally came to her rescue last night. You're husband material, Bruce."

I scoff. "Would you let Farrah know that?"

Andie gives me a sympathetic smile. "Keep doing what you're doing, and she'll see it for herself." She quirks an eyebrow, looking briefly back at the guys in the kitchen. "So, just confirming…you didn't even kiss last night?"

I throw my free hand in the air, rattling Nella, and earning another pout. She jumps off my lap and heads back to her makeshift hockey rink off to the side of the living room. She dive-bombs Noah, who's lying on the rug looking bored. He makes an *oof* sound when she jumps on him.

"You made my little buddy leave," I say to Andie.

"Sorry."

"Dinner is ready," Remy says, startling me. I hadn't realized he was in the living room. He eyes me warily, and there's a beat of awkwardness between us.

The girls get up and make their way into the kitchen, leaving the two of us there in a strange faceoff. I'm unsure what to say to him, since I've already said a million times that nothing happened between Farrah and me—not last night, anyway. If I keep saying it and defending myself, I'll look even guiltier.

Instead, I get up and follow my captain into the kitchen. "Are we good?" I ask quietly.

He glances over at me and nods. "We're good."

Something about the look in his eyes makes me think he doesn't mean the words he just said. My relationship with my teammates is incredibly important to me, more so than the game itself. But this is the year we're favored to win the cup, and we've been working like a well-oiled machine. This is the type of issue that sets a team on its axis and puts the chemistry off-kilter.

My teammates are counting on me, and I cannot let them down.

But what would really be so bad about me being with Farrah? Remy's attitude shouldn't bug me so much since his sister and I aren't even together. But why wouldn't he be happy about it? Doesn't he trust me to be more than just a goalie? Do my teammates only see me as a teammate and someone to further their career?

Why wouldn't they want me to find happiness the way that they have…?

These thoughts niggle, grating at me for the rest of the evening. And what's worse is that Farrah heads straight back to her apartment with her mother once they finally come back downstairs.

THE FOLLOWING week I start working out. And let me tell you, people who say they love working out are big, fat liars. Or, skinny, fit liars, I guess.

I'm *so* sore. But everything I've read said the best thing you can do for PCOS is eat clean and exercise. And my brother has a fancy gym right beneath my apartment, so I don't have any excuses.

Remy told me the soreness will ease as my body gets used to the movements. But he's one of those insane people who enjoys working out, so can I really trust him?

However, working out during Nella's naps is at least a nice reprieve from thinking about a certain tall, blond man who looks eerily similar to Kristoff. I overheard Remy and Amber talking a few days ago, and Remy was telling her he's worried. He said their performance has been off all week ever since the whole *Bruce and Farrah* debacle.

I wanted to scream. There's *no* debacle! It's a moot point. But I also feel guilty. I don't follow hockey as closely as my parents do, but even I know the Eagles are one of the top teams in the NHL this season and they're expected to make it to the final round of the Stanley Cup championship…if not take the whole thing.

But they've lost both of their games this week so far. And I can't help feeling like it's all my fault. In five days, I've gone from thinking maybe Bruce and I could be good together…to believing that if I don't keep my distance from him, they'll lose the Cup and I'll be the number one reason why.

Ridiculous, I know.

I shake my head, trying to remove these invasive thoughts from my mind. I turn up *Since U Been Gone* by Kelly Clarkson on the Bluetooth speakers loud enough that I worry it might wake Nella. And instead, I try to force myself to think about anything but Bruce.

But I *want* to think about Bruce. I want to think about how it felt when his hands wove into my hair and tilted my head to the side. I want to think about the way his mouth tasted, and how it felt to be kissed by such a handsome and wonderful man.

I want to think about what it would be like to watch a movie with him on his couch again, but to cuddle up next to him and feel his warmth this time. I want to know how fun it would be to hang out with him and Jackson for a day and see if they can teach me how to play chess. And I want to daydream about making Bruce all the desserts he wants and having him praise me each time about how amazing my baking is.

I groan loudly, frustrated at my lack of focus today. I look down at the weightlifting workout that Andie printed off and gave me—she's one of the crazies who loves working out—the next move is a curtsy-lunge. I grab two ten-pound weights and begin. I do two sets, and my legs are shaking already, but the pain is enough to finally distract me from everything else in my brain.

My phone—which is hooked up to the Bluetooth speakers—rings, and the sound is deafening since I have the speakers turned up so loud. I glance down at my phone and see my sister's pretty face filling the screen, requesting to Facetime.

I slide it to answer. "Hey, Felicity. How are you?" Seeing her, even through the screen, makes me smile.

"Hey!" She gasps. "Oh my gosh, are you working out in Remy's home gym?"

"Shocking I know." I laugh. "I'm hoping it will give me energy and help the cysts go away."

She wrinkles her pert little nose and leans forward. Her dark ponytail bounces with the sudden movement. "Can exercise make the cysts disappear?"

I snort an undignified laugh. "Probably not, but everything I read about PCOS tells me to eat healthy and exercise. And I'll do anything at this point."

She pouts. "You poor thing. I'm sorry about the drama this weekend. Mom filled me in." she quirks her mouth to the side.

"How much did she tell you?" I shoot her an unamused stare through the phone.

My sister rolls her lips into her mouth, trying hard not to smile but failing. "I heard you spent the night with the hot goalie from the Eagles." She cups her hand around her mouth and whispers, "but she said nothing inapropro happened which is really disappointing."

I roll my eyes. "You're the only one who was disappointed by that. I thought Remy was going to punch him! I've never seen him look so angry."

"Remy?? Really? I can't picture him riled up like that." She sighs. "Everyone's just worried about you. We don't want to see you get hurt again. But a girl needs to have some fun. And I bet Bruce McBride is great at…fun." She waggles her dark brows up and down.

I remind myself never to allow Felicity and Bruce in the same room. They're way too much alike and would cause trouble.

"I don't think I'm a one night of fun kind of person. I'd get attached right away," I admit.

"Have you dated at all since the divorce?" she asks.

I draw my bottom lip into my mouth, considering telling her everything about me and Bruce's history. I've never told a soul, and at this moment, I feel the need to finally confide in someone. "Actually…the night I signed the divorce papers, about a year and a half ago…"

"Yes?" Felicity urges, her voice excited in hopes I'm about to tell her something juicy.

"I went to a bar and had a few drinks…I met a guy there, and he was hot. Like the hottest man I've ever seen. We ate wings together, had a few drinks, and talked for a long time. Then he kissed me."

My sister's jaw drips. "Farrah! I can't believe you never told me that!"

I laugh, remembering that night all too well.

"Was it a good kiss?"

I shake my head slowly…dreamily. "Best kiss I've ever had."

Her eyes go soft, tilting down at the corners. "And you never saw him again?"

I blow out a deep breath. "Nope… I saw him again the next morning when he showed up at Remy's house for a workout."

Her brows draw together. "Wait…what?"

"The man from the bar was Bruce McBride."

My sister gasps again and her arms begin to flail, she's doing this silent scream thing that's freaking me out. Yeah, maybe I shouldn't have told her.

"You're kidding! You didn't know who he was when you kissed?" she says when she can finally speak.

"Nope. The only guy on the Eagles I ever paid attention to was Remy. Bruce looked a little familiar, but I was too distracted with the chaos of my own life to think about it too much."

"And you've never kissed again…ever?"

"Nope."

"Farrah, you naughty girl. I cannot believe you! This is the best thing I've heard all year."

"You can't tell anyone! Nothing can happen with me and Bruce again. I already heard Remy talking about how off the team is this week after the drama."

She rolls her eyes. "I won't tell anyone. And Remy can get over it! Bag the hunk!"

"You're out of control," I tell her with a laugh.

"That's what my husband keeps telling me," she says with a smirk and a dreamy look in her eye.

"How is my favorite brother-in-law?"

Felicity claps her perfectly manicured hands together. "Oh, my goodness, he did the cutest thing the other night!"

I listen happily as my sister goes on and on about her wonderful, adoring husband. It's nice to see her so happy, and it's also nice that I no longer feel a pang of jealousy about it. I can sit here and feel genuinely happy for her, with no lingering negative feelings about my ex are popping up.

What a great headspace to finally be in.

I'M in net for practice and tensions are high. We've lost two games in a row, which always brings morale down…but doing so during the first—and arguably the easiest—round of the Stanley Cup Playoffs? Freaking brutal. There are only seven games total per round, and we're tied three-three. The New York Patriots barely got into the playoffs via a wildcard slot, so they should've been easy to beat.

And with Remy flat out ignoring me, it seems even worse than just a simple losing streak. It's like I'm letting my teammates down *and* losing one of my best friends.

Remy will barely even look at me. I've tried talking to him in the last week and a half and he always just nods robotically and says we're fine. But we're obviously *not* fine.

Right now, we're working on our power plays—when the opposing team has a penalty and we have an extra player on the ice—and penalty kills—when we have a teammate in the penalty box, and the other team has a power play.

We're great at penalty kills, but we all know we could use some work in our power plays. Coach Young informed us we've only scored during twelve power plays all season long.

The end of our three-hour practice nears, and I'm drenched in sweat and ready for a shower. I grab my water bottle and squirt a cool stream of water on my face and neck, but quickly toss it back on top of the net when I see Colby skating toward me. He's on the opposing side for practice and is hoping to score on me. I squat down, getting into position. I have to watch my legs around Colby because he's sneaky with the low shots. Despite being one of the older guys on the team, Colby is still fast as hell. He breaks away from the group behind him and flies toward me. Remy is hot on his heels, his face intense with concentration as he gains on him and tries to keep him from scoring during this pretend power play. I know in his mind this is a real game, and this shot could make or break whether we win or lose. He brings the same intensity and responsibility to every practice, every game.

He manages to catch up to Colby and hits him from behind, knocking him flat on his stomach. Remy swooshes the puck away from my net and almost collides into me in the process. Instead, he stops squarely in front of me, puck in front of his stick.

It's magic, and it's why he's our captain.

I blow out a low whistle. "Damn, Cap'n. Are you sure you're thirty-seven? That was some slick work, man."

He glances at me—barely—and sniffs. It's the snobbiest thing I've ever seen him do. I didn't realize until this very moment that Remy was capable of snobbery.

I grit my teeth together, about to say something about his attitude toward me, but Colby skates up to us with a wide grin on his face. "I can't even be mad about that move, Remy. That was amazing."

Remy smiles easily back at him. "Thanks, Knight." They both pound their hockey gloves together, and before I can chime into the brotherly love, Coach Young whistles and gestures for us all to join him at center ice.

Remy skates off in Coach's direction without so much as a backwards glance at me. Colby, on the other hand, looks back and holds his glove up for a fist bump. I bump it, feeling some of the tension in my shoulders dissipate. At least everyone else is treating me normally, except my team captain.

This treatment is like being grounded when you didn't even sneak out of the house and do anything fun. All the discipline with none of the reward.

Such B.S.

Colby and I skate to center ice side by side and wait for Coach Young to speak. He dives right in as soon as everyone's within ear shot. "All right, boys. Great practice. I know we've taken a few tough losses; you guys have the skills to take this all the way. I hope today gave you the confidence to go with it. I don't have to tell you how important this is. Get your fannies out there tomorrow and give it your all like you did today and we're golden. They've only won three out of seven games; don't let *their* wins get inside *your* head." He swivels his head slowly, looking each of us in the eyes. "Now, go home and relax and be ready to kick butt tomorrow."

We all whoop and yell various expletives and derogatory comments toward the other team. They're nice guys, I'm sure. But this is the playoffs.

With that, we're all shuffling off the ice, through the tunnel, and into the locker room. I'm still taking off my leg pads by the time the other guys are stripped down and heading toward the showers.

"Hey, Bruce. Good work out there today. I don't envy you, being a goalie."

I glance up to see Mitch standing over me. His dark hair is sweaty and rumpled, and he's stripped down to his boxer briefs and shower shoes. Mitch is one of the more modest guys in the locker room. If it was Colby standing before me now, I'd be looking straight at his—well, you know.

"Thanks, man. It's a lot of pressure sometimes, but it's what I was made for."

He nods. "Andie's been on the fan pages, and she says the fans are brutal. I told her not to read that trash."

I snort a laugh and wonder if Andie is on the same fan page I am. Maybe she trolls the haters too. "Emotions are high right now. Not just for us, but for fans. The Cup is so close we can all taste it, but now the stakes are higher."

His expression hardens. "Remy needs to get over the thing with his sister. It's not fair for him to punish you for helping her."

I'm oddly touched by his words. It's nice just to know I'm not imagining him ignoring me. I think I needed confirmation that I did nothing wrong more than I thought I did because something inside me relaxes and calms at his honesty.

"Thanks, man. We'll be okay. I know he's just looking out for her." *But so am I...*is what I don't add.

His permanent frown tugs at one corner in an almost-smirk. "All right, better get those pads off before the rest of the guys use up all the hot water." He nudges his head toward the showers.

I laugh and he stalks toward the room filled with shower stalls, his shower shoes thwacking with every step.

When I finally have all my gear off and a white towel secured around my waist, Colby struts into the locker room freshly washed and stark naked. He stops in front of me and does a little dance. I roll my eyes and scoot past him as quickly as I can.

———

That evening, I pick Jackson up and we head to a local park I found where older gentlemen hang out and play chess. I even brought my chess board along. I've been reading up about chess, and I think I can finally beat him.

He's ten. It'll be easy. Even as I think the words I know it's a lie, because he's already kicked my butt in chess a dozen times.

I pull into a parking spot near the park, and Jackson and I begin walking toward the outdoor tables. My wooden chess board is clutched under my arm. The spring evening is warm, with a cool breeze. I'm glad I wore jeans and a hoodie since it will continue to cool down as the evening wears on.

Two older men with grey hair are already seated at one of the metal tables and look like they're well into a chess match. They're focused on their pieces, deciding their next moves.

Jackson and I sit at a vacant table and set up the board. Right as I think Jackson will start the match, he steeples his hands and eyes me seriously. "All right, before we get into this...I think we need to talk about what's going on with you."

My head jolts back. "What are you talking about?"

He looks around as if worried someone might overhear him. "Listen, I've been watching your games the past week or so, and it's the playoffs, Bruce. You've gotta get your head in the game."

I huff a laugh, but there's no humor in it. Is this kid really telling me how to do my job?

"I know hockey isn't my area of expertise."

I raise my eyebrows, agreeing with him.

"But a few weeks ago, you were a brick wall...nothing could get past you. And then the last two games, something is off."

I sigh heavily, allowing my shoulders to sag. I know he's right—even though I'm shocked he's actually been watching the games for once—but I also don't know what to do about it.

He searches my face. I'm not sure what he's looking for. "So, has something happened in the last few weeks? Is something stressing you out? That can affect my game too, if I'm not in it mentally."

My eyebrows raise up to my hairline. Who is this forty-year-old, responsible man, and what did he do with Jackson?

"When did you become more mature than me?"

He scoffs. "I've always been more mature than you, McBride."

I laugh, shaking my head. "You're not completely wrong. I have been in my head lately."

He nods. "All right, so let's talk it out." He glances down at his lap. "My foster mom does this with me when I'm stressed about something. It always helps to talk about it."

I hold back a smile, his foster parents sound pretty great. "Okay." I blow out a sigh. "Well, Farrah had a...medical emergency. And I was the only one available to help her. So, I did, and she stayed the night in one of my guest rooms, then went home the next morning."

He nods as I speak, clearly following along. "Okay... and?"

"And Farrah is Remy's sister."

He still looks confused. "The team captain?"

"Yes. And he found out she stayed at my penthouse, and now he's not happy with me."

His eyebrows scrunch. "I don't get it. What's the problem?"

I groan and drag a hand through my hair. How do I explain this to a kid? "He thinks something is going on between me and Farrah. He has a 'no teammates can date his sister' policy." I use air quotes. "He's protective of her."

"But you were just helping her, right?"

"Right."

He studies me again. "But you want something to happen between you and Farrah. And her brother knows it."

It's not a question. It's a statement.

I scratch the side of my neck, uncomfortable that a child figured this out before me. Of course, Remy knows I want something to happen. Therein lies the problem. He knows I have feelings for Farrah and he's uncomfortable with it. This isn't about him thinking I'm lying about nothing happening that night…it's him worrying about what happens in the future. Which is so Remy.

"Wow. You're right."

"Of course I am," he says, moving the King's pawn to start the game.

"I really like her, Jackson," I admit. "I can't stop thinking about her."

He looks up at me, screwing his lips to the side as he thinks. "Would your captain prefer you ignore his wishes and win games… or lose games and stay away from his sister?"

"What exactly are you saying?"

"If Farrah's on your mind, you won't play well without seeing her." his eyes widen. "You haven't seen her in the last week, have you?"

I shake my head from side to side, realization dawning on me. Seeing Farrah and spending time with her makes me play better. It makes me happy. *She* makes me happy.

A cocky smirk forms on his youthful face. "Well, there's your problem. Now you have to decide what you're going to do about it."

I roll my lips, pondering his words. What *am* I going to do about it?

For the rest of our game, I consider this dilemma. Jackson beats me easily during the two matches we get through…but just because I'm distracted, obviously. I'll get him next time.

TWENTY-THREE

FARRAH

AFTER DINNER at the big house, I head to my quiet apartment. Remy was in a freaking mood, and I can't with him tonight. I'm also exhausted from watching Nella this morning. It felt like she threw a tantrum every five minutes, and she's not usually like that. The terrible twos are in full force. Amber got home early from working at the salon, thank goodness. I helped her make dinner and then booked it out of there.

I shower and let the hot, steamy water pour over me, washing away the stress of the day. I spend way longer showering than usual but feel better afterward. I don Bruce's sweats again; I've been wearing them every night. Am I proud of it? No. Am I going to stop? Also no.

I'm curling up on my bed, burrowing my face into the tee and catching a whiff of Bruce's manly scent, when a light knock comes from my door. It's so faint, I almost miss it. If I had been watching a show, I wouldn't have heard the sound. I wait for a moment, just to make sure it wasn't the wind or a tree. But another soft knock comes from the door.

I grab my phone from the nightstand and see no new

texts that came while I was showering. And it's also after eight at night. Which is later than my married friends usually want to hang out.

Standing, I pad barefoot toward the door and open it. I'm expecting to see Amber or Remy, but my breath catches when a rumpled Bruce appears before me. He looks distraught, his hair a mess like he's been tugging on it, and his eyes are full of turmoil. The man looks miserable.

"Bruce, what are you doing here? Are you okay?"

He sticks his hands in the pocket of his grey hoodie. "Yeah, can I come in?"

I pause for a second, and in this second, I realize I shouldn't let him in. I shouldn't complicate this even more. I shouldn't want to spend time with him. And I shouldn't want him to kiss me again.

Also, I probably shouldn't want to steal the hoodie he's currently wearing since his scent is wearing off the shirt I already stole.

But even knowing all the reasons I shouldn't, can't keep me from stepping to the side and allowing him inside my small apartment. I do a quick glance, making sure my place isn't a disaster. Thankfully I cleaned last night, and the studio apartment looks tidy. I even made my bed this morning, the emerald-green duvet on the bed pulled up and my decorative pillows neatly placed.

Bruce steps inside, toeing his shoes off and placing them on my welcome mat. He fills the space with his massive form and makes it feel even smaller. I've noticed before that the vaulted ceiling is quite low; Remy has to watch his head when he's up here...but Bruce's head nearly touches the very peak.

I don't have a table or chairs in here, just a cream-colored love seat at the foot of my bed and a circular coffee table in front of that.

"Um, why don't you sit down before you bump your head."

He shuffles on his feet, his eyes turning up toward the ceiling. "Yeah, okay."

He walks further inside the room and sits on one side of the love seat. He then drags a hand nervously through his hair.

Not knowing what to do with myself, I join him on the love seat. I thought there'd be more room for me, but it's pretty tight. I angle my body toward him and study his angular jaw and high cheekbones. He could've been a model or actor if he wasn't such an amazing goalie.

"Bruce," I say, urging him to look at me.

He finally does, and his eyes widen. "You're wearing my clothes."

I glance down at myself and turn bright red. I'd completely forgotten I was wearing his long-sleeved tee and baggy sweatpants.

He swallows, turning to face me. "Farrah, do you want me or not? You look at me like you want me…and you're wearing my clothes, like you want me." He leans in a little closer. "Because I sure as hell want you. And damn it, I missed you this week."

I squeeze my eyes shut, letting his words wash over me. *I want you. I missed you.*

"Bruce," I whisper. "I don't want to complicate things during the playoffs. I feel like everything last weekend already messed up the team dynamic. Remy has been a moody jerk all week. Which is totally unlike him." I shake my head, and Bruce's giant hand comes up and gently curves along the edge of my jaw.

"I've played like garbage all week, and it has nothing to do with my teammates. It's because I needed to see you, talk to you, just *be* with you. I go through my days just hoping you'll text me again, or that I'll see you at Whole Foods. I'm a mess."

I allow my head to fall to the side, enjoying the feel of his hand cradling my face, and burrow deeper into his palm. Bruce takes this as an invitation and leans his forehead against mine.

"If you don't feel the same, tell me now. I'll leave you alone. I'll stop flirting. But if you want me, I have to know."

His words stun me into silence. His words fly through my mind, and my heart. What do I want? I already know. I want him. I want to give into this thing between us. I want to stop fighting it. I should pause and tell him about my infertility issues, but my brain is too fuzzy with the desire to kiss him. It's *just* a kiss, we can talk about everything else later…right?

Unable to speak or even think rationally, I finally answer him by pressing my lips to his. It feels so right, having our mouths fused together again. He doesn't waste a second, crushing his lips to mine and kissing me firmly. His hand slides from my jaw to my neck, and his thumb gently caresses the area behind my ear. I hum approvingly.

His lips feel just how I remember, but even better because now this isn't some random guy from a bar. Now I *know* him. And I like what I know.

Bruce's big hands move to my waist, right above where I've rolled the waistband of his sweatpants. He grips my waist and pulls me onto his lap, surprising me. I inhale sharply at the movement, and we stare at each other for a long moment. I wonder if he's memorizing my features the same way I'm memorizing his.

My hands come up to touch his thick hair, and I run them through the blond strands. His eyes flutter closed, and I make a mental note that he really likes that before looping my arms around his strong neck. I hold on tight, leaning in and fusing our mouths together again.

I feel him smile against my mouth, pulling away just long enough to whisper, "I love seeing you in my clothes." His voice low and gravelly.

Then he's kissing me again. His tongue dips out to taste my bottom lip, pulling a sound I barely recognize from the back of my throat.

The feelings this man can inspire in me while we're kissing are next level. It's an attraction that I didn't realize I could feel, a chemistry so intense I want to melt into it and let it consume me.

A rattle of bars and weights from Remy's home gym—situated right below my apartment—causes me to fly off the Bruce's lap. I stand beside the love seat, my breathing coming fast, and my heart is racing as I stare at Bruce. His lips are swollen and pink from our kisses.

"What if Remy sees your truck?"

He winces. It's subtle, but definitely a wince. "I parked a few blocks down and walked."

I breathe a sigh of relief, but there's still a pang in my chest. Guilt. "Bruce, this is crazy. How are we supposed to… I don't know, date? When you can't even park in front of my apartment."

He stands so he's right in front of me, then pulls me into his meaty arms that make me feel instantly safe and calm.

"Yeux bleus," he croons. "I want to date you; I want you to be mine. But if you're unsure, or not ready, I'll take whatever you're willing to give me. Whatever you're ready for."

"And what about my brother? We just don't tell him?"

His head pulls back, his expression growing serious. "We'll tell him. Let's go tell him right now."

He starts to pull out of my arms like he's going to go tell Remy right this second, but I stop him. I loop my hands tightly around his waist and realize even his torso is solid muscle. This man feels like a literal stone wall. "Bruce! You can't tell him *now*."

"Tell him what?" He arches a brow.

My mouth opens and closes as I try to define what exactly we're doing. What we are.

"I'm teasing," Bruce says. "We don't have to put labels on it, not until you're comfortable. But I don't share, Farrah." His eyes look so intensely into mine; I actually forget about Remy for a few seconds.

I nod. "I don't want to share either. And back to Remy…"

He growls. "I don't want to talk about your brother."

Placing my hands on his chest, I push gently. "We have to."

He sighs and pulls away. "Okay, what to do about your brother. He will barely look at me as it is, so at least we can't make it worse."

He says this sarcastically, but there's a hurt behind those twinkly blue eyes of his.

I think for a moment, considering how to handle all of this. "While you and I are exploring this thing between us, let's keep it to ourselves. We can get to know each other, and then maybe once the playoffs are done, we can tell Remy."

Bruce takes a step closer to me, his chest almost bumping against mine. "You want me to be your dirty little secret?"

His eyes come alive in a mischievous way. Yeah, I think he loves this idea.

I shoot him an unamused look. "If I started dating someone, I'd never tell Remy right away. I'd wait until we'd had time together, and then introduce you. Why should it be any different just because you're one of Remy's best friends?"

He tilts his head to the side and looks at me in a way that says *that's B.S. and you know it.*

"Farrah, I just want to give this a chance. I'll do whatever you tell me to do. And I don't think it would hurt to wait before telling Remy. What I do know is I want to see you as much as possible. I want to get to know you, and kiss you, and see you wearing more of my clothes."

"Okay, I'd like that, too. But only because your clothes are way more comfortable than mine," I tease.

Bruce gasps, and his hands move to my waist where he squeezes and tickles me. I squeal and writhe, trying to get out of his grasp.

My phone pings loudly, and I jump away from him and rush to check it. I want to make sure it's not Remy or Amber coming upstairs for something. But what if they did? Am I supposed to hide this giant of a man somewhere in this tiny apartment? And how ridiculous has my life become that I'd even be in a position to hide a man?!

"Farrah," Bruce cajoles in a calm, smooth tone. "Take a deep breath. You're spiraling."

I listen and take a deep breath, then check my phone.

I gasp when I see it's Remy texting me.

REMY

Are you okay up there? I thought I heard a scream. Is there another spider?

My eyes widen, and I look at Bruce. "It's Remy," I whisper-yell.

FARRAH

Ha! I'm fine. Just watching a scary movie.

REMY

You hate scary movies.

FARRAH

I wanted to try something new.

He has no idea how true that statement is.

REMY

Bruce moves toward me and reads the text exchange over my shoulder. "Do you really hate scary movies?"

I nod. "I don't understand why anyone would want to watch one."

Bruce heads toward the small sofa and sits, patting the spot beside him. "Well, I know what we're doing now."

"Absolutely not."

"Oh, come on," he says. "We can't kiss all evening." he smirks as he says it, knowing we absolutely could do that. But it would certainly lead to more than kissing going by the intensity of the few we've shared.

"We could, actually."

I sit beside him on the couch, allowing our legs to touch. I can feel him staring at my profile when he says, "Am I just a boy toy to you?" I look over just in time to see him drag a hand slowly from his pecs down to the waistband of his jeans. "You just want me for my body?"

I roll my eyes, but my skin is on fire.

Bruce chuckles. "Come on, let's watch a movie. And you got to pick last time, so this one's my choice."

"Fine," I say. "But if I can't sleep the rest of the week, no more kisses for you." I shoot him my best glare, but instead of looking intimidated, he leans in slowly and brushes his lips against mine.

My entire body goes limp, my eyes closing and my body relaxing into him. He pulls away slowly and huffs a laugh. "That's an empty threat. You like kissing me too much to withhold."

My jaw drops, knowing he just tricked me. With a harumph, I lean forward, grabbing my laptop off the coffee table and opening up a web browser.

Bruce quickly scrolls through the movies, and when he hovers over *Texas Chainsaw Massacre*, a chill goes down my spine.

He clicks on the movie, and it begins to play. Bruce wraps an arm around my shoulders and tugs me against his hard body. "It's okay, I'm here to keep you safe."

I sniff. "Yeah, until you leave and I'm all alone and terrified."

"Are you inviting me to stay the night?" He asks, but there's humor in his voice. "It's awfully fast for an overnight. But I accept."

"You're a shameless flirt," I say, swiveling my head to look up into his eyes.

His blue eyes focus on my mouth like he wants to kiss me again. "Only with you."

CHAPTER
TWENTY-FOUR

FARRAH

THE EVENING after Bruce's unexpected visit to my apartment, all the girls come over to Amber and Remy's house to watch the game. The guys traveled to New York for the final game in round one. And Bruce is on fire tonight.

The other team has thirty-four shots on goal—which means shots saved by the goalie—in the final period, but only two goals. The Eagles are ahead by four. A little flip dances through my stomach every time I wonder if Bruce is playing better because he got to see me. Is it cocky to believe his performance during the game has anything to do with me? Probably.

Amber is somber tonight; I can tell something is bothering her. Maybe it's the fact that Remy has been in the penalty box twice tonight, and my big brother never gets penalties.

She stands and heads into the kitchen to grab some popcorn.

When she comes back, she sits beside me again, and I lean over so we're close. "Are you okay?" I keep my voice soft, but not soft enough for the ever-nosey Andie not to overhear.

"Yeah, are you okay?" Andie repeats. "You seem down, Ambs."

Noel and Mel lean forward from their end of the couch to listen.

"I'm okay," she says with a sigh. "Remy just hasn't been himself lately. And he's not playing well tonight...which means he's going to be mad at himself, which means next time he calls he's going to be moody."

Andie pouts. "Sounds like Mitch."

Amber blows out a breath, then adjusts her red Remington jersey. All the girls wore their husband's jerseys tonight so they could get a photo. It made me wish I had a McBride jersey, but it's a little soon for that. Jerseys feel like a girlfriend thing. And right now, Bruce and I are only making out like teenagers and watching horrible movies that make me feel like peeing my pants.

"How do you deal with Mitch when he gets like that?" Amber asks, leaning forward to grab her fruity cocktail, then taking a sip.

Andie sighs dreamily. "Well, when he's home, it's quite fun to cheer him up." She winks. "But the away games are harder. Hearing his frustration and disappointment through the phone honestly sucks." Andie toys with the little pink umbrella of her drink. "Something I've learned is not to bull-shit him. He knows he played poorly, so don't try to sugar coat it. Just add some encouragement, like *you'll do better during the next game.*"

Amber nods. "Okay, that's good advice. Remy would hate if I tried to make it sound like he played great when he didn't."

Noel huffs a laugh. "Can they give Colby some of that humility? That man thinks he plays amazing every game."

We all laugh; then our attention turns back to the TV. since the Eagles are in another power play kill. Colby, Mitch and West are all working defensively to keep the Patriots from scoring on Bruce. One of their forwards slaps the puck with his stick toward the upper left corner and Bruce catches it swiftly in his glove. The camera zooms in on him and a wide grin spreads across his face. Then he notices the camera and winks, sending a swirl through my stomach. The wink was just for me.

The girls crack up, as do I. Bruce is such a big kid sometimes.

The game continues and the other team doesn't score during their power play. The Eagles manage to score one more time before the end of the game, and they officially move on to round two of the playoffs.

Andie sighs and turns off the TV. "I'm so relieved! The guys would've been distraught if they'd lost tonight."

Noel nods. "For sure. Even Colby seemed nervous about this game. It's so important to keep up their confidence and not let the pressure get to them."

Amber slumps back in her seat. "I hope Remy goes back to his normal, calm self soon. He's been so tense and irritable."

Mel grimaces. "I think tensions have been high during practices, as well."

Amber's eyebrows jump up at this. "Really? What are the guys saying?"

Mel's eyes flit briefly to me, then back to Amber. "I don't want to stir the pot, but it seems like Remy is giving Bruce the cold shoulder."

My heart stops, then feels like it falls from my chest to my belly and gets lodged there.

"Oh no!" Amber seems genuinely worried about this and looks over at me. Whatever is written across my face is clearly readable, because Amber slings an arm around my shoulders and hugs me close. "This is not your fault, Farrah. You didn't even do anything. And neither did Bruce."

She squeezes me, and it just makes me feel worse. Little does she know I was harboring the burly goalie in my room last night and savoring his lips. I'm not as innocent here as she thinks. And neither is Bruce.

Mel stands and comes to sit on my other side, placing a hand on my knee. "Oh, sweetie. You look so worried! Like the Stanley Cup rests on your shoulders." She chuckles, and the other girls join her. "Everything will be okay."

I force a laugh, hoping it doesn't sound unnatural.

"It will!" Andie says. "Mitch used to despise West, they even got into a few fights. But now they're close friends. So, trust me, the guys have been through plenty of crap before. And they always get over it."

Amber nods. "Remy has got to move on. Not only for his own sake, but for the team. I don't even understand why he's still so bothered by Bruce helping you."

Noel arches an eyebrow. "I don't think that's it," she says slowly, shooting me a sympathetic glance. "I think it's the way Bruce looks at Farrah. Everyone can tell he has a massive crush on you." She looks at me when she says the last part. "And, maybe it's just me, but you sort of...kind of, look at him the same way." She rolls her lips inside her mouth, almost as if she regrets speaking her thoughts out loud.

The girls nod in agreement. It sends a small thrill through me that they think Bruce looks at me in some type of way, but it's quickly followed by dread that they see I'm looking at him the same way.

I shrug out of Amber's arm, still settled across my shoulders, and lean forward on the couch. "Of course, I notice Bruce. Have you seen him? He's huge, like pick you up and press you against a wall huge. And he's handsome…like really handsome. And he's always flirting, and smirking. How am I supposed to ignore someone like that?" I sit up straight, throwing my hands in the air. "Do you know how long it's been since a handsome man flirted with me? It's addictive."

I know Bruce is more than a flirtatious, hot hockey player. I know he's kind, and helpful, and considerate. I know he goes out of his way to help Jackson. I know he's an amazing person. But I'm only admitting to surface level knowledge, not wanting to say too much. Not wanting them to know I have any feelings for the goalie besides a passing crush.

Maybe after Bruce and I get to know each other, we'll want to go public, or whatever the kids are calling it these days. But this high-stress playoff season is not the time to add this new, fragile thing. Especially when my brother is so butt-hurt about it.

I don't even get it. Bruce is one of his best friends, his teammates, his comrade. Why wouldn't he want us to be together? Is he really that worried about it?

"Oh, Farrah." Mel brings a hand to my back. "No one faults you for noticing Bruce. You're right, he's great. And who could blame him for staring at you? You're gorgeous."

"So gorgeous," Noel agrees. "I'd kill for your hair."

Andie gasps. "Oh my gosh, same. It's so shiny."

Amber nods. "You are stunning, Farrah. Bruce would be crazy not to notice you."

I shake my head, unable to hide my smile. "Stop, I'm going to get a big head." I do a dramatic hair flip, and we all laugh.

"I think you and Bruce would be amazing together. Bruce and Remy just need to fight this out," Andie says. "These dummies have to punch each other to express their feelings."

Noel snorts an undignified laugh. "Andie's not wrong."

Amber looks horrified. "That's awful! Remy would never punch someone."

Andie shoots her a knowing glance. "He might if he thinks Bruce will break his little sister's heart."

Amber seems to weigh these words, then grimaces. "Okay, you have a point."

My phone vibrates from the sofa cushion, and I'm so relieved it's facing downward, because when I check it, I have a text from Bruce right on the screen in clear view.

> BRUCE
>
> I already miss you, Yeux bleus. Can we Facetime?

My heart flutters rapidly.

I place my phone down like there's nothing important on it, then stretch my hands over my head and yawn. "Wow. I'm exhausted. I think I'm going to head to bed, ladies."

"Aw, already?" Mel asks, but then follows her question with a yawn of her own. "Ugh. I guess I'm tired too. This baby is already wearing me out and it's still in utero."

Amber chuckles. "Pregnancy wears you out." She stands up. "Sleep sounds amazing actually. Nella has been a force lately."

I wrinkle my nose but nod my head in agreement. "That red-head temper has been coming out for sure."

The girls and I hug and say our goodbyes; then I'm practically running up to my apartment to text Bruce back.

CHAPTER
TWENTY-FIVE

BRUCE

EXHAUSTED BUT HAPPY, I shower and get settled into bed for my Facetime with Farrah. I'm wearing grey sweats and a white tee but decide at the last second to remove the shirt. My skin is clean and moisturized and camera ready. I hope Farrah enjoys the view. I grab a fluffy hotel pillow and use it to prop up my phone, then lie on my side with one arm under my head.

I pull up her contact and tap on Facetime. She answers quickly, her gorgeous face filling the screen. She has a smile stretched across a face that's clean of makeup. Her skin is pink like she just washed her face, and she has a happy glow about her tonight that makes me smile.

"Hey, you look happy. Did you watch the game?"

She nods, pulling a fluffy blanket up around her chin. "I did. You killed it."

"Did you see me wink at you?"

Her pouty lips tug into a smirk. "That was for me?"

"Of course it was."

I watch as her eyes dip down my chest and torso. "You're very shirtless tonight."

"We could both be shirtless, if you want."

Her head falls back as she bursts into laughter. "You're relentless," she says through her laughter.

I love her like this. Ready for bed, curled up under the covers, relaxed, happy…I wish I was there just curled up next to her, with us talking to each other in hushed whispers and then falling asleep in each other's arms.

And if she was shirtless for all that, even better.

I chuckle. "It was worth a shot."

She shakes her head in reprimand. "Don't you feel great after that game?"

I blow out a breath. "Yes, it felt so good to win. Gave us some confidence. And your brother high-fived me! So maybe things are looking up."

As long as Farrah and I keep our romance on the down low, it should stay that way.

Farrah smiles a sad smile. "Sorry he's been such a weirdo. The girls and I talked about it earlier."

"Really?" I'm curious now, wondering exactly what was said and wishing I would've been there, gossiping with all the wives.

Farrah nods. "Yeah…they think you look at me like you have feelings for me."

I lean in so my face is closer to the screen. "I *do* have feelings for you."

She blushes adorably like this is news to her. Even though I've had my tongue in her mouth several times.

I'm smoldering at the phone screen, giving Farrah my sexiest look, when the door of my hotel room bursts open and Colby and Remy walk inside—damn it, Colby must've charmed the front desk into giving him a key again.

Colby's eyebrows raise as he takes in my shirtless,

lounging form and the phone in front of me. "Dude. I'm so sorry. I didn't know you were having…private time."

"No, no, no! I'm not!" I jump up, flicking the phone so it's face down on the mattress.

"Bruce? Are you still there?" Farrah's feminine voice filters through the phone, but it's muffled by the sheets.

Remy's eyebrows shoot up. "Are you talking to a woman?"

My eyes open wide, and I pull up the screen, wave goodbye to Farrah, and end the call as quickly as possible.

Colby's jaw drops and he places a case of my favorite sparkling water on the hotel desk. None of us are drinking alcohol now that we're moving onto round two of the playoffs.

"Well, well, well," he says with a knowing smirk.

Remy even smiles a little…he looks oddly relieved that I was talking to a woman. I'm guessing he thinks that means I've moved on and stopped thinking about his sister. Little does he know…

"Sorry we interrupted your date," Remy says. "But we wanted to celebrate tonight's win, which was mostly thanks to you."

I drag a hand through my wet hair. "Oh, yeah. It wasn't a date, though. I was just talking to my sister." Sister? Why did I say sister? That's going to remind Remy he has a sister.

Remy huffs a laugh. "You talk to your sister shirtless?"

"And give her sexy eyes?" Colby adds.

I jump off the bed and rest my hands on my hips. "I was not giving her sexy eyes."

"Brucey," Colby says. "You're full of it, and we know it. Now shut up and have some of this awful sparking water with us."

I roll my eyes. "It's not awful. It's pineapple flavored and it's delicious."

Colby shrugs. "If you say so. To me it tastes like a pineapple mixed with water, mixed with water again, mixed with piss, mixed with bubbles."

Remy wrinkles his nose. "That's disgusting, Knight."

Colby removes three cans from the box, throws one to me, hands another to Remy, and keeps one for himself. The three of us open our cans, tap them together, then chug as if it's beer or something stronger.

Colby swallows then pounds on his chest and coughs a few times. "Damn that's gross."

Remy shakes his head and smiles. "You're the most dramatic man I know."

Colby brings his hand to his chest. "Aww, Cap'n. Thank you so much." Colby glances at his Apple watch. "All right, I'm going to bed now. Night Bruce."

"Nighty night, Knight."

Colby snorts a laugh, then turns and leaves the hotel, taking his can of sparkling water with him. I'm sure he'll dump it out the moment he gets back to his own hotel room.

Remy lingers, looking down at his feet. That's what he does when he feels overwhelmed or uncomfortable. "Hey, I wanted to apologize. I've been so worried about Farrah." He clears his throat and finally looks up at me. "I'd never seen her as forlorn as she was after her divorce. That first few months I wondered if she'd ever be the same, you know?" He lifts a shoulder. "I took my worries out on you the past few weeks. But I should've trusted you. I know how loyal you are and that you'd never do anything to compromise our friendship." He blows out a long breath. "Anyway, sorry for being a jerk."

I blink. A twisting, churning sensation claws its way

down my spine and into my belly. I feel like a villain, an enemy. Someone who isn't trustworthy at all. Remy is staring at me, waiting for me to say something.

I swallow, and it's difficult, like there's something lodged in my throat. "It's okay, man. We're good."

His shoulders sag in relief. "Okay, good. I know you had a thing for Farrah, but I'm glad you're moving on. I'll let you get back to that date." He chuckles and tilts his head toward the phone lying on my bed.

I force a laugh that feels like sandpaper. "Yeah, man. See you in the morning."

He smiles his Remy smile. The one that's always put me at ease and made me feel like part of the brotherhood we've created. Only this time it makes me feel sick to my stomach.

CHAPTER
TWENTY-SIX

FARRAH

THE GUYS ARRIVE BACK from their away game this evening. They won, so now the second round begins, and they're over the moon. Amber told me that when she spoke to Remy last night his mood seemed to have gone back to normal. Thank goodness. We can't handle him *and* Nella having an attitude.

Everyone is having dinner here tonight, you'd think they'd all be sick of each other after traveling together, practicing together, and playing hockey together...but they're too hyped up not to celebrate by having some good food—although, they're on a strict eating regime now.

I haven't seen Bruce since he came to my apartment a few days ago, but it feels like it's been weeks. And seeing him tonight is going to be agonizing when I can't even hug him in front of everyone.

Now that he and Remy seem good, bringing any attention to our budding romance would be the worst thing I could do.

I baked a special cake for tonight, it's raspberry flavored with cream cheese frosting and has the D.C. Eagles logo decorating the top. Making it was how I distracted myself from my nerves about seeing Bruce tonight and not pouncing on him.

Remy arrives home with a big smile on his face. Amber, Nella, and Rose greet him at the garage door. Remy kisses Amber for a full minute, causing Nella to throw a tantrum because she's not getting enough attention. He quickly pats Rose's head then picks Nella up and kisses all over her face with his stubbly beard. The guys are officially growing out their playoff beards.

Bruce was clean shaven last I saw him, but I could tell from the footage of last night's game that he has a short beard now. I'm unsure how it will feel to kiss him…if we even find a chance to kiss.

Nella giggles at the prickly kisses and finally burrows into Remy's neck. He carries her into the kitchen where I'm prepping things for dinner and grins at me. "Hey, Farrah. It smells great in here."

Amber bounces in, clearly in a good mood that her man is home. "We made lasagnas." She pauses and adds, "with whole wheat pasta." My brother nods approvingly and she continues. "Salad, and French bread!"

Remy arches a brow, knowing Amber isn't much of a cook. "We?"

She sighs. "Okay, fine, it was mostly Farrah. But I did make the salad!"

She chopped lettuce. I made the dressing. I bite the insides of my cheeks to keep from laughing when my big brother gives me a knowing glance.

"Cake time!" Nella yells from her resting place on Remy's shoulder. "Cake time!"

"No, sweetie, it's not cake time yet," Amber tells her daughter in a cajoling tone.

Nella's face pinches in an angry scowl, and then she bursts into tears. "Cake time!" she wails.

Amber and I cringe in unison, and Remy frowns at the little girl in his arms.

"Can't we just give her some cake?" he asks in a hushed whisper.

Amber shakes her head. "She has to learn to wait, even when it's hard. And our guests aren't even here yet."

That's a lesson I need to learn, too…to wait even when it's hard. I remind myself again not to jump into Bruce's arms the moment I see him.

"Nells," Remy says, running a hand over her red curls. "How about an applesauce pouch instead? We have to wait for our guests to arrive before we have cake."

She sniffs but nods, and he scrambles toward the pantry to get her a pouch.

Glancing at the clock on the stove, I calculate that everyone will be here in an hour, and I'm still covered in flour from baking bread and the cake. I'm pretty sure I have marinara sauce on my face, as well.

"I'm going to go change and get ready for tonight." I smile and excuse myself.

Nella, still in Remy's arms, uses one hand to squeeze her apple pouch into her mouth, but raises the other one in a wave. I laugh and wave back.

When I step inside my apartment, I'm instantly on the hunt for something that oozes sex appeal but doesn't say trying too hard. If it looks like I'm trying to look hot for someone, that wouldn't be good, because Bruce is the only other single person coming tonight.

Rummaging through my drawers, I select a pair of light-wash 90's style shorts, since the weather has been warm all week. I decide to pair the shorts with some leather sandals and a simple, cropped grey top.

My hands are jittery as I move toward the bathroom, so I grab my phone and turn on some music—Chappel Roan. Not the best for calming nerves, but a fun distraction. I don't know if *Pink Pony Club* inspires the sparkly eye shadow and berry-pink lip-gloss I put on, but I'm looking pretty good.

Picking up my phone, I check the time. Everyone should be arriving any moment. I type out a text to Bruce before heading back downstairs.

FARRAH

Hey! If you're early at all, you could stop by my apartment before we head to the big house for dinner.

I worry my bottom lip...was the wink coming on too strong? I chuckle at myself...this is Bruce we're talking about. There's no coming on too strong for him.

BRUCE

Hi, this is Jackson. Bruce made me read and respond to your text. *Face palm emoji* I'm staying with him tonight, kind of a last-minute thing. He had to come pick me up, so we're running late.

I grimace. Okay, the wink was a bad idea.

FARRAH

Okay, no problem! Excited to see you both.

I slump down on my tiny sofa, feeling slightly deflated. No pre-dinner canoodling with my goalie. Okay, *my goalie* might be taking it a little far. We're just really good at kissing each other. We're enjoying this *thing*. We're having fun. No labels.

But I am excited to see Jackson again, and for him to meet the whole gang.

Hearing a few car doors slam from outside, I peek out my small window and see that Mel and West just pulled up, and also Mitch and Andie. I smile and head down to the big house.

Thirty minutes later, the food is ready, the table is set, and everyone is here—minus Bruce and Jackson.

I'm trying so hard not to glance at the front door every five seconds, and it's difficult. I've missed Bruce, I'm dying to see him…and we haven't been together at all since we decided to start seeing each other.

"Farrah, what is with you tonight?" Remy comes up beside me with a quizzical expression. He points to my sandaled foot, which I didn't realize I was tapping on the marble floor. I immediately stop.

"Oh, sorry. Had too much caffeine."

"Aw, I miss caffeine!" This comes from Mel, who comes up on my other side. She turns her attention to Remy. "Remy, should we wait for Bruce, or get started? I'm starving." Mel pats her belly, which is just barely starting to poke out. If you didn't know she was pregnant, you'd probably just think she had a large meal.

"Yeah, let's get started," Remy answers. "I just texted him, and he should be here in ten."

A smile tugs at my lips, but I force it away.

Remy gets everyone's attention and gets them seated at the large table off the kitchen. It's a table long enough to fit everyone when they're here, minus the kids. There's a place setting for Noah and Jackson at the island, and Nella is in her highchair. It's almost her bedtime, and her eyes are looking watery and tired. To be honest, the girl is on the verge of a meltdown. I walk over where Amber is seated beside her and crouch down, so I'm face to face with my precious niece. I need something to do with my hands, and I know Amber is exhausted from Remy being out of town, so I hold my hands out to Nella.

"I'll take her while you guys get food."

Amber kisses her daughter's cheek. "Are you sure? Aren't you hungry?"

"I'm good; I can wait. I wanna hold this one before she goes to bed."

Nella grins at me and lifts her hands in the air. I unbuckle her and pull her out of her chair, squeezing the little drama queen close and enjoying the weight of her in my arms. Nella has always had a calming effect on me, which is the opposite of what I anticipated. She's healed something inside of me. Loving her has brought me a joy I can't express. And right now, when I'm nervous and anxious about seeing Bruce McBride, it's no different. A wave of calm serenity moves over me. Nella lays her head on my chest, and I nuzzle my chin into her soft hair.

"Cake time?" I hear her ask, which makes me laugh.

"Almost. Let's eat some lasagna first."

She whines, and I pat her back to soothe her.

When I notice everyone is seated at the table, I tiptoe toward the cake that's on the kitchen counter. Noah, who's seated at the bar and digging into his lasagna, studies me as I move. I bring my free hand to my mouth in a plea for him to stay quiet. He smirks and keeps watching as I cut a tiny sliver of cake and grab a fork.

I stab a bite and bring it to Nella's face. She gasps and smiles. "Cake time," she whispers, somehow knowing to stay quiet. That's the funny thing about children—no one has to teach them to be naughty; it's an innate sense they're born with.

She gobbles up the bite quickly and rubs her little belly. "Yum!"

Noah and I snicker and peek at the dining table to make sure no one is watching. I give her another bite and she reacts just as excitedly for the second bite.

Amber strides into the kitchen, still chewing. "Okay, I'll take her now! I'm done eating," she says this with food in her mouth. When she notices the frosting on her daughter's mouth, she rests a fist on her hip. "Seriously? You just can't say no to her, can you?"

I scrunch my nose and shake my head. "It's really difficult."

Amber laughs and scoops Nella into her arms. "It's okay, aunt privileges."

I'm laughing and watching her carry Nella back to her highchair when a devastatingly handsome blond man swaggers into the room and takes my breath away. His focus goes straight to me, looking me up and down with a predatory gaze and a grin growing on his face. He winks and starts walking toward me, when he notices Noah for the first time and stops in his tracks. Noah glances between the two of us, his brain clearly working.

He points to Bruce and then to me. "Whatever I just saw, I don't think I was supposed to see it."

Bruce winks and grabs his wallet. He pulls out a twenty and tosses it to Noah. "Hush money."

Noah shrugs and pockets the cash.

Jackson, who's been standing behind Bruce until this moment, pushes the big oaf to the side. "Hey, Farrah."

"Jackson, glad to see you! Want some lasagna?" I ask

him, trying to stay focused on him and not the hunk standing a foot away from him.

Jackson shrugs. "Lasagna sounds good."

"Jackson, this is Noah," Bruce explains. "He's a good kid, great hockey player, and I've heard he's excellent at keeping his mouth shut." He shoots Noah, a look of reprimand and Noah has the good sense to look mildly intimidated.

Noah's eyes move to Jackson, and he nods. "How's it going?" Noah says in greeting. "It's nice to have another person here who's not old."

"Hey!" I say in mock offense.

"Nella's not old," Bruce offers.

Noah's eyebrows raise. "Yeah, but she's violent. I still have bruises from playing hockey with her."

"Aw, did little Nella kick your ass?" Bruce pokes his bottom lip out in a pout, and I remember how it felt to bite down on that lip.

"Keep that up and your secrets will no longer be safe, my guy." Noah arches a knowing brow.

Bruce clears his throat. "Right. I'm really sorry about your bruises, man."

"Is that Bruce?" Remy yells from the dining room before standing up and crossing the space separating us.

"Hey, Cap'n," Bruce tells him with an easy smile.

It's nice to see things back to normal between the two of them. I don't know what made the stick that was up Remy's butt finally come out, but I'm not going to question it.

Remy and Bruce do that half handshake-half hug thing that men do, pounding on each other's backs and then pulling away.

"Grab some food and join us," Remy says. "You too, Farrah."

Remy heads back to the table, and Bruce follows me to the lasagna that's still sitting on the stove top. I grab a plate, and he reaches for one at the same time, on purpose. His hand eclipses mine and he allows it to linger there for a moment. The warmth of his skin and the hungry look he's giving me sends a shiver throughout my body and I want nothing more than to lean back further and press my body to his.

Bruce notices the shiver and leans in close and whispers. "Are you cold, Farrah?"

He presses closer, his front brushing against my back. "This…lasagna…looks delicious," he says it low and slow, and he's not looking at the food. He's looking at me.

Can lasagna be an aphrodisiac? Is this what people mean when they say *talk dirty to me*? Probably not. But it's working.

"If you two are trying to be discreet, you really suck at it."

We jump apart at the sound of Noah's voice, both of us looking over our shoulders to see Jackson and Noah watching us closely. Jackson rolls his eyes and Noah shakes his head.

"I was just serving him some lasagna," I say, my face hot and likely very red.

I quickly grab Bruce's plate and plop a serving of lasagna on it. "There's salad over there." I point to the area of the island where there's a little salad bar set up.

Bruce nods, allowing his bright blue eyes to hold mine for a sweet moment. "Thank you."

Once we both have food, we head to the big table where conversation is loud and lively. There are two spots left, right beside each other at the head of the table on the opposite end that Remy and Amber are sitting at.

I take my seat, avoiding eye contact with Andie, who's on the other side of Bruce. She seems to see everything and sense everything and it creeps me out. There's no way I can look at her without her immediately knowing that I'm thinking of dragging Bruce McBride up to my apartment and stripping his gigantic clothes off. Where does a man even purchase clothing so large?

What has gotten into me?

I don't have to touch my ears to know they're on fire right now. And I can feel Andie's knowing gaze on me. Hopefully she'll think I'm coming down with a cold or something.

When Bruce takes his seat next to me, he conveniently bumps his chair, so it scoots closer to mine. I hear Andie clear her throat but refuse to look up. Instead, I focus on the delicious lasagna I made. Yummy!

Colby, who's sitting on my opposite side, begins to laugh at something my brother said from the far end of the table. "Yeah, so we convinced the hostess to give us Bruce's hotel key, wanting to surprise him."

All the guys start laughing together, and my head snaps up to better listen to the conversation since it's about Bruce.

"But he was shirtless, and laying on the bed all sensual-like," Colby continues, waggling his dark eyebrows. Noel glances from her husband to Bruce, probably searching for his reaction to them telling this story to everyone. Noel is perceptive in a different way than Andie. Noel is all stealth and silent observation, where Andie has more of a honey badger style of communication.

"And he was talking to a woman?" West asks, turning to Bruce. "When do we get to meet the mystery woman, man?"

I carefully glance over at Bruce, not wanting to draw

attention to myself. For a split second, I think he was talking to a woman who wasn't me, until I remember our Facetime and how he was lying on the bed. They're right, he did look very sexy…and it was all for me. This realization calms me instantly, and I remind myself that Bruce isn't Connor. Not that my ex cheated on me—that I know of—but more of a reminder that Bruce cares about me and wouldn't treat me like I was disposable like that. That's not how he treats people.

Bruce's neck is turning redder the longer the conversation continues, and usually he would relish being the center of attention. But he knows he's on thin ice with his captain, and that the woman he was actually on the phone with is the one woman he's not supposed to be with. So, both of us are sitting here with tense spines and our blushes creeping up.

And Andie is still staring at us.

I look down at my food again, poking the lasagna and placing a bite in my mouth. It tastes like nothing. All I can hear, see, and taste, is the uncomfortable story unfolding around me.

"He was in a big hurry to get rid of us," my brother says with a chuckle.

"Yeah, he probably was going to do a strip tease for her. Too bad we missed it!" Colby laughs and stands up, acting like he's going to rip his shirt off. Noel grabs the back of his shirt and forces him back down in his seat.

"So, who was she? Is it serious?" West asks.

I freeze with my fork midway to my mouth.

Bruce laughs, but it's not his big, hearty laugh. It's a forced one. "Nah, it's not serious. You know me."

Remy swallows the bite of food he was chewing. "But you haven't dated in over a year, man. It must be someone special."

"Yeah, don't lie. Where'd you meet her?" Colby asks.

Bruce pulls his bottom lip into his mouth, looking deep in thought. "All right, all right. We met at a bar. She's the most beautiful woman I've ever seen. But more importantly, she's kind and funny and a great cook."

He pauses for dramatic effect, and all the wives glance at me, their expressions worried. I'm sure they're thinking about me admitting my crush the other night and wondering how I'm handling this news.

Little do they know my heart is about to leap out of my chest. The frenzy inside me grows faster and faster the more he goes on about me. But I'm the only one who knows he's talking about me. I shoot Amber a small smile, letting her know I'm fine.

"Honestly?" he continues, holding everyone's attention —including mine. "I'm pretty serious about her. It took me a long time to convince her to give me a chance."

I glance briefly to my left, giving Bruce a friendly, neutral smile. Something that I hope everyone in the room is reading as me being happy for him and not at all bothered.

The girls are all shooting me quizzical looks, likely surprised Bruce met someone when they thought he was so into *me*. Suddenly, it feels wrong to hide this thing brewing between Bruce and me. But I never thought it would get so out of hand, that we'd have to lie this much, and that we might hurt some of our favorite people in the process.

I force my focus back on my food again, picking up some salad with my fork, when I feel a warm hand rest on my thigh under the table. Bruce squeezes gently and I release a breath and relax into my chair. Everything will be okay. We're in this together.

"When can we meet her?" Remy asks.

Another squeeze from Bruce's hand on my thigh. "As soon as she's ready."

Remy nods, seeming to be fine with that answer.

Finally, the subject is changed, and soon everyone's done eating. The group of friends shuffles inside the kitchen for dessert and Remy excuses himself to put Nella to sleep.

Needing a moment to regroup and compose myself after holding it together all throughout dinner, I make sure Amber is fine cutting the cake for everyone and head to the guest bathroom downstairs. It's just a half bath with a small cabinet, countertop, sink, round mirror, and toilet. It used to be bare, but Amber recently decorated it in golds and pinks.

I close the door and rest my back against it, inhaling a deep breath and closing my eyes. I startle when a soft knock comes from the other side.

I wait for a moment, and another knock comes. "Busy!" I say.

A deep throat clears. "Farrah, it's me."

Opening the door, I find Bruce. He pushes inside the small room and closes the door and locks it, pinning me quickly against the door. He leans in, kissing me roughly, like he's been waiting years for this moment.

He hums, a deep sound in the back of his throat that sends goosebump along my arms. "I missed you, Yeux bleus." His lips move away from mine, but only to run along my jaw and then down my neck.

"I missed you too. But we can't both be in here; it's too obvious." I give a very weak attempt at pushing him away and he doesn't budge.

But I didn't really want him to.

He kisses my neck, tasting my skin. My hands stop pushing against him and instead grip his T-shirt tight to bring him closer. Bruce's mouth comes back up to tangle with mine, and we're lost in each other for a glorious moment until the door handle rattles.

I gasp, my eyes widening and searching Bruce's. "Oh no, what are we going to do?"

Bruce brings a hand up and presses a finger against my lips. I refrain from dipping my tongue out and licking it. That wouldn't help our current predicament one bit.

Bruce clears his throat. "This bathroom is occupied."

"Hurry up," Noah grumps from the other side. "I have to pee."

Bruce rolls his eyes and reaches down to hold onto my wrist, then tugs me behind him. He cracks the bathroom door open and looks out. Determining it's safe, he opens the door wider, and we both step out.

Noah eyes us with keen judgment, making him look much older and wiser than his thirteen years of age.

"Wow," he says dryly, holding a hand out. "Your ass is mine, McBride."

Bruce growls and grabs his wallet, pulling out another twenty and slapping it into Noah's ready palm.

Noah shakes his head like a father who's disappointed in his children. "I'll never have to work a day in my life at this rate."

Bruce rolls his eyes as Noah disappears into the bathroom.

"That was close," I whisper. "Too close." I sigh heavily. "I'm going back to the kitchen, but you should wait at least five minutes. Then no one will know we were both back here."

"Except Noah."

I grimace. "You think he'll tell anyone?"

He shakes his head. "Nah, all he cares about is playing hockey."

I nod, then start walking back down the long hallway into the main area of the house. But before I get too far, Bruce gently grabs onto my hand and brings it to his lips for one final kiss.

The D.C. Eagles #1 Fan Page On Hockeyisbetterthanfootball.com

Craig Nottingham: Okay, okay. I've got to admit…after that last game, McBride is going to kill it in this second round.

Todd Ferguson: I TOLD YOU HE WAS THE BEST GOALIE IN THE LEAGUE.

Craig Nottingham: Okay, that's taking it too far.

Harry Johnson: Craig, if the Eagles win the cup this year, you'll be eating your words.

Todd Ferguson: And I can't wait to see it!

Craig Nottingham: Yeah, yeah, yeah. Let's just focus on winning round two for now.

"SO, are we just not going to talk about what's going on between you and Farrah?" Jackson asks.

I glance over from my spot on the couch to look at him. He's watching me instead of the movie playing on my TV. I shrug. "What's there to talk about? We're friends."

Jackson rolls his eyes. "Yeah, okay. So, I guess you decided to go for it and deal with the consequences from your captain later?"

I sigh. "Something like that." My chest hurts at the reminder of how Remy will inevitably react when he finds out. And I do plan on him finding out, because this thing between me and his sister will last forever if I have my way. "I think I'm falling for her."

Jackson nods, like he already knew, and I think back to seeing Farrah earlier this evening.

Am I still annoyed Noah interrupted our bathroom rendezvous? (there's a sentence I never thought would go through my head.) Yes. But was it for the best so someone else didn't catch us? Also, yes.

I would've parked around the corner after dinner and spent the rest of the evening in her apartment making up for lost time, but Jackson's social worker called me about respite care the moment our plane landed earlier today. I enjoy spending time with him and knowing he's safe, so I didn't hesitate to accept.

I toss my phone far away from myself, so I'm not tempted to zone out again. We turned this movie on to watch it together, and he obviously noticed I wasn't paying attention.

"Okay, man. Sorry for getting distracted. Let's watch the movie. Which one did you pick again?"

An annoyed sigh comes from Jackson's end of the sofa. "The Mighty Ducks. It's been playing for forty minutes."

"That's one of my favorite movies!"

"I know, dumbass, that's why I picked it."

"Language, mister." I raise an eyebrow. "Do all the chess club kids have potty mouths?"

He blows out a breath. "Oh yeah, we're basically a bunch of gang members."

I chuckle. "Buncha rebels, those chess guys."

"You know it," he teases. "Do you have popcorn?"

"Yeah," I answer, beginning to push myself off the couch.

Jackson raises a hand to stop me. "Start the movie over, and I'll get it. I think I know where it's at."

I sit back and smile, liking that he knows his way around and that he's comfortable here. It's also nice having him around, even though that meant I couldn't get extra time with Farrah. I like that I'm not sitting home alone tonight.

I start the movie over, and soon Jackson comes back with a big bowl of popcorn, one can of sparkling water, and a can of Coke.

"Thanks, kid," I say.

He holds up his can, and we tap the brims together.

"Now pay attention this time," Jackson warns. "Maybe you can learn a thing or two from Greg Goldberg."

———

Early the following morning, I drop Jackson off at school and then heading to an early morning skate. We have a two-day break before our first two games in the second round against the Texas Spurs. These two home games are our best chance to get ahead for round two.

And if we choke this round…we're out.

As I arrive at the Eagles ice plex where our practices take place, I find myself looking forward to hanging with my teammates, and thankful there's no more awkwardness between us.

For now. Those two words keep running through my head and taking away my joy, replacing it with a tight feeling of dread in my gut. This peaceful harmony between teammates is a vapor in time; it's fleeting. And no matter what I do, I can't ignore that fact.

My heart is feeling heavier when I walk inside our locker room to get my gear on. I'm going to need a hell of a romcom to get my head in the game on Wednesday. Maybe Farrah can come watch it with me...in my truck. Triple the luck.

I shake my head. That's the stupidest idea I've ever had.

I'm pulling on my padded shorts when Mitch strides into the room and stops in his tracks the moment he sees me. He glances around before crossing the room, each step manufactured with malice, and I'm gonna be honest—I'm terrified.

He stops right in front of me, his nostrils flaring. "Are you seriously trying to hide that you're with Farrah? In the middle of playoffs?"

My eyes widen, and I open my mouth to speak but nothing comes out. "Wh—what?"

"Don't lie to me, Noah tells his sister everything."

I groan and slump down on the bench. "That brat owes me forty bucks." Resting my elbows on my knees, I attempt to rub away the stress by pressing my fingers into my temples. "What am I supposed to do, Mitch? I think I love her."

I glance back up and find that Mitch's pinched expression relaxes—barely—at my admission. "Really? It's not just a fling?"

My head whips up to glare at him. "Is that what you think of me? That I'd lead her on and use her?"

He drags a hand through his hair. "No. I don't know. Damn it. I've just never seen you date anyone more than once. This is Remy's *sister*, man. You better be sure you're in it for the long haul."

"I am. I swear." I bring my hands up and bury my face in them. How have I mucked this up so bad? With a deep breath, I look back up at my teammate. "Over the last two years I've watched as all my friends found their person. I've watched you all fall in love and become better men for it. There hasn't been one second where I've wondered if any of you missed being single. You guys are annoyingly happy. And your wives are all incredible, way too good for the lot of you. Do you really think I could have a front row seat to all of that and want to keep dating random woman after random woman? No way."

Mitch narrows his eyes at me, but not in a menacing way, more like he's contemplating what to say next. "All right. I get it. I mean, you're going through life like normal, and then all of a sudden, on a random Tuesday, a woman walks into your life and changes everything." He shakes his head like he's remembering back to the day when he met Andie. "And you can't stop thinking about her or picturing a future with her…it's wild." At some point while he was talking, my grumpiest teammate began to smile.

I smile back. "See? That's Farrah for me."

He rests his hands on his hips and blows out a long, deep breath. "I won't say anything, seeing as we're nearly halfway through the playoffs, but I hope you know what you're doing."

I sober at the reminder. "Me too, man. Me too."

TWENTY-EIGHT

BRUCE

AFTER PRACTICE, I shower and change then drive as fast as I can over to Farrah's apartment. Parking several blocks down the street from her place puts a twisted feeling in my gut. It feels dishonest and cold. All I want is to come clean, to tell everyone that Farrah and I are together. But one—she's not ready. And two—I can't risk upsetting our team dynamic in the middle of the freaking playoffs.

So, I'm walking a tightrope, and every time I see my team captain it feels like that tightrope's about to snap, and send me tumbling to the ground.

I sneak around the side of the house, hoping Remy hasn't installed any new security cameras I didn't know about before and feeling ridiculous. I'm a grown man sneaking into a girl's window—er, apartment.

As I'm creeping up the steps to her apartment, she opens her door and peers out. Her pretty face brightens as soon as she sees me, a wide grin appearing. If I could put that look on her face for the rest of my life, I could die a happy man. Stanley Cups or no. It's her smile that has the guilt in my stomach withering away, replacing it with a warm sensation of contentment and happiness.

Her thin tank top and little pink pajama shorts are enough to drive a man wild, and I bound up the steps faster. When I reach her, she throws her arms around my neck. My hands slide around her waist, holding her steady as I kiss her and walk us back inside her apartment. I kick the door closed with a snap of my heel, making Farrah laugh against my lips.

We exchange a smile and chuckle in between kisses and roaming hands. Farrah's fingers press against my chest, then glide slowly down my stomach. She takes her time, like she's counting every muscle there. While she savors the planes of muscle on my body, I enjoy the softness of hers beneath my own hands. Her mouth moves from my lips to a spot right on the pulse point of my neck that until just now, I didn't know was an area I like being kissed. But I like it. A lot. My blood feels like it's thrumming throughout my body, every nerve ending coming alive with the desire to touch her.

She moves to my earlobe, the pierced one, and tugs gently with her teeth. I groan, using my hold on her waist to push against her and put some distance between us. She whines and tries to come closer again.

I bring my hands to her shoulders and hold her at arm's length. Once I'm sure she'll stay put, I move backward across the room until my butt hits the kitchen counter.

"Okay. Here's the thing. We know we have incredible physical chemistry...like, out of this world, insanely hot chemistry. But..."

Her lips twist to the side in a sassy expression, waiting for me to finish the sentence. She crosses her arms over her ample chest, briefly drawing my attention there. I close my eyes and try to remember what I was talking about.

"But I want us to get to know each other. When we're kissing, we're not talking."

She holds her hands out to her sides. "Haven't we been getting to know each other for the last year and a half?"

I cross my arms this time, mirroring the sassy pose she did a moment ago. "Oh, is that what we were doing? Do you mean the year and a half that you were completely ignoring me and pretending I didn't exist? I guess I didn't get to know you very well, seeing as you would barely look at me."

Her pout lifts into a hesitant smile, and she takes one small step toward me. My arms uncross and I brace my hands on the countertop behind me.

"When I looked at you, I remembered our kiss. And when I remembered our kiss... I wanted to repeat it." Her eyes go from soft and sweet and innocent to dangerous and sultry.

I swallow as she prowls toward me. She's the cheetah and I'm the...what do cheetahs eat? Don't know and don't care right now. But it's amusing watching her move like she's the one with all the power, considering how much bigger I am. But just this once I don't mind being the hunted. As long as she's the huntress. Who'd have thought this sweet little baker could be such a minx?

She continues her slow prowl toward me, not stopping until her chest brushes against mine. She's close enough that she's forced to tilt her chin to meet my gaze. I'm sure my eyes are as dark as hers currently are.

Farrah's hands come up to rest on my waist, right above my hips and she leans against me. "What do you want to know about me, McBride?"

I look into her eyes, really trying to see her. Not just who she is on the outside, but her soul. I reluctantly remove one hand from where it's braced for safety on the counter behind me and move it to her chin. My hand cups her gorgeous face.

"Everything," I say, my voice deep and low.

I kiss her softly, then pull back. My hand moves down to hold hers, and I lead her to the couch. We sit down close to each other, our hands still linked.

"Let's play a game." I search the dark blue eyes I can't stop thinking about. "Twenty questions."

She laughs. "I'll give you three."

"Five."

She glances upward, considering this. "Okay, fine. Five questions."

"And you can ask me five in return." I shrug. "Or twenty. *I'm* an open book."

Farrah rolls her eyes. "I didn't limit the amount because I'm closed off, I just wanted to get back to the kissing faster."

I shoot her what I hope is a roguish look. "You ladies always have one thing on your minds."

She sighs like she's annoyed, but she can't wipe the smile off her face. "Let me get us some drinks before we start this. What do you want? I have seltzers, wine, Coke Zero, water."

"Nonalcoholic seltzer?"

"You got it. Pineapple?" Farrah arches a knowing eyebrow.

"You took note of my favorite, eh?"

She gets up and starts to walk away, but glances back at me over her shoulder. It's hot. Very hot. "I wanted to be prepared."

Goodness, I love this confident side of her personality.

Farrah smiles at me, then heads to the fridge and pulls out a seltzer and a Coke Zero and comes back to sit beside me.

"Not a seltzer girl?" I ask, watching as she snaps the top of her can and takes a sip.

"No, that stuff is disgusting. No offense."

I shake my head. "More for me, I guess."

"Okay, enough small talk, McBride. Ask the first question." She leans forward to place her can on the coffee table, the motion causing the bottom of her tank top to pull up, exposing a sliver of the bronze skin on her back. I just know that area of her back must be smooth and soft, and I'd do just about anything to run my hands along it.

I blink a few times, reminding myself we're getting to know each other. And I'm supposed to ask a question. I try to think of one to start us off that's not too invasive.

"Did you play any sports growing up?"

She smiles, like she thought of a happy memory. "Volley-ball. I loved it."

I roll my lips with my teeth, trying not to whimper. Farrah in those little volleyball shorts? That's my new fantasy.

"Really? Volleyball is what gets you going?" She asks, obviously seeing the desire written across my face.

"I think everything about you gets me going."

"You're the one who put a stop to the kissing."

"Huge mistake," I say, leaning toward her with a grin that I can't hide.

She pushes me away with a hearty laugh. "Stay focused! I want to know what your other questions are."

"All I really needed to know was that you own a pair of volleyball shorts."

Farrah playfully slaps my shoulder. "Okay, it's my turn. What's your most embarrassing moment?"

Groaning, I slump back against the sofa cushions then

smack a hand over my face. "I changed my mind! I want a dare!"

Farrah laughs. It's loud and unreserved and the sound of it could pull me out of the darkest mood—if I was in a dark mood.

Uncovering my face, I watch her in fascination, loving all the different facets of her personality.

"This isn't truth or dare. Just truth," she finally says through her laughter.

I release a half-laugh, half-groan. "Fine. When I was ten, I was in net for a hockey tournament. I'd spent all summer going to goalie clinics and camps…then all fall doing extra ice time on top of practices. We were about to win the tourney, our team's first ever championship. But I was nervous, it was my first big success playing goalie. I was so nervous; I drank a water bottle throughout each period. Whenever I was nervous, I took a sip."

She gasps and her hands cover her mouth.

I run my tongue along my front teeth, remembering that day like it was hours ago. "And as you can probably guess, I pissed myself. All over the ice. It was a big puddle…enough for my teammates to notice when they rushed to congratulate me when we won. One of the kids slipped in the puddle."

Farrah wrinkles her nose in disgust. "Okay, that's pretty bad."

"So, are you still attracted to me now that you know that?"

She smirks. "Is that one of your five questions? Choose wisely."

I bite my bottom lip and place a hand on her thigh, then slowly slide that hand up higher and higher. Her breath hitches and goosebumps break out along her smooth, tanned legs.

I exhale a cocky laugh. "Nah, you're definitely still attracted to me. So, my second question is—"

"You're the worst." Farrah gasps and tries to scoot away from me, grabbing one of her colorful throw pillows and tossing it toward my face. It misses, and I lunge forward, gripping her around the waist and holding on tight then pulling her onto my lap like I did the last time I was here.

"Come back here."

She shakes her head but doesn't push me away. I keep my arms around her waist, and she lays her head down on my shoulder. I could sigh happily, but I refrain, not wanting to be too cheesy. But it feels so good to hold her like this.

"What's your favorite childhood memory?" I ask, keeping my voice low as to not ruin the moment.

Farrah moves her head, getting more comfortable. I can feel her smiling against my shirt, like she instantly thought of a good memory, something that has stuck with her through the years.

"It might sound silly, but we used to go to a quiet beach in Michigan every summer. We stayed in the same beach house every year. It had white siding, and a wraparound front porch with a swing. The front gate opened to a private beach and us kids would run and laugh and build sandcastles while Mom and Dad rested in lawn chairs, always holding hands and grinning at each other. I always thought to myself that that's exactly what I wanted someday. To have a family with my soul mate. I thought even the simplest things would feel lovely if I had the right person by my side." As she trails off, her voice grows softer, a sadness burrowed within.

She pulls away from me, and I miss the heat of her body

pressing against my chest. Farrah slowly scoots off my lap and sits beside me, her back resting against the couch, and her shoulder pressing into me. I'm thankful she left that tiny bit of connection.

"I'm sorry your ex wasn't that person, but that doesn't mean he doesn't exist."

She tilts her head to look up at me, and her sad eyes break me apart. "You really think so?"

I nod. "I have a pretty good feeling your soul mate is still waiting for you."

Her eyes become glassy, and the sight causes something to snap inside of me. The things that idiot ex of hers said and did…they still affect her. They might always.

But I'll do everything I can to assure her she's wonderful, beautiful, and worthy of love. And whatever else that man might have convinced her that wasn't true.

I look into her eyes and the tears that were brimming there a moment ago, are gone. I breathe a sigh of relief. Not because I can't handle seeing a woman cry…but because she's crying over someone that doesn't deserve her tears, her love, her anything.

"Your turn," I say lightly, hoping to brighten the mood.

Farrah worries her plump bottom lip in a way that tortures me. "Who's your favorite Disney princess?"

I chuckle but her expression stays serious, I grow somber.

"Take it seriously; your answer is very important." Her face is so stoic it's almost scary. And it makes me nervous because I would usually just say Ariel since she's wearing the skimpiest outfit…but Farrah wants me to put some thought into this. So, I do. I take a few minutes to really mull it over, while she sips on her Coke.

"Tiana," I answer finally, nervous it's not the correct answer.

"Okay," Farrah says, dragging out the y sound. "Why her?"

"That's two questions, but okay."

She rolls her eyes.

"Tiana is strong, kind, and hard working. And she's a baker. Bakers are hot."

Farrah laughs again and I join her. "I'm surprised you even know who Tiana is. Everyone forgets about her even though she's arguably the best princess."

"I watched *The Princess and the Frog* before a game last year. And I got a shutout that night, so I think Tiana might be another lucky charm."

She shakes her head, causing her shiny dark hair to fall over her shoulder. I reach up and thread my hand through the silky strands. It's so damn silky.

Farrah closes her eyes, savoring the moment. "You like to have your hair played with?" I ask.

She nods.

"Sit on the floor, between my legs."

Farrah's eyes widen but she obeys, taking a throw pillow with her and sitting on it. She rests her shoulders on the back of the couch and my legs surround her. Once her head is nestled between my thighs, I'm wondering how smart of a decision this was, but I push the thought away and grab the pink brush I see on the coffee table. I begin brushing her hair with smooth, long strokes. When it's free of tangles, I replace the brush with my hands. First, I run them through the tresses, then I focus on her scalp, digging in gently with the pads of my fingers. She closes her eyes and allows her head to fall back with a contented sigh.

I continue the massage until she's fully limp and relaxed. I slowly bring my hands to a stop and rest them on her shoulders. She doesn't move. I lean forward so my face is hovering over hers and her eyes flutter open. They're hazy like she just woke up from a deep sleep.

She doesn't look away when her hands move up to my face, and she pulls me closer until my lips are on hers. It's strange at first, kissing her upside down, but our lips seem to fit perfectly at any angle.

She parts her lips, and I take our kiss deeper, enjoying the soft sounds she's making.

I realize then that I'm never going to get my other three questions in tonight. But I can't bring myself to be mad about it.

TWENTY-NINE

FARRAH

I'M GOING to Bruce's game tonight. And it feels weird.

All the girls are meeting at the arena, all of them wearing their WAG (wives and girlfriends) jackets. These jackets are the dream. They're customized, blinged out, and completely fabulous. The wives and girlfriends go all out for the play-offs, sometimes they'll have a different look for each playoff round. It's my favorite part of the hockey season, seeing what all the girls wear to the playoff games. Silly I know, but it's art. Like the icing on a cake…the WAG playoff jackets are that for me.

And I'll be the only person without one…because Bruce isn't my boyfriend, and because whatever we're doing is a secret. But suddenly I want to tell everyone so I can snag one of those jackets.

Amber has a sitter for Nella, a sweet teen who lives down the street, since the game will run late. Especially if it goes into overtime, which playoff games tend to do. That's what happens when the teams are so equally matched.

I study myself in the bathroom mirror for the millionth time, even though I might not even get to see Bruce tonight.

My dark hair is in a high ponytail with a red ribbon tied around it. I'm wearing black leggings that look like they're made of leather, white high-top sneakers, a red crew neck shirt, and a denim jacket over the top so I won't get cold. I might not match the other girls tonight, but at least I'll blend in.

My doorbell rings, but I take a second to apply another coat of my cherry-red lipstick. Red is the color of the Eagles home jerseys, and all the girls are doing a red lip tonight. With my lips perfected, I rush to answer the door.

Amber stands before me in a black mini skirt, heeled boots that pull up over her knees, and an out of this world red satin jacket. It's bedazzled with blue and white rhinestones and has my brother's number on the tops of the sleeves, kind of like a military dress uniform. She grins at me, her red lipstick perfectly in place, then spins so I can see the back where the jacket is emblazoned with 'Remington' in more blue and white rhinestones. Right under my brother's name is a gorgeous, embroidered eagle. The eagle is soaring, hopefully right into the final round of playoffs.

It's the best WAG jacket I've ever seen. I'm raging with jealousy on the inside, but it quickly subsides because Amber looks incredible, and I know we're going to have the best time tonight.

I allow my jaw to drop as I take her in. "Amber! You're a babe! Wow."

She flips her hair that's curled in loose waves and winks. "You think Remy will like it?"

"He'd be crazy not to."

"You look amazing too! I wish you had a jacket. I should've had an extra Remington one made." Her mouth turns down at the corners.

"Absolutely not; that would be so weird." I grab my

small handbag from my table. "Okay, let's go meet the girls. I have a feeling it's going to be a very good night."

Amber squeals and does a little bounce—impressive in those boots. She grabs my hand and hauls me outside.

An hour later, we're walking down to our seats in the corner behind Bruce's net. This is where the wives tend to sit—aka, where the general manager, Tom Parker, gives them cheap tickets. Andie paired her jacket with velvet, flared pants and red heels. Noel wore high-waisted trousers and vintage saddle shoes with hers. And Mel opted for a skin-tight black dress that falls around her ankles but has a slit up to her thigh. She's wearing adorable red sneakers with the dress—she said she wanted to be comfortable. They all look amazing. They had me take a bunch of photos for them earlier, and they asked me to be in a few, too. I smile to myself, loving that they always include me.

The five of us shuffle into our row. Another row of WAGs sit right behind us, dressed equally cute.

I'm on the very end of the row, and Andie is beside me. Mel and Noel are next to her and then Amber. Soon, the guys file out for warmups and the ladies go crazy…and not just the WAG section. Literally every woman in this place is whooping and blowing kisses. I wish I could say it's fine, and it's all in good fun, because deep down I know that it is. But three rows in front of us there's a whole row of women with McBride jerseys holding posters they made in hopes to catch Bruce's attention. Bruce—to his credit—doesn't seem to notice anything happening behind the glass. He's in net, blocking shots like the talented goalie he is. I wish I could see his face, I bet he's smiling. But it's better that he can't look at me, we've already been too reckless.

Bruce slides out of his area and starts shooting pucks into the empty net, and now I can see his face. I was right; it was better the other way, before I could see his handsome, happy face. I swallow, my heart thumping wildly in my chest.

After playing around with the guys, Bruce starts stretching. First his arms and shoulders, and then his legs and hip-flexors. When the guys stretch it's completely innocent, part of their job. But it doesn't look that way…it looks like they're grinding against the ice, their hips moving in rhythm with the music. Watching Bruce's hips moving and sway like that…it makes me think about him doing things that have nothing to do with hockey. Before I realize how far my imagination has taken me, I'm tugging off my denim jacket and feeling rather warm.

Andie sighs. "Oh, girl. You've got it bad."

I glance over at her. Bruce already warned me that Noah told her about finding us in the bathroom and Bruce trying to pay him off—unsuccessfully.

"Can't you two just tell everyone? Then you can wear the WAG jacket I got you." She shakes her head like her words are no big deal.

"You got me a jacket?"

She snorts an undignified laugh. "Of course, I did. I thought you two would be halfway down the aisle by now and wanted to be prepared. The way he looks at you…it could melt this entire arena. But you really dug your heels in trying to resist him. And now I have a McBride jacket hidden in my closet when you should be wearing it." She raises her chin as if to ask *why were you so stubborn?*

How has she seen all that just by watching us over the last year and a half? I've basically ignored him. I was so careful. And they ordered these jackets a year ago. Suddenly, it dawns on me how Bruce got my number.

"You knew. All this time." I shake my head. My skin has cooled, and my thoughts are now on throttling the giant man and not on dragging him into bed. "He told you about the bar, and you gave him my number."

"Don't be mad! I didn't tell anyone. The poor guy was desperate. Kissing you altered his brain chemistry, Farrah." She smiles at me, soft and knowing. "I'd never insert myself in someone else's love life—"

I gape at her. "Andie, yes you would. You live for that."

She considers this and then nods. "Okay, you have a point. But I just wanted to help. I could see how Bruce changed after each of his friends met someone and got married…some guys would brag that they still got to be single and out on the town, but not him. He's a family man at heart, and I could see he wanted that for himself."

Sighing, I turn my face forward. "I thought he was too young and immature, especially after everything with my ex. But he's different than I thought."

I swivel my head back in Andie's direction when she whispers, "He's changed. You brought out the best in him."

I gaze out onto the ice, to find the man in question looking right at me. He's frozen in place, staring with a dumb grin on his face. I shake my head but smile back. Just two fools falling in love no matter how little they make sense on paper. No matter how much drama they might cause. I guess that's what love—er, feelings—will do to you—you'll fight for it no matter the cost. And I know it will cost us.

Bruce lifts his hand that's covered in a massive goalie glove, and waves. My brother, Colby, Mitch, and West notice him and join in the waving. All the guys wink and blow kisses at their wives, not noticing exactly where Bruce's attention is directed—thankfully.

Amber runs down the aisle and up to the plexiglass, placing her hands on it, and Remy skates close and covers her hands with his. Only the glass separates them. The

Eagles photographers eat it up, snapping photos rapidly. Amber finally notices the flashes and blushes. She blows her husband one final good luck kiss and bounds back up the stairs.

Warmups come to an end, and Bruce disappears, with one last glance in my direction, along with his teammates.

The girls and I run to get concessions for the game, and by the time we wait in line and get our food, we're back just in time for puck drop.

The first period passes quickly with the Eagles ahead two-zero. I think it's going to be an easy win for our boys, until the second period comes and goes. The Texas Spurs move into the lead, with a score of three-two. A loss tonight could be devastating to the team's confidence. The stakes are high and all the relaxed, jovial vibes we experienced walking into this arena are now dashed. Instead, as the third and final period begins, the girls and I are literally sitting on the edge of our seats. Andie is biting her nails, Noel is tugging on her short curls, Mel is anxiously rubbing her non-existent belly, and Amber is closing her eyes like she can't bear to watch. And I'm just staring at the back of Bruce's head, willing him to block more goals.

I know he'll beat himself up if they lose tonight. I've always thought being a goalie would be the worst position in hockey. You're blamed for everything, and it's the position with the most pressure. But I never thought about how anxiety inducing it might be to be the person who loves the goalie. Well, maybe not *love*. Love seems like a strong word... The person falling for the goalie? The person who occasionally makes out and watches movies with the goalie.

Nine minutes into the third period, the Spurs get a tripping penalty, giving the Eagles a power play. And thanks to

West's powerful slapshot, he scores and ties up the game. The power play ends, and the game is ties up the game.

None of us girls can even breathe at this point. I've known Andie for almost two years now, and I never knew she could be this quiet. I wish she'd make a funny quip to distract us like she usually does, but I know she can't focus on anything but the game right now.

As both teams faceoff on the offensive end of the ice, Bruce takes a moment to stretch his neck from side to side. He grabs his water bottle—which I know is filled with yellow Gatorade—and squirts it on his face and neck. I cringe, that's going to be sticky. But if I was in net and sweating as much as he probably is, I might spray myself with Gatorade as well.

Andie audibly gasps, and my focus sways from Bruce to what's happening with the other players. The Spurs captain has sped away from the rest of the pack and is gaining rapidly on Bruce's net. Bruce crouches down, getting ready for him.

I hold my breath as the Spurs' captain gains on Bruce and acts like he's going to shoot down low, then switches at the last second and slaps the puck in the left corner. I have no clue how—some kind of goalie magic, I suppose—but Bruce's hand goes up in the nick of time and catches the puck deftly in his glove.

I jump up from my seat, screaming at the top of my lungs, "Yes! Bruce! You made that puck your bitch!" But no one can hear me except Andie, because the entire arena is on their feet, cheering so loud it feels like it could crack the ice.

Andie cackles at my statement and pulls me into an embrace. "Yeah, he did, girl! Let's put that on a T-shirt!" We both jump up and down laughing hysterically from how excited we are.

Bruce gets high fives and head taps from his teammates; then the arena quiets down in hopeful anticipation. The teams faceoff once more with only two minutes left. Colby wins the faceoff and skates quickly in the direction of the Spurs' net. West and Mitch follow closely, and Colby waits for just the right moment to pass the puck to West. West is the highest goal scorer on the team, so the defensemen for the Spurs are all over him. He passes to Mitch, and Mitch catches the puck, but it ricochets off his stick. One of the Spurs forwards takes advantage of the mishap and snags it, moving it back out of the offensive zone. But Remy is ready for him, snagging it deftly and skating it back toward the net.

I bring my hands up to cover my mouth as I watch, thinking he's going to shoot it.

Thirty seconds left.

At the very last second, he passes the puck to Mitch, it's smooth and easy, like they've practiced this play a million times—and they probably have. The goalie wasn't expecting the trade off and isn't prepared for Mitch when he pulls his stick back and shoots the puck so hard I'm surprised it doesn't slice the thing in half. The puck shoots into the net right under the goalie's legs.

The buzzer goes off marking the end of the game only a few seconds after Mitch scores his goal. Everyone's up again, screaming and cheering. It's deafening, but in a glorious way.

Andie is going berserk to my left, cupping her hands over her mouth and yelling the most inappropriate things into the air around us.

I guess when her husband scores a goal, she becomes even more unhinged than usual...which is concerning because she's pretty unhinged on a daily basis.

Smiling so wide my face hurts, I turn my attention to the ice once more. I expect to find Bruce McBride hugging and celebrating with his teammates, but what I find instead quiets everything around me. The noise seems to silence, and the crowd seems to disappear as I find Bruce standing by his net but facing me.

He's staring at me with a wide smile again, like a puppy greeting his best friend after being separated all day.

Like a hero coming home from war.

Like a man who loves a woman.

CHAPTER
THIRTY

BRUCE

AFTER THE GAME the hype in the dressing room is loud and proud. Coach Young gives an epic speech, with a lot more happy-profanity than usual, and Remy follows his speech up with his own praise for us. Mostly praise for me. I relish in it—I'm a words of encouragement man. But the pride in his eyes as he tells me how honored he is to have the best goalie sitting right here in this room causes my stomach to wave and sway uncomfortably. I'm beginning to know this guilt all too well; this pit in my stomach is just a foe who resides inside me now, even thought he was uninvited.

I just want to come clean and tell him about me and Farrah. But I also want to know that he'll be happy for us, and I know he won't be. These thoughts lead me to ask myself the same question that has gnawed at me for weeks. Why doesn't he trust me with Farrah?

I stare blankly at the area right behind Remy's head. I don't even realize the guys are chanting my name until West slaps me hard on the back.

"Bruce, Bruce, Bruce!" he cheers, his eyes twinkly and happy in the bright overhead lights.

I stand, dragging a hand across the back of my neck. "Thanks, guys," I say to my teammates, needing to raise my voice to be heard over their noise. "I couldn't have done it without you all there to have my back, eh?"

The room erupts again, and this time, I can't wipe the grin from my face. I cling to that joy, trying desperately not to let my sour feelings toward Remy back inside my head.

Eventually, the group calms down and heads to the showers. I take mine quickly, ready to get outside of this smelly dressing room and into the orbit of one Farrah Remington. She smells a helluva lot better than these guys.

I finally heading out of the locker room, dressed again in the game day suit I arrived in—black and white pinstriped with a royal blue shirt and tie beneath—my eyes scanning the broad hallway for Farrah. I spot her standing and laughing with all the wives. She looks beautiful, but I can't help but notice she's the only one not wearing a jacket that matches the other girls'.

My hands flex at my sides, itching to pick a fight. But the only one I could fight with is my damn self. Or Remy. But he doesn't fight.

I want Farrah to be mine, openly. I want her to wear a WAG jacket—with my name on it—to every single game. I want her to share that last name someday, if she wants to. And I want to hold her and kiss her no matter who's watching.

And you know what else? I want to park my stupid, old truck smack in front of her apartment and not care who sees it and knows I'm inside with her—probably making out on her couch.

And I could have all those things, if only we weren't nearing the final round of playoffs and if only my team captain wouldn't throw a gasket about it.

Last week I was so happy that Remy was talking to me again, that our friendship was right once more. But now I'm pissed. Because he has no right to tell me, or his sister, who to date. And there's an ache in my chest that he doesn't trust me the same way I trust him. We've been teammates and friends for five years now.

I've babysat his daughter, for shit's sake. If he can trust me with her, he should be able to trust me with his sister.

Farrah glances over her shoulder like she feels me nearby, and a coy smile plays on her lips. I unclench my fists, wanting nothing more than to wrap her in my arms and burrow my nose into her hair. There's a desperation to the way I want her arms wrapped around me, embracing me. *I need her.*

My skin itches with the urge to go to her and kiss her. But I stay glued in place.

Farrah's face falls, and she moves like she's about to walk toward me, but then Remy appears by my side. He doesn't seem to notice me; his eyes go right to Amber. Her face lights up and she runs to him and throws her arms around him. I have to move to the side to get out of their way.

I've never felt bitter while watching my teammates with their wives. Ever. Not until right now. The unfairness of it seems stifling in this moment.

Before I know what's happening, Andie is walking toward me. She pulls me into a big hug. One of my arms reluctantly comes up to hug her back. But she's not the one I want to hug.

"If you can hug me, you can hug Farrah. Now stop pouting," she whispers before pulling away.

I blink, wondering if I heard her correctly. But then Mel comes up and hugs me as well, then Noel. Noel is great, but this is definitely the first time she has *ever* hugged me. Next, Farrah walks over.

When she hugs me and whispers *great win, McBride*, I don't hesitate to hug her back. I squeeze her tight and smell her hair, savoring the sweet, floral scent I've come to know and love. She pulls away too soon and I hesitate before letting her go.

"I'm glad you came tonight, Yeux bleus," I say in a low voice so no one else can hear.

"I'll see you all at practice in two days!" Remy yells through the crowd with a wave, then wraps an arm around his wife's waist and gives her a look that says *let's go home, Baby.* Amber rests her head on his shoulder, and they walk toward the parking lot together.

Farrah looks up at me, smiling shyly. "They're my ride." She jabs a thumb in their direction then turns to follow them. Her steps are slow, like she doesn't really want to leave.

I watch until she's all the way down the hallway and through the doors that lead outside, before sighing and taking in who's around me for the first time since spotting her in the crowd. I'm surprised to find Mitch, West, and Colby staring at me and shaking their heads. Their wives are giving me similar looks as well.

"Dude," West says. "You might as well just tell him if you're going to look at her like that."

Colby nods. "What about the girl on the phone?" His eyes widen as soon as the words are out of his mouth. "Ohh-hhh. You're in for it."

I nod slowly. "Yep. She *is* the girl."

Mitch emits some sort of growl. "I told you this would happen."

Andie pats his chest like she's calming a wild bear.

"Bruce, you two care for each other, so just tell Remy. He'll understand."

Mitch, West, and Colby all nearly snap their necks to look at her, all of them clearly unhappy with her idea.

"That's the worst thing he could do," Mitch argues. "It needs to wait until after playoffs."

I groan, not wanting to hear this and not wanting six people involved in my dramatic love life.

I walk away from the group, leaving them arguing in my wake.

THIRTY-ONE

FARRAH

I HAVEN'T SEEN Bruce since the last home game I went to, the one where he looked stricken and miserable when I saw him after the game.

Over a week ago.

It broke my heart seeing him like that, and again when he called that night and explained it was torture not to be able to celebrate with me the way he wanted to. And that it was starting to not feel right to hide it, but that telling Remy could ruin everything for the team. He sounded frustrated with my brother, and I'm feeling the same way. If it was any time other than playoffs, I'd march up to my brother and tell him right this moment that I'm falling for his goalie—yes, I'm falling for him, I can't deny it any longer.

Plus, the Eagles' schedule has been insane now that they've moved onto round three after powering through and winning four games in a row. The fast pace, and the intensity of it all has Remy on edge. He's always struggled with shutting down when he's overwhelmed—part of being neurodivergent—but I haven't seen it this bad since he was a teen.

He can only focus on one thing right now, and that's

winning this next round. Poor Amber has to deal with his moody butt every evening while I excuse myself. It's hard to be around him when he gets like this…stressed and hyperfixated. Especially when I'm harboring feelings of resentment that he's keeping me and Bruce apart.

Bruce and I have Facetimed in between his practices, work outs, away games, and two Melarrah Events. But we haven't had a moment to see each other.

Mel and I had one event this past week while the guys were away, a ninetieth birthday party for a sweet grandma that was planned by her twenty grandchildren. This woman hadn't just built a life…she built a freaking legacy. I felt a little jealous of her. It was a reminder that I might never have that. Something I need to talk to Bruce about, if we ever have a moment to see each other.

I was hoping to see Bruce when he got back from Texas, but he ended up with Jackson for a few nights. Jackson takes precedence over me, as he should. I know Bruce takes his responsibility there very seriously, and that's something I respect about him. He seems like this big, silly goofball, but he's the most loyal and caring person I've ever met. He's going to be the best dad someday, and the weight of telling him about my infertility issues is pressing hard on me, along with everything else. My memory of finding out the fertility issue was with me and not with Connor comes back full force. The indignation inside of me at not being able to do what should come easily…the sadness of feeling less than other women. There's a heaviness in my heart I can't shake.

My heart longs to see Bruce and talk to him about all of this, but I can't even see the one person who could make me feel light again.

And—on top of all of that—today my parents, sister, and her husband just arrived in town for Remy's two home games this weekend, the first two games of round three. I can't get away without having a good excuse, and I don't want to set off my mother's curiosity. Especially after the talk she gave me about Bruce last time she was here.

I'm rolling my sister's suitcase into one of my brother's upstairs guestrooms when I turn and see her and her husband, Harvey, having a silent conversation back and forth with only their eyes and eyebrows.

I study them both as they communicate. Her husband, Harvey, is kind and unintimidating, but maybe I only feel that way because he's about the same height as me. His features are soft too, like his demeanor. He has rounded cheeks and a nice smile, light brown hair, and bright blue eyes.

My sister is the opposite of me in every way—minus her dark hair—with her chocolate brown eyes and petite figure. She gives my brother-in-law one last eyebrow raise, then he glances at me and excuses himself to go to the bathroom. I have an inkling he doesn't need to use the bathroom.

Felicity shuts the door as soon as he's gone and locks it. "Okay, spill. Tell me everything that's happened with the goalie. I looked him up by the way! Wow. Am I crazy, or is he a hotter version of Kristoff?"

My head falls back with a laugh, and it soothes something inside of me. I needed my sister more than I realized. I miss having someone to talk to who's in no way connected to the D.C. Eagles. All my girlfriends here are way too emotionally invested in this whole thing and knowing how it affects the team. Felicity probably hasn't even thought about that, she just wants the tea.

I pull her into a long hug. "I missed you."

"I missed you too," she says, hugging me back before shrugging away and sitting on the guest bed. It's made up neatly with fresh white linens, but Amber added some fun, pink throw pillows and a hand-painted floral art piece above the bed. "Now don't change the subject. Any new developments with him?"

With a sigh, I sit down beside her. "Well, we gave in and kissed again. And then again...and again."

She squeals and claps then quiets down and waits for me to continue.

"So, we decided to see where it goes, and we've been seeing each other more, whenever we could. But it's hard with playoffs." I sigh heavily, and then my mind goes back to my brother. "And Remy was kind of a jerk to him when he thought there might be something going on, so now we're keeping it just between us, but it's getting harder and harder. I just want to tell Remy and be done with it, but he's such a mess right now. Like he can handle the playoff pressure... barely...and nothing else."

She nods, hanging on every word I'm saying. "You think Remy would be upset if you told him?"

I nod.

"And then he and Bruce would play poorly and lose the playoffs for the whole team."

"Yep," I say, popping the p.

She blows out a raspberry, a few long tendrils of dark hair flying up in the process. "Yeah, I can see how that's complicated. Can you just wait until the end of playoffs? Remy will be on a high from winning the cup and everything will be hunky-dory."

I blink. Felicity sees the world in a very positive way, which isn't a bad thing, but she can seem out of touch with reality. I love her brightness, and never want it to dull...but also, she could be a little more realistic.

"We have at least three more weeks of playoffs, Felicity. That's starting to feel like a long time."

She shoots me a soft smile and touches my shoulder. "It'll go quick! Then everything will be fine."

I snort a laugh, and she shrugs. "I'm staying positive."

"As usual."

She bumps my arm with hers. "So, how serious is this? You sound serious."

A smile spreads across my face, I try to tone it down, but I can't. "I'm really falling for him." I roll my lips. "But I need to talk to him about the fertility issues before it gets too far. I'd rather end things sooner than later if that's going to be an issue, you know?" My heart hurts just thinking about it.

Felicity wraps an arm around my shoulders. "Not every guy is an idiot like Connor, Far."

"I hope not."

A knock comes from the door and Felicity jumps up to answer it.

It's Harvey. "Can I come in now?" he asks.

She steps out of the way to make room and Harvey steps inside, but he hardly has time to move out of the way before the rest of the Remingtons barrel into the room.

"This is where you've all been hiding!" My dad's voice booms, filling the cozy guestroom with his big personality. Nella is in his arms, and she giggles at his loud voice.

He and my brother might look just the same, but their personalities couldn't be more different.

My mother chuckles, cozying up next to him the way she always has. She kisses Nella's cheek quickly before saying, "We talked about ordering pizza for dinner, does that sound okay to you guys?"

Remy sticks his hands in his pockets, not seeming

thrilled with the idea, but he stays quiet. I know no matter what we order, he'll be eating one of his healthy, macro specialized meals. He and all his teammates are being very strict with their diets during the second half of playoffs, making sure their energy and performance isn't hindered by junk food.

Amber pats him on the shoulder knowingly. "Pizza sounds fine to me," she tells my mom with a smile.

An hour later we're all downstairs eating pizza—except Remy, who's grumpily munching on his grilled chicken, whole wheat pasta, and steamed broccoli.

My family is seated around Remy's large table, country music playing low on the Bluetooth speakers—I believe it's Jake Owen. One of my brother's favorite candles is lit at the center of the long table and everyone is happily eating and catching up. Nella is loving all the attention, and the pizza, and for once she doesn't even seem on the verge of a breakdown.

Between her and Remy, I'm not sure who's wound tighter lately. Is it terrible comparing my brother to a two-year-old? Not if it's an accurate comparison. I silently narrow my eyes at him, even though he's not looking at me.

Sibling relationships are a funny thing…you spend your whole childhood together and they know you better than anyone else on the planet during that time. And no matter how much you bicker or how awful you are, you know at the end of the day you'll still love each other. Until one day you grow up and live apart and then your bond changes.

Unless you grow up, and they still think they know what's best for you. Then you revert to bickering again, I guess. Only Remy doesn't realize how badly I want to lay everything out in the open and fight with him. I'm not sure who's going to snap first, me or Bruce. Hopefully neither of us.

Three or four weeks until playoffs are over. Or sooner if they lose…but I don't even want to think about that.

I'm simmering silently in annoyance, nibbling my pepperoni pizza but barely tasting it, when I hear my dad loudly whisper to my mom. Did I mention he's not a quiet man?

"Have you told her yet?"

Mom pretends she didn't hear him, taking another bite of her slice.

"Have you told her yet?" he repeats, louder this time.

Mom's eyes move up to my dad's in a look that says *would you please shut up?*

Her eyes flit to me, and I know the *her* in his question means me.

"Tell me what?" I ask, setting my pizza back on my paper plate.

Mom sighs and shoots my dad a glare. He grimaces and takes a drink of his Coke.

"Nothing, sweetheart. Let's enjoy dinner." Mom's gaze drifts to Amber. "This pizza is delicious."

Amber looks between me and my mom with a worried expression. "Um, thanks. It's from our favorite pizza place."

"Mom, just tell me. What's going on?"

"We'll talk about it later," she answers without looking at me.

Felicity drops her pizza onto her plate with an annoyed sigh. "Oh, my gosh. Just tell her whatever it is, and we can move on. I want to play a game!" She grins, and her husband kisses her temple.

Mom looks at Dad and he shrugs. "Rip off the Band-Aid," he says.

My mother purses her lips and tucks her shoulder-length hair behind one ear. She looks at me, her face serious enough that I'm not looking forward to whatever it is she has to tell me.

"I wanted to tell you this later, without a crowd." She gives Dad an annoyed look. "But I'll get on with it, I suppose." She clears her throat. "I ran into Connor's mother at the grocery store. He's getting married next week."

My entire body freezes for a long moment. Too long. I feel like my blood is frozen. My mind goes to the photos I saw of Megan and her husband with Connor and his girlfriend. The woman next to him in the photo looked so young I assumed it wasn't serious, and that he was just enjoying his newfound singleness. I mean, the blonde from the photo must be barely out of college. Slowly, I inhale a deep breath. It's okay Connor is moving on. So am I. I'm just feeling surprised by it is all. I don't love Connor anymore; I don't want him in my life.

Best of luck to the young, fresh wife he will have.

"Okay," I finally say. "He should move on with his life. I know I have."

The look on Mom's face as she studies me can only be described as trepidation. She hesitates before speaking again. "There's more. They're getting married quickly because she's pregnant."

My stomach roils, and I have to wrap my arms around my middle and swallow down the bile rising in my throat. This revelation makes it hard to breathe, hard to think. All that runs through my head is that Connor gets to move forward with his life with a new wife and a *baby*. He gets to live the life *I* wanted. The life I'm not sure I can ever have.

I don't want Connor... but I also don't want him to be happy. Is that awful? I want karma to give him early male-pattern baldness and an erectile dysfunction for making me believe he'd love me forever just to cast me away the moment things didn't go as planned.

I'm not sure how long I sit there, reeling from this news. But when I finally look around the room, everyone's eyeing me with worry, waiting for me to speak. I stand up and push my chair back.

"I'm sorry; I just need a minute," I rush the words out, I don't know if anyone can understand me or not. Everything around me seems to blur, my brain and vision is fuzzy. All I can think about is my ex-husband happily holding a newborn baby.

I flee to my apartment. I don't think I even take a breath until I'm up the stairs and through the front door of my quiet space.

Locking the door, I let the tears come. My knees buckle, and I lean my back against the front door and slide to the floor. I stay there, hugging my knees to my chest, until there are no tears left inside of me.

I wouldn't want Connor back in a million years, but it's all just so unfair. My thoughts wanders to Bruce. He's so kind and caring and attentive. But so was Connor at first.

I can warn Bruce ahead of time, unlike Connor, about my…issues. But who's to say he won't change his mind down the road? How do I know he won't give up on me like my ex did, then throw me away for a newer, younger model. Just like he'll eventually do with his pickup.

And not only that, but Bruce is *so* young. Does he even know what he wants? Or is he just chasing the fantasy of true love and marriage after watching all his friends get married?

My head—and my heart—ache from crying and worrying. I can't even seek refuge in *Frozen* because it will only remind me of Bruce.

And Bruce McBride would be better off with someone who isn't me.

I WALK into the Eagles Arena with a Starbucks coffee in hand—black and boring, not the caramel mocha I wanted. The Eagles' social media team snaps photos of me and I force a smile on my face. I may look sharp in my game day suit—a rich purple with a black shirt and tie—but I feel like trash. Farrah has completely stopped talking to me in the past twenty-four hours.

I can't sneak over there when her entire family is visiting. And I haven't had a minute to spare even if I could. This morning, we had an early skate, then I went to Jackson's chess meet—which he won—and then I had to take a nap before the game. I realize most grown-ups don't nap, but I always nap before a game, it saves my energy and it's part of my routine. A pregame routine I don't stray from. Especially not during the playoffs. Plus, I slept awful last night after worrying about Farrah. I finally texted Andie to see if Farrah was okay, and she said she's probably just busy with her family in town.

But for almost a month, Farrah and I have been texting

all day and late into the night...or we Facetime. It's too strange for her to just outright ignore me. There's more going on and it's driving me crazy that I don't know what it is and how to help.

I've been tense and on-edge all day, and I tossed and turned during my pre-game nap, which isn't making me feel great about my performance tonight. I'm exhausted, stressed, and feeling off kilter as I walk past the photographers and into the dressing room.

I spot Remy as I enter the room, and instantly prickle when I see his frown. The moment my tired eyes meet my team captain's something inside me snaps. That tightrope I've been walking on...it frays and comes undone. Just like my temper.

He doesn't even smile at me when I cross the room towards him, which makes my temper flare even hotter.

This has to be Remy's fault. He probably took her phone away like she's thirteen and banned Farrah from talking to me.

By his expression, he's obviously not happy. And in my exhausted and frustrated state of mind, I twist that into a reason to fight with him.

At this moment, my bitchy attitude wins out. I'm itching to stir up a fight, something a goalie rarely gets to do. I want to take out my frustration on someone, and who better than Remy? The man who's been keeping me from the woman I love, whether he realizes it or not.

"Hey," I say, my voice strained and irritated. I ignore the heads that snap toward us at me using a tone so rare for me. "What's the deal?"

His dark eyebrows draw together. Ah, so he's playing dumb. "What are you talking about?"

I step closer to him. He's tall, but not as tall as me, and I like that he has to tilt his head slightly to look up at me.

"Why won't Farrah talk to me?"

I hear a heavy sigh from somewhere behind me…it sounds like a Mitchy sigh.

Remy's head snaps back like I hit him. "Why would Farrah be talking to you at all?"

My hands come up to rest on my hips. "Why *wouldn't* she?"

"Because I made it clear you need to leave her alone." His expression is colder than ice as he speaks. "Are you telling me you didn't respect me enough to comply with that one simple request?"

My tongue glides over the front of my teeth as I try to contain my anger. "Maybe you should respect *me* enough to treat her right. I'm not her ex."

His nostrils flare. "What are you saying? You've been seeing her?"

"We're adults, Remy. We can see each other if we want, even without your permission."

His back straightens, he's trying to make himself appear bigger, but I still have the size advantage. This is weird, facing off with Remy. I've actually never seen him look this angry, but in turn, I don't think *I've* ever been this angry.

I want him to punch me, or push me, or spit in my face. I want to escalate this and have it out. Get it done with. But Remy's eyes are growing distant, and sweat is forming on his brow. I know this means he's shutting down. The anger inside me is quickly replaced by regret. I handled this all wrong. I could've taken him aside and spoken with him alone, or I could've waited until I could go see Farrah. Hell, I could've just waited until the game was over.

"Remy," I say, the anger gone from my voice. "Can we go talk outside? Please."

His brown eyes are still distant, but he gives me a barely perceptible nod. It was only a year ago Remy told us he has autism, and it's helped us understand him better. Like how he gets quiet sometimes or needs time alone, especially after doing any kind of interviews.

When I stormed in here itching for a fight, I also didn't take into consideration how much pressure he's under right now as the team captain. And that he's already over-whelmed on top of finding out I've been seeing his sister… and I did it in front of the entire locker room.

Remy looks numb as he turns and walks out the dressing room doors. I follow closely behind him. He stops in the quiet hallway that leads to the offices and takes a few deep breaths.

"Listen, I'm sorry you're hearing I'm in love with your sister in such an abrupt way. I was just…" I drag a hand through my hair. "I was pissed and stressed, and I took it out on you."

His eyes snap wide open, his mouth slightly agape.

"What? Why are you looking at me like that?" I ask, crossing my arms.

He shakes his head like a dog shaking off water. "Sorry, can we take a step back to you being in love with my sister?"

I relax. "Oh, yeah. What did you want to know?"

He blinks slowly and huffs an annoyed laugh. "Umm, for starters, how the hell did you fall in love with her when, as far as I know, you two haven't even been on a date."

Damn it. I really backed myself into a corner here.

Remy's nostrils flare. "You can say that again."

Oops, I didn't realize I'd said that out loud. I raise my hands up in front of my body for protection, even though

Remy wouldn't hurt a fly. "We've sort of been seeing each other in secret, because we didn't want to stir up drama." I use my arm to gesture between myself and Remy, and the drama happening. "But I'm crazy about her, Remy. I'm sorry for hiding it from you, but you were so pissed about her spending the night after I took her to the ER. The tension with the whole team was off after that, man. We barely made it through to round two. I couldn't risk being honest about me and Farrah and chance that happening again." I can't read his expression, his nostrils are still flared, but his stance is relaxed. It's confusing. "I'm committed to this team. I'm not going to be the reason we lose the Cup. But I also wanted to give me and Farrah a chance. I guess I wanted my cake and to eat it too, you know?"

He growls. "Terrible choice of words, McBride."

I grimace. "Yeah, sorry."

Remy looks up at the ceiling and exhales a deep breath before speaking. "I don't even know how to feel about all of this. I can't believe you two snuck around behind my back."

"I mean, in all fairness…you didn't tell us you married Amber until after the fact—" his intense glare has me snapping my mouth shut before I say more.

He glares for another few seconds before his mouth pops open like he just thought of something. "Wait, if you're together, why isn't she coming to the game tonight?"

I throw my hands in the air. "That's what I was saying in the locker room! She won't talk to me. Won't respond to my texts or answer my calls. I thought you had something to do with it."

He rolls his eyes. "Well, clearly she doesn't listen to me." Remy grows somber, shuffling on his feet. Deep in thought, his eyes grow distant, and I know he's deep in thought. It feels like five minutes go by while I wait for him to speak. "Actually, I think I know why she's shutting you out."

"Really? What did I do, man? Tell me and I'll fix it. I'll do anything."

He twists his mouth to the side. "It's not about you. It's about her ex. It's Farrah's business, so you'll have to hear the rest from her." His eyes shift from one side to another, like he's considering if he wants to say his next words. "Are you really serious about her?"

"I've never been more serious in my life," I answer honestly.

He shakes his head, fighting a smirk. "She's been so happy this last month, humming and floating around. Like she was back to her old self. I can't believe I didn't see it."

I smile, then remember she's currently ignoring me. "What do I do?"

"Farrah needs someone to fight for her. Someone to show her she's *worth* fighting for. If you're really serious about this, you've got to keep fighting. You have to break down her walls and show her over and over again that you're a much better man than the last one. If I know my sister, she's probably feeling like she can't trust herself anymore."

I nod, soaking up every word and mentally making a plan.

With another heavy sigh, Remy slaps a hand onto my shoulder. "I know you're distracted with this. Honestly, so am I. This is weird for me." He quirks a brow. "But we both have to suit up and win tonight. We owe it to our teammates and our fans to compartmentalize this for the next three hours or so, you hear me?"

"Yes, Cap'n. Loud and clear."

With one last pat to my shoulder, Remy turns and starts walking back toward the dressing room.

"Are we good, Remy?" I ask. "I need to know you and I are good before we suit up."

He stops in his tracks, pausing before turning to glance at me over his shoulder. "We're good. But if you break my sister's heart... I won't hesitate to strongly suggest to our owner and general manager that they should trade your ass to the coldest, snowiest place in Canada."

"Noted."

THIRTY-THREE

FARRAH

I'M in my apartment feeling miserable and watching the game on my tiny laptop screen. How am I supposed to keep Bruce McBride off my mind when he's literally blocking every shot and moving like the beautiful beast he is. The third period is almost over, and the Eagles are winning four to one.

It's also not helping that I'm wearing his sweats again. I couldn't stop myself. They're so comfy and they still smell faintly of whatever shower soap he uses.

Tired of wallowing, I pick up my trash from the food I had delivered and throw it away. Connor and his new wife and baby deserve no more of my tears, no more of my emotional energy. He's already taken years from me; I won't dwell on him and his seemingly perfect life anymore.

I will also stop resenting the fact that some women grow babies while I grow cysts. Actually, that's probably a lie… I'll always be a little bitter about that.

Moving to my door, I slide on my fuzzy slippers and pad down the steps and into the big house. I turn on Remy's oven—wishing it was Bruce's La Cornue—and start whipping up a celebratory cake for tonight's win. Maybe Bruce will come over for a slice…no. He can't. We can't.

They say it's better to have loved and lost than never to have loved at all, but whoever said that is a liar. Because the pain of being thrown away might never subside. But I could've lived happily forever as a single woman with cats.

Rose whines at my feet like she knows I'm thinking about cats. I pat her fluffy head and smile.

Tonight, I let my creativity take me away in the kitchen. This cake isn't for an order, no one requested it. I can do whatever I want.

And where does my heart lead me? A yellow three-layer cake with ice blue frosting and silver sprinkles on top. The yellow of the cake is almost the exact shade of Bruce's hair, and the frosting matches his eyes. And those silver sprinkles capture the light with a twinkle just like the stud in his ear.

I heave a sigh and cut myself a thick slice, then sit on the countertop and devour it like I haven't eaten in days. Rose whines and wags her tail, so I drop a big bite of cake on the floor. Remy will never know since she licks it right up, not leaving a single crumb behind.

With a glance at the oven clock, I realize with a start it's nearly midnight and everyone will be home soon from the game. It takes a while once you wait for Remy to get out of the dressing room and get through traffic.

I cover the cake and leave a note on top that says *congrats on the win!* Then head back to my apartment for some rest. Hopefully I'll sleep better tonight, but probably not since I just inhaled a pound of sugar.

———

I wake up with a start the next morning. I don't even know what time it is, but just that someone is knocking on my door, repeatedly.

If that's one of my family members, they're about to see just how grumpy I can get. I was finally sleeping good after not falling asleep until three in the morning. Those jerks.

Throwing off my covers, I stomp to the door and swing it open. "What do you want?" I seethe, my eyes still bleary from sleep.

"Ummm," A very deep voice says from above me. "So, I take it you're not a morning person?"

I wipe the sleep from my eyes and look up to see Bruce McBride. He probably didn't get much more sleep than I did last night, and yet he looks as fresh as a bouquet of wildflowers. Speaking of wildflowers… he's actually holding a bouquet of wildflowers.

I can't explain why, but seeing him standing here, all soft and smiley for me…brings tears to my eyes. Maybe tears of relief because I've wanted to see him so badly but didn't feel like I should. Or maybe the tears are because I know we've run our course, and I need to end this, but I don't want to.

Bruce's warm hand moves up to cradle my cheek and he uses his thumb to brush away tear that escaped. "Yeux bleus, don't cry. I'm here."

The poor, handsome idiot doesn't realize that's part of the problem. I sniff, crossing my arms over my chest since I'm not wearing a bra.

"What does that mean, anyway?" I finally ask. It doesn't matter now if it's something stupid that will piss me off. Our clock is ticking by the second. "It's something dumb, isn't it? It means stinky feet in French?"

He drops the flowers to the ground with a thump and brings his other hand up. My face is cradled in his large hands, and the feel of it is intensely comforting. I never want him to remove those hands.

"It means blue eyes. Because your eyes were the first thing I noticed about you."

Okay, that's really sweet. Too sweet. I want to be annoyed at him, so this is easier.

He smirks. "Okay, in all honestly, your eyes *and* your butt were both fighting for my attention. But calling you *great butt* in French isn't very romantic."

I snort an unbecoming laugh, unable to help myself.

"Can I come in?"

I bite my bottom lip, feeling unsure. We need to talk, but being in an enclosed space with him typically leads to a lot more than talking.

"You can come in, but just to talk."

He arches one eyebrow. "Okay." Bruce steps past me, and I close the door behind us.

I point to the sofa. "You, over there."

He obeys.

I run to the bathroom, needing to make sure I don't have drool all over my face or anything. I'm a drooly sleeper. Closing the bathroom door behind me, I nearly shriek when I see myself in the mirror. Dark circles under my eyes, folds from the blanket I was lying on imprinted in my face…and my hair. Oh, wow. It's basically a nest.

I splash some cold water on my face and apply a dab of moisturizer, then brush my hair and secure it into a braid with an elastic. I'm about to leave the bathroom when I spot my deodorant on the bathroom counter. I swipe my pits a few times, then head back out for my dreaded conversation with Bruce.

His eyes do that soft, gooey thing they do when he looks at me. "I kind of liked the sleepy look."

I sigh, wishing he'd stop being cute. Silently, I stand there in the middle of the room. I'm looking down at my feet and thinking that I don't know what to say, or how to start this conversation. I don't *want* to talk about any of this. Can't I just go bake something?

Not realizing Bruce had left the couch and crossed the room, the nearness of his voice surprises me and my eyes snap up to meet his.

"Let me in, Farrah. Talk to me."

I swallow down the lump in my throat. He's being so patient despite me not responding to him for days. He left me alone and gave me time, gave me space. He's truly so different than Connor…maybe he wouldn't end up breaking my heart. Maybe I'd be enough for him, even without babies. I shake the thought; I need to get that out of my head. That sounds too much like hope.

"I'm sorry I didn't answer your calls," I say, finally.

"Or texts," Bruce adds with a raised eyebrow. His hands slide into the pockets of his dark jeans, and he rocks on his feet. "I'm a pretty good listener, you know."

I smile but it feels sad. "I know. I haven't felt ready to talk."

His eyes search my face. I'm not sure what he's looking for, but his eyebrows scrunch in concern. Probably because of the dark circles under my eyes.

"The truth is," I say, taking a deep breath. "My ex left me because we couldn't get pregnant. He was the person who swore to love me forever, unconditionally. But there was a condition on it, apparently…my ability to bear children." I pause, feeling the emotion well up inside of me and trying my hardest to tamp it down. With a shaky voice, I start again. "And that didn't happen quickly enough for him, so, he kicked me to the curb, and now he's marrying a younger, hotter woman who obviously has better ovaries, because she's already pregnant." My eyes burn and I can hardly see Bruce's face through the tears I'm trying not to shed. "Everyone seems to be able to accomplish the one thing I can't...getting pregnant. Amber, Mel, and someday Andie and Noel will have babies, too. Everyone will have a baby to hold. And I'll have to watch them, and I'll hate that there's a piece of me that's bitter about it. Because I'll want so desperately to be happy for them, and I will be, but it will be tainted. It will be tainted with a desire to hold my own baby."

Bruce wraps his arms around me as I release a sob. Tears are rapidly streaming down my face and soaking his shirt. But he keeps holding me and allowing me to cry. It feels good to say my horrible thoughts out loud, and it feels good to be in his arms. But nothing will fix this.

I might never be enough for this man, for any man. I'd rather end things now than find that out later.

Bruce slides his hand up and down along my back and makes quiet *shhhh* sounds. I relish in his embrace for a moment longer, before reluctantly pushing away from him. I sniff and wipe my face on the sleeve of the sweatshirt I'm wearing—his sweatshirt.

"Farrah, everything you're feeling is understandable. Your feelings are valid. I think you might not know that, and it's important that you do. Your feelings and your grief...it's valid. And you can also have more than one feeling at a time. You can be happy for someone you love, and sad for yourself at the same time. Those emotions can coexist together."

His words soothe me in a way nothing else ever has. I've never heard anyone put it like that before, but he's right. I'm thrilled for West and Mel, and even love seeing her growing belly, but it's also a reminder of what I couldn't have. I'm happy and sad, together. One doesn't negate the other.

"Do you—" Bruce starts to ask a question then stops abruptly.

"Do I what?"

"Do you wish you were still with Connor? Are you upset he's getting married?"

I snort a laugh through my tears. "No. I wouldn't take him back in a million years." I shake my head. "I just hate that he gets to live *my* dream."

The pesky tears are back, flooding my eyes once more. I allow them to stream down my face, releasing all the pent-up emotion after days of repressing it. "This has nothing to do with my ex, but I don't think I can be with you, Bruce," I say it gently, but his face still falls.

"You've been so sweet, and our time together has brought me so much joy." I try to muster a smile through my tears, but it's as unsteady as my emotions. "But you're young. You'll meet someone who can give you a family. You were meant to be a dad more than anyone I've ever met."

Bruce steps closer to me and brings his hands up to grasp my upper arms and holds me gently but firmly. "Farrah, I don't want to build a life with you because of what you can give me someday. I don't cherish you for your ability to have children or not. And I don't love you based on any conditions."

My eyes widen in shock at his confession.

"I love you because of who you are. I love your kindness and your loyalty. I love your Frozen obsession and how passionate you are about baking. I love that you support everyone around you even if you're having a hard day. And I want to build a life together for just that…to be together.

And if it's just you and me, that's okay. All I need is *you*, Farrah."

I choke on a sob. "You say that now, Bruce. But you don't know. You don't know how you'll feel in five years, or ten or twenty. What about when we're old and grey and everyone has grandchildren but us?"

"If you're by my side in the nursing home, it doesn't matter."

I huff a humorless laugh. "Connor used to tell me that we'd be together until we'd need to clean each other's dentures."

Bruce's jaw ticks, and his shoulders straighten. "I'll say this to you as many times as I need to, but I'm not Connor. Connor might be older than me, but he was just a boy. A real man would never let you go. A real man would never walk away from you."

Bruce is saying all the right things, all the things that should console me and make me confident in us. And I believe he means what he's saying, I really do. But that doesn't change the fact that people change their minds. Every single day. And I can't allow myself to fall harder for this man with the risk he'll change his mind later.

Bruce's hands fall from my arms. "What can I do to change your mind?"

I raise my chin and look into his fervent gaze for a long moment. "Nothing."

His shoulders droop and gorgeous mouth turns downward. "Farrah," he says my name like a plea. "I love you. I can't just let you go."

For the first time since I met him, Bruce McBride looks small, like he's turning in on himself. And I hate that I'm the one causing this big, happy, confident man to crumble.

"I'm so sorry," I say, my voice so low I'm not certain he can hear me. "It's better this way."

His eyebrows knit together, but his eyes don't leave mine. "There's no world where a life without you is better."

I feel one lonely tear stream down my face. Bruce brings his hand up, wipes the tear away gently, then slowly turns and walks toward the door. His hand rests on the door handle for what feels like a full minute, before he turns and gives me one last look.

He leaves and I crumple to the floor. I somehow feel worse now than I did when I found out about Connor's baby. Everything feels bleak when I think of my life without Bruce's smiles, or his teasing, or his hugs. When I compile a list of my happiest moment over the last year and a half, they're all somehow attached to Bruce McBride.

This is for the best.

D.C. Eagles #1 Fan Page on hockeyisbetterthanfoot-ball.com

Craig Nottingham: I bet you're all regretting your hype for McBride after tonight. The guy was a DISASTER.

Todd Ferguson: It wasn't pretty. But everyone has an off game now and then. He'll pick back up next game!

Craig Nottingham: No one has an "off game" at the end of the $^@&* playoffs!!!

Todd Ferguson: It's not ideal, but I'm holding out hope. His save percentage for the season is .927. It doesn't get better than that.

Mandie Banderson: You know what, CRAIG. Maybe he's going through something. Have you ever thought about THAT? Maybe he had a really tough day. Go outside and touch some grass.

THE RANDOM WOMAN'S comment has me almost

smiling. The tenacity behind it reminds me of someone I know, but I can't put my finger on who it is.

The comments on the fan pages are awful, ripping me to shreds, really. But this time, I deserve it. The Thunder Bay Lightning destroyed us last night, and it was mostly my fault. I was slow, and slow goalies don't keep pucks out of the net.

I've barely slept in days, and it's wearing me thin. My energy feels depleted, mentally and physically. I've kept up with my healthy diet. I've worked out more to distract myself; I even tried taking a sleeping pill the night before the game to get some rest. But no. My mind wanders right back to my conversation with Farrah two mornings ago.

I can hardly even stand to be in my own home. Everything reminds me of her. When I walk through the living room, the couch makes me think of the morning we watched a movie…then when I go upstairs and head to my room, I pass the guestroom she slept in. Hell, I can't even be in my kitchen anymore without staring at the oven and wishing she was there happily baking something.

How could she doubt my feelings for her? How could she doubt they'll last? What I want to do is find Connor and ream him for making Farrah feel like no one could love her for more than her ability to have children. The idea is absurd.

A long life with Farrah Remington is all I need. We could be the cool aunt and uncle who spoil our friends' and relative's kids, we could travel whenever we wanted—outside of hockey season—we could have pets…a cat might be nice. And, down the road, if we decided—mutually—we wanted kids, we could adopt. Adoption is a wonderful thing that I'm very grateful for. Even just helping out with Jackson has added so much joy to my life.

But Farrah is the only thing I need. That's it. There will never be anyone more attractive and wonderful to me than her. Now how to make *her* see that, because I'm not giving up. Remy told me to fight to make her see she's worthy of love, and I plan to do just that.

We don't have another game until tomorrow night, which means tonight I'm a volunteer lackey for Melarrah Events. The event is a birthday party for our general manager's six-year-old daughter. I spoke to the GM, Tom, about it before the game last night. He and his wife wanted to make sure she didn't feel neglected in the midst of all the playoff madness, and I respect the hell out of them for that.

Jackson is coming with me for our big brother night this month. It probably wasn't his first choice of activities, but it's a birthday party…he can at least have some delicious cake.

I smile, feeling hopeful for the first time since leaving Farrah's apartment a few days ago. She will see she can't get rid of me no matter how hard she tries. She can give me her worst, and I can handle it.

No more wallowing for me—it's time for action.

———

"So, you're going to show Farrah you love her by setting up chairs and a bouncy house?" Jackson asks as we pull up to my general manager's mansion outside of Alexandria. His voice sounds skeptical.

I withhold an eye roll as I tousle his hair and usher him toward the back gate where I know the girls are already getting started with the décor. Mel filled me in.

"Sometimes it's the small things, my guy. Showing up every day, no matter what. Big or small. I'll be there every time she turns around, waiting for her to see I'm the love of her life."

He shrugs. "I hope so. I like Farrah. You guys make each other happy."

I tousle his hair, and he pushes my hand away. "Aw, you little softy!"

"Get off of me," he says, but there's humor in his tone.

When we reach the wrought iron black gate, I unlatch it and swing it open, allowing Jackson to walk through before me.

He glances around, jaw agape. "Wow. This is the fanciest yard I've ever seen."

I'm impressed as well; I've never been here before. Tom has an expansive backyard with lush, green grass and expert landscaping. At one end of the yard there's a massive covered pool, and on the other end there's an inground trampoline off to one side and a big, wooden playground beside it. Mel and Farrah are on the patio unloading boxes, West is with them making sure Mel doesn't overdo it. Farrah is wearing a black sundress that hits just above her knees and has little straps over her tanned shoulders. Her hair is down and curled and I know what it smells like without even being close enough to inhale the scent. The sight of her sends a jolt through my chest. I'm happy to see her and yet still devastated by our last conversation.

West spots us first and waves. "Finally, some more muscle!" he yells.

I force a smile on my face and flex my arm. "Happy to be of service."

"I was talking about Jackson!" he yells back.

Jackson grins.

Mel smiles at us, not noticing the shocked expression on Farrah's face.

As we get closer, Farrah avoids eye contact altogether. For a second, I wonder if I shouldn't have bombarded her. Maybe she genuinely doesn't want to be with me and wants me to stay away.

I shake the thought. I've seen the way she looks at me, I've felt the way she kisses me. I saw the agony written all over her face when she told me we'd be better off without each other.

No, Remy was right. I need to show up; to show her I'll stick in there through the hard times. I'll be her rock when times are tough, and I'll be her soft place to land when life is challenging.

This is the only way I know how to show her that.

"How can I help? Put us to work."

Farrah briefly glances up at me, her sad blue eyes give me the urge to pull her into my arms, the desire to do just that almost overwhelming. But I stand firm where I'm at.

Mel points toward a giant pink bag in the middle of the yard. "You can set up the bouncy house."

"Done." I shoot one last glance at the dark-haired beauty I can't get out of my head and walk toward the bouncy house. I wore my black athletic shorts, the ones that show off my quads, I hope she notices my legs when I'm expertly setting up the most important part of the party.

Thirty minutes later, I'm drenched in sweat. I feel like I've just repeated last night's game. Setting up a bouncy house that looks like a princess castle is harder than I imagined. But it's done.

My grey tee is plastered to my pecs, I glance down and try to pull my shirt away from my body, but it just adheres right back to my skin. When I look up again, I notice Farrah staring at my chest from across the room. Her eyes move up my body to find me staring at her and she instantly looks away, turning bright red.

A few days ago, before she tried to break up with me, I would've loved the blush. I would've teased her until she smiled and then I would've pulled her into my arms and kissed her breathless. But now, I hate that she feels ashamed and embarrassed to look at me like that. It's like she believes we've actually broken up.

West strides over, his back is turned toward the girls. He raises his eyebrows and grimaces in a *this isn't going well for you, is it?* kind of way.

He pats my shoulder. "Give it time."

I shake my head. West could've been with Mel much sooner, but he convinced himself he was doing her a favor by staying away. He also had some kind of idiotic pact with her older brother about not dating her. Actually, that's a lot like my predicament, but Farrah is the West here.

"Hey, what made you finally man up and seal the deal with Mel?"

He blows out a breath, causing the front of his dark blond hair to fly up in the air. "I think I just realized that if years had gone by and my feelings for her still hadn't faded, they never would. I knew I wanted her and didn't care what it cost to achieve that. Even my relationship with my best friend."

I listen, silently mulling over his words. "Yeah, I'm gonna be honest, that doesn't help me at all."

West chuckles. "I think if you give it time and keep fighting…she'll see in you what I saw in Mel. It's already there, she's just choosing not to acknowledge it to protect herself."

"I can't really fault her for protecting herself after all she's been through."

He shakes his head. "Nope. You just have to be patient. And be ready to jump when she comes around."

"Oh, I plan to be ready."

He smiles. "You're nothing if not persistent. Maybe Colby would give you better advice." West cups a hand over his mouth so the girls won't hear, even though they're all the way across the yard. "He built Noel a library to win her heart."

I scoff. "Farrah would rather I build her a bakery." The words have my mind drifting to how impressed she was with my oven…hmm.

"I see your wheels spinning, but you can't actually build her a bakery, man."

Jackson slides out of the bouncy house and strides over to us. "So, what next?"

To my surprise, Farrah starts making her way to where we're standing, nervously touching her arm as she walks. She focuses on West, trying to ignore me, just like she used to.

"Hey, West, could you get the birthday cake from the car for me?"

"I'll get it," I say, forcing her to look over at me.

She gives me a resigned look and starts walking toward the gate. I follow quickly. As soon as we're through the gate and out of sight, she whirls on me.

Farrah crosses her arms and settles an icy gaze on me. "Bruce, what are you doing here?"

I hold my arms out at my sides. "Helping. Obviously."

She closes her eyes, and her mouth moves like she's counting. "Don't make this harder than it needs to be." Her eyes meet mine, and for the first time today I see vulnerability there. "Please."

"I'm not letting you go without a fight, Farrah."

Something sparks in her eyes, something more than annoyance. It's so brief I wonder if it happened at all. Before I can analyze it too much, she whirls again, this time away from me and toward her car. She unlocks it and opens the back end where a tall cake box is surrounded by items to keep it from sliding around.

Farrah taps her foot impatiently as she waits for me to get the cake out. That's fine, I can deal with her sass as long as she doesn't give me those sad eyes again.

When I lift the cake box, I'm surprised by how heavy it is. "This is just a cake for a tiny little girl… right?"

"Yes. But it's filled with pudding between each layer."

My eyebrows shoot up. "Your first one like this?"

She meets my gaze, giving me the faintest hint of a smile. "Yeah."

"I'm so proud of you."

She seems to bask in my praise for all of point-five seconds before she remembers she's 'better off without me.'

"Bruce," she reprimands. "Stop." She looks away again and stalks off, like she can't get away from me fast enough.

With a sigh, I stride carefully back into the yard. Tom Parker is standing on the patio now. It's very seldom I see the man in anything but a suit and tie. But today he's wearing linen pants, leather sandals, and a knit polo. His hair is combed neatly and there's a little girl beside him wearing a yellow dress. Her curly, dark hair is braided back into pigtails. She looks like her father but the cuter version.

"McBride," Tom greets me with a smile. "Is that the cake?"

I nod.

He chuckles and glances at Farrah. "I can't believe you trusted this guy with the cake," he teases, shooting me a wink.

"Farrah can trust me with anything," I answer quickly.

Farrah blushes, and Tom looks between the two of us curiously.

"Here," he says, holding his arms out. "Let me take that inside."

I carefully transfer it to him, and he disappears through the back doors and into the large house.

His daughter takes advantage of his absence and runs toward the bouncy house.

"Bruce," West calls from a few yards away where a cart holding white wooden chairs is sitting. "Help me set up the chairs and tables."

I glance over at Farrah to see her crossing the yard where Mel is assembling some kind of balloon arch with a floral backdrop. There's a table setup in front of the arch and I wonder if that's where they'll put the cake.

She doesn't even look back at me as she walks away.

The ache I felt after she ended things is suddenly feeling stronger and more permanent. Maybe this really is over.

Jackson comes to stand beside me. "You okay?"

"Not really," I say with a sigh.

THE DAY after our birthday party event, I'm up early in the morning and heading to the big house to watch Nella for the day. I'm exhausted from the party…. Six-year-old girls are not all sugar and spice and everything nice, okay? They're actually rabid.

Mel and I agreed we're only doing events for adults from now on. And we also agreed to hire some help. There's no way we can continue doing setup ourselves, especially as her belly grows. And I cannot mentally handle Bruce McBride showing up to help in his little black shorts when I'm trying to move on.

It's literal torture. His sweat soaked shirt adhering to his chest was practically pornographic.

The guys have a game tonight, and they're on a flight as we speak. I'm just happy for a four-day reprieve from running into Bruce. He can't pop up and remind me how adorable and handsome he is when he's all the way in Canada.

I breathe a sigh of relief as I walk into the kitchen, knowing I can erase Bruce from my mind for the rest of the week. When I enter my brother's kitchen, I stop in my tracks. My eyes are so wide I worry they might fall out of my head.

Amber strides into the room with Nella and Rose trailing behind her. I barely register the large dog and my niece though. I'm too busy taking in the most gorgeous piece of kitchen equipment I've ever had the privilege of seeing with my own eyes. Even prettier than the one in Bruce's penthouse.

"Is that a?" I manage to form a few words.

"Yep," Amber says with a knowing smirk. "There's a note that came with it."

I take another step toward the stunning La Cornue stove and swipe the handwritten note on top that's attached to a gigantic bow.

Yeux bleus,
Saw this and it reminded me of your eyes.
(Your brother already knows if you ever move, the oven goes with you.)
From,
Your petit gâteau

I huff a laugh at just how outlandish this gift is. Most men would find a gemstone that reminded them of a woman's eyes, or a flower...but Bruce McBride? No, that's not his style. He goes right for the fourteen-thousand-dollar oven.

I drop the note like it's on fire. No, I can't have my mind

so easily changed by an oven. Albeit a very impressive one…that I will absolutely use every day.

This oven is the best gift I've ever received, but it doesn't change any of the reasons we can't be together.

What were those reasons again?

I pick the note back up and read it again. *Your petit gâteau.* Pulling my phone out my shorts pocket, I tap on the Google app and type it in. *Your cupcake.*

Nella claps her hands, reminding me I'm not alone. She patters over and runs her hand along the glass of the shiny new oven, leaving a streak of little fingerprints. Somehow, that makes it look even better.

I glance over to find Amber watching me curiously. "Are you okay?"

I hadn't realized I was crying until she asked me that. But now I feel the tears on my face. "Why does he have to make this so difficult?" I ask with a sniff. "I can't get hurt again, Amber."

She walks toward me, dressed in black skinny jeans and cute wedge heels. She's ready for work and will need to leave soon. Unworried about the time, she gives me a hug, then pulls back to look at me. "I know it's hard to trust again. But it might be worth it."

I groan. "Not you, too. I already got this talk from Mel yesterday."

Amber smiles. "We just love you both and want you to be happy. And Bruce seemed to make you happy."

"I don't think I can trust myself," I admit. "Connor made me happy, too."

"When you look back at your marriage, do you see any red flags? Things you might have brushed off or ignored?" she asks the question gently.

Nella pulls on my oversized tee, and I pick her up. She

wraps her arms around my neck and gives me a sloppy kiss on the cheek. Rose trots over wanting to be part of everything with her tail thwacking against my legs.

"Yes. That's what worries me. I was so in love I was willing to look past the way he treated me. How we always did what he wanted and never what I wanted. I did all the compromising, and he did none. What if I repeat that again?"

"Nobody is perfect. I think the best way to know someone's character is how they support you. Are they there for you when things get hard? Are they passionate about your interests? Do they show up?"

When I think about Bruce, my answer is yes to all those things. "But Amber, he's so young and has so much to learn. He will probably want kids someday, even if he thinks he'd be fine without them now. And what if I can't give him that?"

"Okay, I'll play devil's advocate. What if you give Bruce a chance and you're unable to have kids. What about other options, like IVF, or adoption?"

I weigh the options for a moment, even though I've considered them all before. "I think I'd really like to adopt."

"Do you not think Bruce would be on board with that option? He's so great with Jackson. And he *is* adopted himself."

"I don't know," I admit. "We never talked about it."

"And I'm not saying you have to. If you're sure he's not the one for you, then you should let him go. But if you're unsure…maybe it's worth a conversation?"

Not wanting to think about all of this before I've even had a cup of coffee, I squeeze my eyes shut and blow out a breath. "He bought me an oven."

Amber chuckles. "I think he might be in love with you."

I open my eyes and hold my sister-in-law's gaze. "I'm just...confused."

She glances at the clock on the shiny new stove. "I have to go, but we can talk more about this later if you want?"

I nod.

"Oh! And the girls are coming over tonight for the game. We'd love for you to join us...if you want to."

She's giving me the opportunity to skip out since I'd have to watch Bruce for three hours. But I can't lose my girlfriends over this. And I've missed them. "Okay. I'll be there."

"Yay!" She does a little dance then kisses Nella and heads out through the garage.

I look over at Nella, who's still happily settled on my hip. "Well, kiddo. Just you and me for the day."

She grins and points to the new stove. "Cake?"

I smile back. "Okay, you twisted my arm. Let's bake some cupcakes."

―――――

When the girls come over that evening, I have freshly baked cupcakes ready and waiting. The oven is immaculate. Total perfection.

The desire to text Bruce about it is almost too much to resist, but I'm too mixed up about my own feelings to confuse him, as well. I don't want to give him hope that I'll change my mind when I don't even know if I've changed my mind.

Everyone is dressed down tonight, thank goodness. Because all I wanted to do was throw on some pajamas and chill. And I'm wearing my own pajamas tonight instead of Bruce's sweats. I even washed them so I can return the items to him. They no longer smell like him, which made me tear up. But I'm fine. Totally fine.

While Amber is putting Nella to bed, the girls and I get settled on the couch with blankets, popcorn, wine, and cupcakes.

Your cupcake. The signature on Bruce's note runs through my head for the millionth time today. Here I thought I could erase him from my mind for a few days, then he goes and buys me a La Cornue.

I settle in on the couch, Bruce's face filling the TV screen. He removes his helmet, then shakes his hair out. I can't tell if he's frowning, or just focused. But something about his expression looks strained and unlike the grinning version of himself that I love.

The cameraman stays focused on Bruce as he grabs his water bottle and squirts a long stream into his mouth. His strong throat works as he swallows it down, then the camera finally moves to Remy and the other team captain, number seventy-nine, at center ice. The referee drops the puck, and the Thunder Bay Lightning captain snags it right away.

The game takes off in a fast pace, but I'm still thinking about the sadness in Bruce's eyes.

Number seventy-nine takes the puck across the ice and into the Eagles' zone. He passes it to another teammate, Mitch tries to steal it, but it gets away from him, then the Lightning right wing shoots it straight between Bruce's legs.

Bruce's head sways back and forth, like he's lecturing himself. A pit forms in my stomach. We hid our relationship so it wouldn't affect the team during playoffs, and yet, our relationship *still* affected the team. I broke their goalie's heart, and everything we tried to prevent ended up happening, anyway.

For the rest of the first period, I watch with bated breath

as Bruce allows shot after shot into his net. He's like a completely different goalie tonight.

The first period ends with the Eagles down one to four. A terrible start to the game.

Usually, us girls chat and laugh and cheer, but tonight we're all quiet. And I feel like I'm the elephant in the room. I feel like this is my fault.

As we sit in silence and watch the commercials before the next period starts, I finally can't take it anymore, burying my face in my hands. "Girls, I'm so sorry."

A second later they're all surround me. I can feel arms draping across my shoulders. "Oh, Farrah. This isn't your fault," this comes from Andie. "Life happens, and the guys have to set it aside and play their best. Do you think Bruce is the first guy to go through a breakup during the season?"

I remove my hands from my face and find all four of them beside me. Noel and Andie on my left, Mel and Amber on my right.

"And it won't be the last, either," Mel adds.

I wipe my tear-streaked face on my shirt sleeve. "But not during playoffs!"

"You can't stay with Bruce just so he'll play well during playoffs," Noel says. "If you don't want to be with him, you were right to end things."

I do want to be with him. The thought pops into my head before I can stop it. Whether I want to be with him or not isn't the issue. It's that someday, inevitably, he'll change his mind about wanting to be with me.

Mel leans in. "We're here for you, no matter what. We love you *and* Bruce. And we love you whether you're together or not. You're not a package deal."

Until that moment, I didn't know how badly I needed to hear that. I never expected to lose all my friends during my divorce, but it was eye opening. Connor and I *were* a package deal for them. And after we split, they cut me off like a dead limb.

"I love you guys," I say.

"We love you, too," Amber says, leaning around Mel to hug me. The embrace quickly turns into a group hug, and I do feel moderately better now.

When the second period begins, we all stay huddled together. I gasp when Bruce doesn't come onto the ice, instead he's been replaced with their backup goalie, O'Malley.

Andie uses her arm that's still around me to give me a squeeze. "It'll be okay."

But it's not okay because the Eagles lose game three of the third round of the playoffs, three to eight.

The D.C. Eagles #1 Fan Page On Hockeyisbetterthanfootball.com

Todd Ferguson: Well, Craig. Maybe you were right after all. I don't know what's going on with McBride. Why'd he wait until round three of the playoffs to choke? 🧑

Craig Nottingham: I just have a sixth sense about these things. I can tell if it's going to rain if my eyes are twitching, too. My mom always said I had a prophetic nature.

Mandie Banderson: Craig you're full of it. 😳 McBride has two off games, and you two dickheads are freaking out. Calm your tits, guys.

Craig Nottingham: Full of it? Then why is my eye twitching right now and it *is* raining?

Mandie Banderson: Anyone would know that by simply looking out the window.

Harry Johnson: I think after being benched last night, McBride will be motivated for tomorrow's game. Being benched can serve up some humble pie pretty quick.

Todd Ferguson: I sure hope you're right, Harry. The backup goalie isn't up to par, he'll be better in a few years, probably, but he's not at playoff level.

Harry Johnson: O'Malley is a great goalie; he's just young and still learning.

Craig Nottingham: Maybe McBride and O'Malley can go back to youth training camp this summer.

Mandie Banderson: For the love, CRAIG! SHUT UP.

I CHUCKLE at Mandie's comments as I turn off my phone and lay it on the squat rack beside me. I'm working out at the hotel gym, trying to distract myself from this shitshow I call my life.

My phone pings, and I glance down at the screen, expecting it to be a hockeyisbetterthanfootball.com notification. My eyes widen when I see Farrah's name pop up.

FARRAH

You can't just buy me a 14,000-dollar oven.

My mouth lifts at the corners. Even if she's being sassy, at least she's speaking to me.

BRUCE

I can. And I will. Are there other colors you'd like, too?

FARRAH

You're impossible.

FARRAH

But...thank you.

It's not much, but her texts are enough to lift my spirits through the rest of my workout.

When I get back to my hotel room, all the guys are waiting in front of the door. They're dressed like they're going out and leaning against the walls.

"What's going on?" I ask.

"We're taking you out," Remy says. "You've gotta stop working out every spare minute. You need to save that energy for tomorrow's game. And we think you need a steak…and dessert."

I perk up at that. "Dessert? Really?"

Remy reluctantly nods. "If Alexander Ovechkin can play how he plays while inhaling Flaming Hot Cheetos and Coca-Cola, you can, too."

Alexander Ovechkin is every goalie's worst nightmare, he's almost broken Wayne Gretzky's goal scoring record.

My shoulders slump, I don't even bother hiding how pathetic I feel. "I could really use some dessert," I admit. I was so tempted to go out and find some Tony's chocolate bars last night.

Colby rushes over and pulls me into a hug. "I know, Brucey, I know." He pulls away quickly, his nose wrinkling and a gagging sound coming from his mouth. "But go shower first; you smell awful."

An hour later we're at some fancy restaurant in downtown Thunder Bay. It's one of those ultra-modern places that feels European and has the prices to match the vibes. We're seated at a large, round table at the very back of the place, hidden away from prying eyes. It's nice to be out but not noticed or bombarded.

Colby, Mitch, West, and Remy all order grilled chicken salads with a side of whole wheat pasta and organic butter to substitute the pasta sauce. They're also drinking water. Just water. Meanwhile, my team captain has given me permission to order whatever I want. Probably because my performance on ice can't get any worse, so to hell with it all.

I take advantage by ordering a steak smothered in onions and gravy, with a massive side of loaded mashed potatoes, and another side of mac & cheese. I pair it with a glass of Moscato. Yeah, the sweet stuff. I also ordered devil's food cake for dessert and requested a scoop of vanilla ice cream on top—Mitch called me a child for asking for the ice cream.

When the server brings the food out, one whole tray is for me. She scrunches her face as she hands me each item.

Once she leaves, Colby starts to laugh. "That poor girl thinks there's something wrong with you."

"It's just a broken heart," I say, trying to play if off like a joke, but my voice is too sad for any of them to believe it wasn't serious.

Remy pushes his bland-looking salad away. "You're giving up already?"

I blow out a breath. "I don't know what to do. I don't want to be desperate. But I feel desperate for her."

He prickles at that. "Wow. This whole time I worried if you guys got together, you'd break her heart, but my sister is the one who did the breaking. Maybe I should ship *her* off to a blistering cold place in Canada."

"Please don't; then she'll have to find a way to move that giant oven."

Mitch shakes his head. "I still can't believe you bought her an oven. That's the least romantic thing I've ever heard."

"Says the man who gave his wife a platter of sub sandwiches," I mutter under my breath.

Mitch narrows his eyes at me.

I shove a bite of mashed potatoes into my mouth, and they all look at me with jealousy clouding their vision. Remy stabs a few pieces of lettuce and eats the bite with a scowl on his face.

Washing my potatoes down with a sip of Moscato—a terrible pairing, by the way—I study each of my teammates. "I'm really sorry, guys. I know I'm sucking it up out there. I'm trying to put it out of my head during games, I really am. But I think it's the lack of sleep that's getting me. When I'm lying in bed each night, all I can think about is Farrah and what I'll do if she never loves me back."

Remy nods as I speak. "I know you're exhausted. What have you tried for sleeping?"

I tick off each item as I say them. "Sleeping pills, a sleep mask, a weighted blanket, magnesium, a warm bath…"

West's face lights up with an idea. "Have you tried essential oils?"

I scoff. "No."

"Mel swears by them, she sends me with sleep oils for every trip. You wanna try some tonight? You put a few drops in coconut oil and rub it on the bottom of your feet."

Shrugging, I reply, "Sure. I'll try your witchcraft."

He beams like he solved world hunger. "I'll bring them by tonight."

"All right, hopefully you'll sleep better tonight after this feast, and Mel's witch magic," Remy says. "We need Bruce McBride back, the one that's a beast on the ice. The backup goalie doesn't cut it."

"Poor O'Malley," Colby says. "He needs more training."

The rest of us nod.

"But if I can't get my head in the game…he's all we have." I slump back in my seat, the delicious food suddenly not looking so great.

"You've got this. You're a professional," Mitch says.

"This is why they pay you the big bucks. Once playoffs are over, you'll have time to figure things out with Farrah and send her more ovens."

Remy takes a sip of his water, and the look on his face tells me he wishes it was something stronger. "We believe in you."

THIRTY-SEVEN

BRUCE

WALKING into game four of seven, I'm feeling more like myself. Mel's essential oils, and probably the incredible food, helped me finally sleep last night. The best night of sleep I've had since Farrah tried to break up with me. Yeah, I'm still not acknowledging that we're broken up. For one, we never labeled what we were…so there's nothing to break from. And two, I still haven't given up on us.

I even manage a grin and a finger gun for the photographers who are snapping photos of my royal blue suit and crimson red tie combo. There's still an ache in my chest, but the ability to mask it and go into tonight's game seems easier today. Maybe I'm getting better at compartmentalizing.

Walking into the bland dressing room, I take in the scuffed white walls, plastic and metal benches, and simple cubbies. It's nothing like our Eagles' dressing room, but this is what Thunder Bay gives the away teams, apparently.

My eyes meet O'Malley's, and I cross the room and sit next to him. He's tense, and his eyes look intensely worried. "You okay, man?"

He looks down, his shaggy brown hair falling onto his

forehead as he fastens his shoulder pad. "Not really. They chewed us up and spit us out the other night. The pressure was unreal. Like during a normal season game, I'm nervous at first but it wears off…but a playoff game? I don't know how you handle it."

I snort laugh. "Obviously not well. Remember how I was benched?"

"Please don't get benched tonight," he whispers.

"I'm feeling good tonight," I say. "But you're in the NHL for a reason, kid. You're a talented goalie. I know the pressure is a lot, especially right now, but you have what it takes if you get out of your head." When I finish talking, I realize I'm preaching to the choir.

O'Malley's dark eyes meet mine in look that tells me he was thinking the same thing.

"We're wiping the floor with these guys tonight, I can feel it."

He nods. "I hope you're right."

An hour later, I'm crouched in front of my net and the first period is starting. Remy gets possession of the puck straight away, which is always a great way to start off a game. We want to stay on top all throughout, not be playing catch up.

I stretch to stay limber and alert while the guys are at the other end of the ice, until their team captain gets a break-away and is racing towards me. I get in position, ready for him. He flies straight at me, and I try to guess where he'll shoot the puck. At the last second, I see his stick move and my instincts tell me to get down low. He tries to shoot it between my legs, but the puck bounces off my pads.

I breathe a sigh of relief, but it's short lived because the Lightning captain crashes into me and my net. I fly back with a thud onto the ice, and the net slides away.

The other guys have made it over to us by now and I feel the Lightning's captain being lifted off me. When I glance up, I see it's a very angry looking Mitch yanking him up by his jersey.

The Lightning captain looks just as furious at being manhandled and throws a punch at Mitch. Although Mitch 'The Machine' Anderson has gotten better about staying on the ice instead of in the penalty box, he's not a perfect man. He throws a punch back, hitting the captain's nose and drawing blood.

I squeeze my eyes shut in frustration. Drawing blood is an automatic four-minute penalty.

Sure enough, the dreaded whistle blows from the ref, and Mitch is hauled away—seething—to the penalty box. Now we have one less player on the ice for four minutes.

I love that my teammates are fiercely protective of their goalie—me—but this game is too high stakes to be racking up penalties and giving the other team a power play.

Remy looks ready to burst; I'm not sure I've ever seen his jaw so tense. It looks like he's gritting his teeth so hard his molars might break.

A faceoff starts to the left of my net, and a right winger who replaced the captain while his nose stops bleeding, wins the faceoff. He passes the puck to a defenseman, and he takes it around the back of the net. Colby and West are working hard to cloud their access for any decent shots, but then the defenseman passes the puck to their team's top goal scorer, and he shoots the puck deftly into the top corner of my net.

And we still have three minutes where we're down a player.

A bead of sweat trickles down my forehead and the

bridge of my nose. I can't take my eyes off this puck for even a second until this power play is over.

As I watch the puck move from stick to stick, player to player, I pay no attention to the men on the ice. It's just me and the puck. Someone shoots, but I'm ready, and deflect it away with my stick. The puck flies free again, bouncing from man to man and skidding across the ice. It flies toward me, this time it's a higher shot, I extend my glove to catch it and miss by the smallest fraction. It finds it's mark in the top left-hand corner of my net making the score zero to two in the first period.

A stream of expletives leaves my mouth. When we're back at full man advantage, Coach Young calls a timeout, and I can finally take a deep breath. Coach Young motions for me to stay put, which is a relief. This timeout isn't about me; it's about everyone else. It's nice not to be the one causing the issues tonight.

The rest of the period passes and we're not able to score on the Lightning, but thankfully, they don't score on us again, either.

Going into the second period, we're all amped from Coach Young giving us the ass chewing of a lifetime. I've never seen the vein in his forehead protrude so dramatically. Spit flew from his mouth as he berated us. But we needed it.

West scores in the first five minutes of the second period, which gives the guys some much needed confidence. After that, everyone is passing more smoothly and skating faster. Colby lands another goal in their net toward the end of the period, tying up the game.

The vibes in our dressing room are more positive between the second and third periods. Coach Young has calmed down, he offers us encouragement and tells us to keep doing what we did in the second.

When we head back out again, we're feeling ready to win this thing. But unfortunately, the Lightning are feeling the same way. It's a fast-paced period from the get-go, all the men on the ice determined to go home with a win.

One of the forwards gets into a scuffle with Mitch, it looks like their sticks are tangled up. He falls to the ground dramatically, and Mitch glares at him. The forward is trying to make it look like Mitch tripped him. The ref buys the performance and sends Mitch to the penalty box for a two-minute minor penalty. Mitch resists, and Remy skates over to defend him. Mitch is smart enough to stay quiet, not wanting any time added to the penalty, while Remy yells at the ref for the ridiculous call.

The ref doesn't back down, and Mitch heads to the penalty box—again—with steam practically pouring out of his pores. Remy looks just as angry.

The Lightning captain high sticks Remy and he clasps his hand over his mouth where the stick hit. There's no blood, and the whole thing goes unnoticed by the refs. Convenient. The Lightning captain passes the puck to one of his centers and he scores on me while we're basically playing three on five since Remy is clutching his face.

Now we're down two-four. We spend the rest of the game trying to catch up, and the refs appear to be kissing the Lightning's butt tonight. Remy has a fat lip from the high sticking but manages to score one more goal during a break-away in the last minute of the game. We lose three-four, and it sucks.

My teammates and I trudge to the dressing room, every-one, including Coach Young, is quiet. He stands by the exit door with his hands on his hips and his head down. "The refs sucked tonight. I admit that. We started the game off in poor form," Coach narrows his eyes at Mitch. "But I'm proud of the way you played after that. But now they've got three wins. One more and they beat us out for a slot in the final round." He sighs, closing his eyes briefly. "If you guys want this…really want this, you have to give it your all and then some. One hundred and fifty percent. You hear me? Our next game is at home. That's *your* game. Those are *your* fans. That's our chance to tie up this third round."

Everyone nods and agrees, then Coach leaves through the exit letting the door slam behind him. The rest of the administrative staff lingers awkwardly, no one knowing what else to say. Jeff, our equipment manager, quietly stores our gloves in the background, trying not to make a sound.

But sometimes silence is the worst sound of all.

That night as we're on our red eye back to D.C., I pull up hockeyisbetterthanfootball.com to see what fans are saying. Tonight's loss wasn't just my fault, but everyone loves to complain about the goalie anyway.

The D.C. Eagles #1 Fan Page On Hockeyisbetterthanfootball.com

Craig Nottingham: Well, well, well. Another loss! Who wants to have an Eagles jersey burning party?

Todd Ferguson: It's not over yet, Craig, I'd hold on to those jerseys. Unless they're signed, then I'd be interested in buying them from you.

Todd Ferguson: But McBride played well tonight! Not even you can deny that.

Craig Nottingham: He did okay. I still think we should trade him.

Mandie Banderson: Tonight's loss was completely due to the refs and had nothing to do with McBride's skills.

Todd Ferguson: PREACH.

Craig Nottingham: Was the loss the ref's faults, or

Anderson's? That idiot can't stay out of the sinbin for more than ten minutes at a time.

Mandie Banderson: I know you didn't just call MITCH THE MACHINE ANDERSON an idiot. You whiny little biotch.

Craig Nottingham: Is there an admin in here? Can we remove Mandie for bullying?

An admin has disabled comments on this post

I smile at my screen, now knowing why this woman with the big mouth sounds familiar.

I'M at the big house this morning, spending time with my oven. The air in the house is warm and smells of freshly baked bread. It's my favorite scent…besides whatever Bruce smells like. But I'm pushing that thought from my mind.

Amber took the day off since Remy is home from his away trip today. He's currently in bed sound asleep after arriving home around four in the morning, so I'm baking up some whole wheat bread for him to have when he wakes up.

Amber stalks into the kitchen and smiles when she spots me staring at the gorgeous piece of baking equipment that I'm still in awe of. She slowly shakes her head.

"What?" I ask.

"If you don't know, I'm not telling you."

I turn and rest my butt on the oven. "Just spill."

She waves me off. "You're not ready to hear it."

I cross my arms. "Yes, I am."

She crosses her arms and quirks a brow. "Fine. You're in love with that man, and it's frustrating to watch you torture yourself by staying away from him."

My jaw drops and I let out a little huff. Deep down, I

know she's right, but I'm not ready to admit it. Her flippant way of saying it makes me prickle, but I've been strangely emotional all day. I think it's just the stress of the entire situation, but something feels…off kilter. "We're better off—"

She interrupts me. "Bruce isn't Connor, and you know it."

I tsk, my eyes burning, and I don't understand why. "I'm not sure I like this sassy side of you." This is the thing about living in close proximity with your sister-in-law and seeing her almost every day—your relationship becomes sisterly. It's great because I feel close to her, but complicated because we speak our minds more often than not.

My niece runs into the room, breaking the tension. She sees how her mother is standing. Nella mirrors the pose, sticking out her bottom lip and crossing her arms.

Amber glances down at her daughter and smirks. "Well, get used to it because there are two of us," she says with a teasing lilt.

Unable to help it, I crack a smile. "My brother has his hands full."

Amber's expression grows serious. "You know I just love you and want you to be happy, right?"

"I know," I tell her.

"Wose made a mess," Nella says. Wose means Rose. Amber and I look at each other wide eyed.

"Uh-oh." Amber rushes into the living room to see what the mess is. Nella scurries after her, and I'm left alone with my thoughts.

Am I in love with Bruce? And am I really just making this unnecessarily hard for both of us? I hate that I don't trust my own judgement. And I hate that I'm worried about the crushing weight of being rejected again. I want to go back in time before Connor, when I was full of hope and trust. And I want that version of me to meet and fall in love with Bruce.

But that's not the version of me he fell for. And he loves *this* Farrah. As impossible as that seems to me.

But instead, I'm fighting the deep-seeded fear that I'm taking something away from him by letting him love me. A life with me would be more complicated than it might be with someone else.

I allow myself to picture us together, and to wonder if I could allow myself to love him and trust him completely—the way he deserves to be loved—when a dull ache thrums in my stomach. My hand comes to rest on my belly button, and I rub at the area through my shirt. It's probably nothing.

Ten minutes later, the oven timer beeps, and I bend to remove the bread. The pain grows, moving lower now, and I wince. I use oven mitts to pull the bread out, turn off the oven and rest my back against the kitchen counter. The pain is familiar now, just like that night I was tearing down our event, and Bruce came to take me to the hospital. Only this time, I think it's even worse. And it's intensifying rapidly.

I slide to the floor and even though there are crumbs on the tile from Nella carrying her waffle through the house earlier, I lay down in hopes to ease the pain.

My phone is on the counter, and I don't feel like I can stand back up to get it, so I just lie there with my cheek against the cool tile, waiting for someone to find me.

Rose finds me first, whimpering when she sees me and pressing her wet nose to my hairline in a loving sniff. She lays down beside me and I lift my hand to pet her soft head, but even that movement adds to my discomfort. It hurts everywhere, it hurts to breathe, it hurts to think.

"Farrah!" I hear Amber's voice, finally. "What's wrong?"

She kneels on the ground so I can see her, her expression is frantic with worry.

"I think it's another ovarian cyst." I barely can get the words out, and just the effort of speaking has a cold sweat breaking out along my chest and face.

"Oh no. What can I do?"

I consider her question through the pain, unable to articulate what I truly want. All I can think about is how Bruce showed up last time this happened, and how safe he made me feel. How careful he was, and protective. I think of him sitting in the waiting room for hours when he could've gone home. And what I really want, is him to be here again. Nothing else seems to matter in this moment. I want Bruce. I need Bruce.

"I'll get Remy," Amber says, her voice stricken. She stands up to get my brother, but I stop her.

"No," I say, the panic in my voice surprising me. "Bruce. Please. I want Bruce."

She nods before rushing off to another room. I faintly hear her on the phone but can't make out the conversation. A short moment later, my brother is in front of me. He slides a small pillow under my head.

"Farrah, I think we should get you to the hospital."

"It would be a waste," I say hoarsely. "They'll just tell me cysts shouldn't cause this much pain."

His dark eyes are full of worry, and I see his mind working, trying to figure out what to do. "Can you move to the couch? You'd be more comfortable."

"Don't you dare touch me," I say through gritted teeth.

He takes a deep breath. "Bruce is on his way; he should be here soon."

I lower my chin in a nod, and an overwhelming sense of relief washes over me despite the pain. I wasn't sure Bruce would come to me after everything I've put him through. Hopefully he doesn't change his mind on the way here. I wouldn't blame him if he did. I force my eyes closed again but I hear him moments later when he comes through the front door.

"Farrah," his voice is close and the softness in his tone soothes my aching soul. I think this man is a balm to me, a medicine. Bruce McBride could heal me in ways I never imagined.

When I force my eyes open, the light from the kitchen makes my head throb. But I can make out his large form. He's on the kitchen floor, shuffling himself onto his side. His warm, calloused hand comes to gently rest on the side of my face and tears spring to my eyes at how comforting it is. "Yeux Bleus," he whispers. "I'm here."

His soft, simple words are what allow my tears to finally release and roll down my cheeks. I feel the warm liquid pool against my nose and ear, but Bruce wipes the tears away.

"Is the pain worse than last time?" He asks.

I nod, trying not to move too much. "Yes." Swallowing, I force my eyes open wider to take him in. His scruff covered jaw and messy hair are the best thing I've seen all week. "I wasn't sure you'd come."

His hand slides from my face to my hairline, cupping my face a little tighter. "I'll always come to you. Don't ever doubt that."

"I'm so sorry, Bruce. For everything."

"Shhhh, we can talk about everything later, okay? Right now, we need to get you to the hospital."

"No." I hear the alarm in my voice. The thought of being moved right now is the worst thing I can imagine. "I can't move."

"Baby, you're so pale. And you feel feverish. I want to

make sure you're okay. Remember last time? We'll count to three and I'll pick you up. That'll be the worst of it, then you'll lie in the truck, and we'll be on our way."

"Okay." My chin wobbles. I know he's right. This time is different than last time. And much, much worse.

I brace myself for him to pick me up, and like last time, it hurts so bad to be moved that I think I might pass out. But soon, I'm resting on my side in his pickup that I've come to love, and we're on our way to the hospital.

When we get to the ER and the nurses transfer me to a bed, I finally pass out from the pain of being jostled around. When I wake up, I have no idea how long it's been, but Bruce is in a chair in the corner of the small hospital room. He jumps up and crosses the room when he notices my eyes are open. His hand comes to rest on top of mine as he looks me over. "Are you feeling better? They gave you some strong pain meds."

My belly is sore, but I feel tingly and warm all over from the medication. "Yes. Much better. I can't believe they let you come back with me." My voice is groggy and barely recognizable.

Bruce blushes. "Um, I told them I was your husband. Sorry."

A dry laugh comes out of me and Bruce turns to get me a water cup that has the hospital's logo on it. He holds it up and I take a long swig from the bendy straw.

"Thank you."

"The doctor is supposed to be in soon; they did some scans while you were out."

As if summoned, a doctor wearing black scrubs and a white lab coat knocks on the door frame and steps inside the room. It's a woman this time, and she has kind eyes. I'm relieved it's not the same doctor as last time.

"Farrah?" She asks and I nod. She has brown skin and short, dark hair. I'd guess she's only a few years older than me. "I have some unfortunate news; would you like your husband to stay in the room?" She looks from me to Bruce and then back to me again.

"I'd like him to stay," I say, nerves assailing me at her words. But I don't want Bruce to leave me. He sits carefully on the bed beside me and takes my hand in his.

She takes a breath and sits on the roller stool that was pushed to a corner in the room "I looked at your scans," she says, jumping right in without small talk, which I'm grateful for. "Your cyst was quite large, six centimeters. Sometimes, unfortunately, when cysts are that big, it can cause complications and affect the area around it. In this case, the ruptured cyst caused a torsion and twisted your fallopian tube. We'll need to perform a laparoscopic procedure to straighten it out. But there's a chance the damage could be worse than we feared and then we would need to remove the fallopian tube completely."

It takes me what feels like a full minute to comprehend what she's saying. Bruce squeezes my hand and the reminder that he's here bolsters me. "Okay," I say slowly. "If you do have to remove the fallopian tube, what are my chances of having kids after that?"

The doctor's eyes flit to Bruce. "Some women can have children down the road after they've healed, but the chances are small. About seven out of a thousand women."

A sob gets trapped somewhere in my throat, and I gasp for breath. The motion is painful, and I remove my hand from Bruce's so I can wrap both arms around my stomach. Bruce quietly stays by my side, placing an arm around me and kissing the top of my head.

"But there are other options, if it came to that," the doctor continues. "A lot of women have great success through IVF." She pauses like she's giving me a chance to catch up. "We need to prep you for the procedure right away to restore blood flow to the area." I barely make out the doctor's voice through the muddle of my own thoughts.

I feel numb.

But what I can register is that Bruce never leaves me. Not while the doctor tells me what to expect before and after the laparoscopic procedure. And he doesn't leave me once I'm back from surgery.

Bruce also never leaves me when the doctor tells me they *did* have to remove the fallopian tube. He doesn't just stay; he holds me afterward while I cry myself to sleep, his hand gently moving up and down my back as I sob.

CHAPTER
THIRTY-NINE

BRUCE

I STAYED the night with Farrah after her surgery, not wanting to take my eyes off her and refusing to leave her side. What if she needed help in the middle of the night?

She did, by the way. And I was the best nurse of all time.

We're in bed at her apartment, with me lying on my side and one arm curved beneath my head. Soft morning light filters through the curtains and onto her face. Her dark eyelashes fan out along cheeks that now look rosy and healthy again, unlike how pale she looked when I found her on Remy's kitchen floor yesterday morning. Although her skin looks better, and I'm glad she's healthy again, I know her heart is breaking over the surgery. But I'll be here when she wakes up, and I hope that will bring her some comfort.

Farrah's eyes eventually flutter open, slowly and sleepily. The whole of those blues that I love are visible, and I bask in them. Not wanting to break the peaceful morning fog, I quietly take her in, memorizing all the features that I've missed in the last several days. Features I wasn't sure I'd ever get to study this closely again.

"You stayed," she whispers.

"I keep trying to tell you, I'm not going anywhere."

She reaches out and grips the back of my neck, pulling me in and placing a tender, heart aching kiss on my lips. I scoot closer, until our bodies meet beneath the covers. I'm still wearing my athletic shorts and black tee from yesterday, and she's in pajamas that have little cupcakes all over them. But even though we're not skin to skin, I still feel closer to her than ever. It's a connection that has nothing to do with how physically close we are. I feel like our minds are finally in sync, like she's finally trusting me to stay. Trusting me with her heart.

I slide a hand into her hair and kiss her deeply, tasting the sweetness I've missed desperately. I pull back slowly, because we need to talk, and I don't want to hurt her. The doctor said she'd be sore for a few weeks.

She allows her hand to fall from my neck, but it doesn't go far, moving to rest on my bicep. "I missed these," she says, giving the muscle a pat. Farrah smiles and it lights up my world that was starting to feel too dark. "I missed *you*."

I lean in to run the tip of my nose along the bridge of hers'. "I missed you too."

"And I'm sorry. I'm sorry for bringing my baggage into this amazing thing we have, and not believing what your actions have told me over and over again."

"It's okay. I know we have some barriers to work through, and I'll be patient as we break through those. But let's do it together, okay?"

She nods. "Okay." Farrah looks away, her eyes growing misty. "Being with me means giving up on some of your dreams. Like being a dad. Are you sure you're okay with that?"

I kiss her softly. "Farrah, *you* are my dream."

Farrah blinks back tears. "Bruce, I love you."

"I love you too, Yeux bleus."

She smirks, humor filling her eyes. "My handsome Petit gâteau."

I don't tell her she pronounced it wrong.

Farrah's expression grows serious, worrying her bottom lip. "I have a question for you, and it might seem too soon to ask it, but—"

I hold a hand up. "I plan to spend my life with you, so nothing is too soon."

She smiles. "Okay, here goes. I'm not sure I'd want to go through IVF...trying to get pregnant the first time around was so hard, mentally. Month after month of negative pregnancy tests. I'm not sure my heart could handle it again." Farrah pauses, not looking away from me. "Would you ever want to adopt?"

I don't even need to think about my answer. "I would love to adopt."

I grin, the thought of fostering warming my heart. So many kids out there need good homes and I'm so grateful I was adopted by incredible people who loved me. Giving that to another child...what could be better?

Farrah and I slowly drift back to sleep, together, in each other's arms.

That afternoon, I pry myself away from Farrah's bed to get ready for the game. I told her I could skip it, and she told me she'd never speak to me again if I did. She looked deadly serious, and I wasn't about to take any chances. Also, her mom and sister drove down today after hearing about her surgery, and they're going to stay with her tonight. I don't think I could've left her all alone, but I know she's in good hands.

Farrah is sitting up in bed, with a tray of food over her lap. I kiss her on the forehead and start toward the door.

"Bruce! We didn't watch a romance. What about your good luck ritual?"

I stride back over to her and kiss her on the mouth, lingering there until it's hard to pull away again. "Baby, you're the only good luck charm I need." I wink and she laughs.

"What about your truck?"

"Actually, I thought about finally trading her in. I think it's time for a fresh start."

Her jaw drops. "But I love that truck."

"An SUV would be better for hauling large cakes around."

She smiles at that. "True."

I check the time. "Will your mom be here soon? I should probably get home and change into my suit."

A knock comes from the apartment door and Farrah shrugs. "You summoned her."

I open the door and Sally Remington beams up at me with her blue eyes and grey hair. "Well, if it isn't the second most beautiful girl in the world," I say.

She hits my arm lightly. "Oh, you rogue!" Sally laughs heartily and I realize that's where Farrah got her amazing laugh from.

"Bruce, this is my youngest daughter, Felicity." A small woman who looks like a younger, dark-haired version of Sally steps forward, grinning the same way her mother does.

"I finally get to meet the infamous Bruce McBride," she says, resting her hands on her hips. "I've heard you're the best kisser my sister has ever experienced."

"Felicity!" Farrah yells in horror. I look back, and she has her hands over her face.

"Is that right?" I ask, waiting for Farrah to uncover her face. When she does, I wink at her. "I try my best."

I wrap Sally in a one-armed hug then pat Felicity on the shoulder. "I hate to rush out, but I've got a Stanley Cup to win."

"Good luck!" The three women yell in unison.

And as I trot down the stairs and head to my pickup, I've never felt so damn lucky in my life.

"OH, SWEETHEART, I'M SO SORRY," my mother says from where she sits curled up beside me in my bed. Felicity is on the other side, and I'm in the middle. "We came as soon as Remy called us."

I ease into her, savoring the comfort only a mother could offer. A mother who has been with me through all my struggles while trying to conceive, and then my PCOS diagnosis, and who held me after my divorce. A mother that taught me what it is to be a mom, even though I may never be one. My heart aches at the thought. But if I ever adopt, and I really hope to—someday—I'll know how to show any child the same love my mother has always shown me.

"Thanks, Mom. It means a lot that you're here." I place my hand over hers on top of the blankets and allow my tears to flow freely.

"And I'm sorry for saying what I said about Bruce before. He's done so much for you and treated you with such care." Mom kisses the top of my head.

"It's okay. I doubted him, too," I admit. "But I'm so lucky to have him."

"I can see that," Mom says with a smile. "In spite of everything going on, you don't look beaten down, there's a hope in your eyes I haven't seen in a long time. I think we have Bruce McBride to thank for that?"

"And he's a tall drink of water, too!" Felicity says, fanning herself. "He almost doesn't look real."

I shake my head but don't disagree with her.

"I'm devastated they had to remove one of my fallopian tubes, of course. But I'm reminding myself there are good things happening too, and I want to focus on the good things. I think the entirety of this will hit me at other moments in time, you know? Like watching other people's pregnancies and knowing I'll never experience that." I sigh. "Bruce reminded me of something, though."

Mom and Felicity wait for me to continue. "He said I can feel more than one thing. I can be happy for someone and sad for myself at the same time."

"Bruce is wise beyond his years," Mom admits with a soft smile. "I like you two together."

Felicity swings her arm around both of us, so we're locked in one comforting mother-daughter hug. "I'm sorry, too, Farrah. I don't know what to say, other than I'm so sorry and I love you."

I sniff. "Thank you. Having you both here is enough, honestly. You don't have to say anything."

The three of us stay curled up in my bed like that for a long while, simply enjoying being together.

Felicity finally breaks the silence, "So, what should we order for dinner while we watch the Eagles kick butt?"

An hour later, we're devouring Chinese takeout and Tony's chocolate while we watch the Eagles wipe the ice with the Lightning. The game is insanely fast, and Bruce has never played better. He's in the zone tonight and I'm so proud of him. I wish I could be there in person.

When the game ends and the Eagles win five to one, I want to jump up and down, but instead cheer sitting down, with a pillow over my stomach for extra comfort. They only need to win one more game to make it to the final round. My stomach flips with excitement at how far they've come and the awareness that their dreams are in sight.

Mom and Felicity chant *Eagles, Eagles, Eagles* and run around the room as I grin and watch them.

"This is their year to win, baby!" Felicity yells into the air.

My heart swells with hope for all the possibilities the future holds, for the first time in a long time, I feel like my dreams might come true. Maybe not in the way I pictured, but in a beautiful way, nonetheless.

FORTY-ONE
BRUCE

WE WON our fourth game in round three yesterday, officially moving us forward to the final round of playoffs. So tonight, we're celebrating at Remy and Amber's.

Jackson is with me, of course; he's part of the gang now. And Farrah is feeling much better from her procedure. Her mom and sister stayed with her until we got back from Thunder Bay.

Walking up to Remy's front door with Jackson right beside me, I've never felt happier. When the door opens, my stomach does a flip. Just knowing I'll see Farrah soon does that to me. That, and knowing we don't have to hide. I can hug her and kiss her and give her attention all night, and no one can say a word—I'll also save a lot of money not having to pay Noah to keep his mouth shut.

Farrah opens the tall front door with a smile on her gorgeous face. Her makeup is done nicely, and she's wearing a blue top that makes her eyes pop with little denim shorts with fashionable holes worn in them. They show off her thighs in a very sexy way. It's the beginning of June now, and her skin already looks slightly tanned.

She grins up at me, and I know I'm smiling just as big. My hands itch to touch her.

Jackson groans and slips past us into the house. "You guys are gross; I'm out of here."

Farrah covers her mouth to stifle a laugh, but I take advantage of our brief moment of alone time and slip my arms around her waist, pulling her close until our bodies are pressed together.

Her arms slide around my neck and then into the back of my hair, which is longer than usual since we all stopped cutting our hair or shaving our faces a few weeks ago. It's a playoff thing.

I kiss her, fusing our mouths together in a dance of lips and tongues and passion. A dance that makes me want more. She grunts in a way that makes me pull back. "You okay?"

"Yes," she whispers with a laugh. "I'm still a little sore, but not too bad."

"Sorry, I got carried away."

"So did I," she says, looking up at me through her dark lashes.

I loosen my grip on her and place one more kiss on her lips. The clearing of a throat has us looking up to see Noah standing awkwardly behind us in the entry way. "They sent me to tell you guys dinner is ready."

"Sorry, Noah," Farrah says. "We're coming!"

I reach into my wallet and pull out a fifty, and when I pass Noah, I shake his hand and leave the money behind. "For old time's sake." I wink.

Noah shrugs and follows us into the open concept living space.

"Ahh," Colby says when he spots us. "There are the lovebirds."

I'm holding Farrah's hand and use the contact to draw her closer to me. She's blushing and all I want to do is kiss her again, but I don't have a death wish. I'm not about to push Remy too far.

Andie squeals and claps her hands. "Oh, my gosh. You guys are so cute. I've been waiting for this moment forever."

"*You've* been waiting forever?" I roll my eyes. "You're ridiculous, Andie Anderson." I pause and narrow my eyes at her. "Or should I say…Mandie Banderson?"

She gasps, and Mitch, who's standing next to her, whips his head in her direction. "What's he talking about?"

She grimaces. "It's nothing, I just have an online persona where I troll the fans that are trolling you guys."

Mitch sighs heavily, bringing his hand to his face and massaging his temples with his thumb and index finger.

"But wait!" she says. "How'd *you* know?" She stares at me, waiting for my answer.

I crinkle my nose, trying unsuccessfully to hide a smile. "I troll them, too. I'm Harry Johnson."

Andie's head falls back as she cackles. Not laughs, cackles.

Remy shakes his head. "Really? Harry Johnson?"

I shrug. "So, Noah tells me the food is ready?"

"Changing the subject…nice tactic," Farrah says, keeping her voice low.

"Your brother is great, but he can be scary when he wants, and I don't want him to tell coach," I whisper back.

She stands on her tippy toes and plants a kiss on my lips. Right in front of everyone. I'm stunned and have to blink a few times. Farrah bites her bottom lip and strides into the kitchen, leaving me unable to speak in her wake.

When Mitch passes by me, he slaps me hard on the back. "Glad you finally met someone who stuns you into silence."

"Ha, ha, very funny."

Remy and Amber have dinner arranged on the table tonight. The table is set with pretty, white dishes and there's a big bowl of whole wheat pasta and grilled salmon. There's a large platter of steamed broccoli as well, and then one more dish with fried chicken for the non-hockey players. My mouth waters at the sight of breading, but we're too close to being done with playoffs to ruin my diet now.

I notice Farrah's in the kitchen fussing over whatever dessert she made for tonight and sneak in there while everyone else is getting seated around the table—I note that they squeezed in two extra chairs so the younger boys can sit at the table with us—Jackson sits by Noah and the two of them start chatting. I smile.

"Do you need help?" I ask Farrah, trailing one hand down her spine then settling it on her hip.

She finishes spooning a thin frosting on what looks like sweet buns. I whimper. "Sticky buns?"

"Sorry," she says, her voice apologetic. "But all the girls requested them."

I nuzzle my nose into her neck, and she giggles. "It's okay, those aren't the sticky buns I really want anyway."

Farrah laughs, ducking to get out of my grasp. "Noah is going to walk in here when you're doing that."

She's standing in front of the oven now; I'd almost forgotten about the La Cornue. She looks perfect standing in front of it, a true baker with a top-of-the-line oven. She notices what I'm staring at and grins. "I love this thing. It's the best gift I've ever received."

"The best gift you've ever received *yet*."

"Would you two get in here?" Remy yells from the dining room.

"We better sit down," Farrah says, grabbing onto my

hand and pulling me into the dining room, even though I'd rather flirt with her in the kitchen all night.

Once we're seated, Amber stands up, clutching her glass of wine and raising it in the air. "To the final round of the playoffs!" she says.

Everyone makes a ruckus, cheering and standing up to clink their glasses together—wine for the ladies and water for the rest of us.

Remy slowly stands, holding his water glass up for his own toast. We all watch him in surprise since he's not one to draw attention to himself. He clears his throat, looking mildly uncomfortable with all eyes on him, then he turns to look at me. "I'd also like to toast to Bruce and Farrah. I know I wasn't encouraging of you two getting together, and for that I'm sorry." He rolls his lips inside his mouth as he considers his next words. "But I saw how you took care of her, Bruce. You're one of the best men I know, and I shouldn't have doubted you." He lifts his water glass higher. "So, to Bruce and Farrah."

The group of friends, now a little teary, clinks their glasses again. Farrah lays her head on my shoulder, and I kiss the top of her head.

Everything feels right as we start eating, passing food around and filling our plates. I notice Rose noses her way in between Noah and Jackson, and the two of them feed her small bites of their chicken.

Nella is in her highchair between Amber and the two boys, she squeals with glee at the dog and drops a piece of her own chicken for Rose.

I don't say anything, letting them have their fun.

"So," Colby says. "Not sure if anyone noticed...but the house two down from me in the cul-de-sac has a for sale sign in the yard."

I perk up. "Really?"

"Yeah," Noel says, looking at her fingernails like she's bored, but I see the twinkle in her eyes. "It'll go fast. Hope someone jumps on it soon."

Slowly, I turn my head to look at Farrah. I find her grinning at me. "You think it'll fit the La Cornue?" I whisper.

"There's only one way to find out," she whispers back.

TONIGHT IS the final game of the Stanley Cup final against the Sacramento Fire Cats, and it's at home in D.C. The girls and I have made it to all the home games this round, and I've worn my WAG jacket that Andie had the forethought to get for me. But tonight is extra special because Bruce's family is here, my family is here, and Jackson came with his foster parents.

Everyone is jittery with nerves and excitement as we take our seats in the stands to the left of Bruce's net. During warmups, he finds me and waves his goalie sick in the air, then removes his gloves to form a heart with his hands.

His mother is sitting in front of me, and she turns back with a wide smile on her face. "It's such a treat to see him so smitten."

My face heats at her comment, and she laughs.

Jackson and his foster parents are wearing McBride jerseys and Jackson looks awfully hyped up for someone who says he doesn't like hockey.

Noah is with Andie, and he appears very tense and nervous for the guys.

My family is seated in the row below Bruce's family, and they've all donned Remington jerseys, except Felicity who decided on a McBride jersey at the last minute, which Remy will likely grumble about later.

During the first period, we're on the edge of our seats, barely speaking to each other at all. The period ends with the Eagles down one to two.

The second period, everything amps up. The guys seem faster than ever out there as they fight to get ahead, and they do. The period ends with the Eagles ahead four to three.

When the guys come back out for the third and final period, you can tell they're tired, but still laser focused. Bruce doesn't even smile at the cameras; he's in his net and stretching his legs before the puck drops.

The third period feels like it goes by in slow motion. The captain of the Sacramento Fire Cats gets another goal, tying up the score with five minutes left. Every player on the ice is ultra careful tonight not to get a penalty, which means there's a serious lack of fights. I find that I miss the action a little but understand why everyone's playing it safe tonight. Both teams would give anything to win this.

I blow out a breath as the game moves into the defensive end, with Bruce crouched and ready in front of the net. Someone tries to shoot a puck between his legs, but he brings his pad down just in time to send the puck flying off it and away from him.

Remy snatches the puck and takes it across the ice and away from Bruce. I breathe an audible sigh of relief and Amber, who's beside me, gives me an empathetic look. I know she's feeling just as nervous as I am.

I scoot to the edge of my seat, like that will help me see better. Remy expertly passes the puck to West. West takes it around the back of the net and then shoots it. It ricochets off the side bar and the entire arena groans at once.

Mitch gets the puck from a defenseman on the opposing team and he's surrounded quickly. He passes to Colby and Colby finds an opening and shoots. We wait with bated breath; the entire arena feels frozen as we wait to see if the shot hits its mark…

And it does. The buzzer goes off, and the arena goes wild. We're all up and hugging and jumping up and down. But there's still one minute left in the game. It's not impossible for the Fire Cats to tie it up again and send it to overtime.

The Fire Cats captain takes possession of the puck in the next faceoff and drags it quickly down to the defensive zone again. I can't imagine the pressure Bruce feels in this moment, keeping the puck out of his net in this next minute is possibly the most important minute of his entire career.

The captain shoots it, and Bruce knocks it away with his glove. Another Fire Cats player snags it and goes for a rebound, but Bruce is ready and knocks it away with his stick.

The defenseman grabs the puck again and slides it to his captain. The captain takes one last shot, in the top left corner with seven seconds left in the game.

Bruce catches the puck in his glove and the buzzer signaling the end of the game hums loudly throughout the arena. Everyone's up again, screaming.

I look over at Amber, and we hug each other close. "They did it!" I scream over the noise.

"They won the Cup!" She yells back.

I turn to look at Bruce and tear up when I see his teammates giving him hugs and lifting him into the air.

The Eagles ease Bruce back onto the ice then line up to

shake hands with the Fire Cats players. The other team looks deflated and heart broken. I feel bad for them; it has to suck to get so close and not win in the end.

Amber grabs my hand and yanks me. "Come on! Let's go congratulate our guys!" The row of us wives and girlfriends head through the chaos of bodies in the stands to get to the bench and onto the ice.

We make it there just in time for the red, white, and blue balloons and confetti to be dropped from the rafters. It rains over us like a shower and makes it difficult for me to find Bruce, but he's the easiest one to find with all that goalie gear on. When I find his beaming, bearded face, I run to him —careful not to slip on the ice—and throw myself into his arms. He catches me and holds me as I wrap my legs around his waist. "You did it! You were amazing!"

Bruce rips his helmet off, letting it fall onto the ice and gives me the sweatiest, happiest kiss of my life. He smells terrible, and I don't even care. The only thing that matters in this moment is kissing my man and letting him know how incredible he is. "I love you, Cupcake," I tell him.

"I love you too, Yeux bleus." He smiles wide and kisses me again.

EPILOGUE-ONE YEAR LATER

FARRAH

I'M at George's Bar again, but this time I'm not sad, or overwhelmed, or trying to forget. No…I want to remember all of this—my wedding reception.

Bruce and I are on the makeshift dance floor, swaying to our first dance song that he picked out. Bruce is wearing a white tux with a black tie, and I'm in a simple but lovely white, lace gown with delicate straps, and we're surrounded by only our closest friends and family. Only the people who matter.

I said if I ever got married again, I wanted my groom to look at me like I was his entire world, and I am have no doubt that's how Bruce is eyeing me right now. His icy blue eyes are glued to mine, as he softly sings the words to "La Vie En Rose" to me.

My vision blurs with happy tears, and he leans in and kisses my forehead, then continues singing. He has a surprisingly good voice, deep and soothing.

Our song comes to an end sooner than I want it to. The DJ makes a chaotic shift from our slow, tender love song to Macho Man by Village People. I cringe at the song change, but not my husband. The man starts breaking it down like an expert. I laugh as I watch him; Bruce doesn't skip a beat and does the robot with surprising skill.

"Come on!" He yells, grinning at me.

I wince at the blister my shoes are creating. "I'm giving my feet a rest! And getting more cake!" I yell back.

All I can think about is taking these shoes off and devouring another slice of white cake with champagne frosting.

"Okay, but you're mine for the next dance!" He winks and continues dancing.

Felicity, however, loves Village People, and she and Harvey join Bruce on the dance floor. I watch for a moment as Bruce, Felicity, and Harvey boogie without any embarrassment whatsoever. I laugh and shake my head. I knew Felicity and Bruce were kindred spirits; she played this song during her wedding reception as well as Y.M.C.A.

I sit in a wooden chair and give my feet a break. Jackson is in the chair next to me, his shoulders moving with the song.

"You and your mom should get out there!" I say.

His mother, who is working hard to get her parental rights back, chuckles from his other side. Today is one of her visitation days with Jackson today. "Come on, Jackson! Let's go!" she says, standing and tugging him along with her.

He grins at her, and they're off to join Bruce and my sister on the dance floor. I take advantage of the extra chairs and put my feet up. The strappy, silver heels are gorgeous, but not made for dancing the night away. I think it's time to go barefoot.

Mel walks over toward me, her little baby girl cradled in a sling carrier on her chest and she's holding a slice of cake in one hand. She sits beside me and hands me the cake. "Need this?"

"God bless you," I tell her, taking the cake and forking a bite into my mouth, then closing my eyes to savor it. I've outdone myself with this champagne cake.

She chuckles. "We've gotta head out soon and get this one home and put to bed."

West comes up behind her and places a hand on her shoulder. "Tell your husband I said goodbye; he's a little busy right now."

The three of us look at the dance floor where Bruce is on the dirty bar floor doing the worm. "Oh boy. I'll let him know."

We laugh and I stand to hug them before they leave.

After a few more songs, all our friends and family start to say goodbye. Jackson and his mom head out, and our parents left a few songs ago along with Ford and Amber and a reluctant Nella—she wanted to stay for more dancing and cake. Now the only ones left are Felicity and Harvey, and the rest of Bruce's teammates and their wives. Everyone is on the dance floor, but they're slowing down as the night comes to a close. Andie smiles at me from where she's swaying with Mitch a few feet away.

Bruce pulls me close during our final slow dance, picking me up off the floor and giving my feet a nice reprieve.

"I want to take you home, Mrs. McBride," he whispers against my ear.

"Then take me home, Mr. McBride."

He pulls back, a handsome smirk on his face. "First, there's something we need to do."

I arch a brow, and he puts me back down on the ground, raising a hand to get George the bartenders' attention.

"George, can you get us an old fashioned and a Long Island iced tea?"

George nods, and Bruce turns back to me. "For old times sake." He winks.

———

BRUCE

"It's nice to carry you like this when you're not in immense pain," I tell my bride as I carry her over the threshold of our new home, one in the same cul-de-sac as my teammates.

She giggles, a little tipsy from her Long Island Iced Tea. Her rosy cheeks and giggly spirit take me back to two and a half years ago when we met and drunkenly made out in a corner booth at George's. Which is why George's was the only place that felt right for our reception.

Even if we hadn't just won the Stanley Cup last week—for the second time in a row—I would feel like the luckiest man on earth. No Stanley Cup could compare with having Farrah as my wife.

Ma femme.

My wife.

A low growl makes its way up my throat, bringing another giggle from my wife.

"Okay we're inside; put me down so I can see how the oven fits!" she says, wiggling to get down.

I pause, not really wanting to let her go, but knowing she'll be distracted until she sees that her beloved La Cornue is safe and sound.

She runs across the wood floors, the rooms still mostly empty even though I've lived here for several months. It's still missing that cozy, homey touch that I know Farrah will bring with her. We need rugs and throw pillows and art, all the stuff I suck at, but she'll add effortlessly.

Farrah comes to a halt in front of the kitchen, her simple lace wedding gown fluttering around her bare feet and her strappy heels in her hands. "Oh, Bruce. It looks perfect."

I come to stand beside her. "Yes, it does." But I'm not looking at the oven…I'm looking at her.

She slowly glances up at me and crosses her arms. "You didn't even look at it, did you?"

I bring my hand to her chin, angling her head where I want it. "I'm not interested in kitchen appliances at the moment."

Farrah opens her mouth to speak but I kiss her instead, swallowing her words. She can tell me whatever it was later. She leans into the kiss, clearly forgetting whatever she wanted to say. Her tongue sweeps in along mine for a moment before she pulls back.

She rests an index finger on my chest, right between my pecs. "Wait right here."

With a smile, she runs upstairs, and I don't move a muscle.

When Farrah appears again at the bottom of the stairs, her updo has been taken down, allowing her long, dark hair to flow freely around her shoulders. And she's wearing nothing but a crimson red McBride jersey.

I swallow, unable to do anything else. I'm in a caveman state of mind. My brain sees her in my jersey, and it tells me to throw her over my shoulder and have my way with her. I told myself I wouldn't go caveman on her until she wanted me to, and it sure looks like she wants me to.

My bride stalks toward me slowly, and I watch wordlessly as her hips sway.

She stops right in front of me, bringing her hands to my

black bow tie and undoing it, then unbuttoning my white dress shirt. When the shirt is open, she rests her hands on my pecs, and slowly trails them down my torso. I close my eyes and savor the way she's touching me.

She moves up to her toes and presses her lips to my neck. I feel her tongue peek out to lick the sensitive area, and then she kisses it again. Her perfect mouth takes a path to my collar bones, then the top of my chest.

"You can touch me, too, you know," she whispers.

I blink. I was so lost in her caress I'd almost forgotten I had hands there for a second. I've always been grateful for my hands, as they allow me to do what I love. They made me an NHL goalie—a two-time Stanley Cup winning goalie—but I've never been more grateful for these hands than right this damn minute, when they rest on my wife's thighs and move their way up her body, removing the jersey at the same time.

Hands are a very, very cool thing indeed, is my last coherent thought as I make love to my wife on the kitchen counter, right beside the oven she loves so much.

ALSO BY LEAH BRUNNER

Under Kansas Skies Series

Running Mate

House Mate

Check Mate

Cabin Mate

D.C. Eagles Hockey Series

Passion or Penalty *West & Mel*

Desire or Defense *Mitch & Andie*

Flirtation or Faceoff *Colby & Noel*

Betrothal or Breakaway *Remy & Amber*

Secret or Shutout *Bruce & Farrah*

ACKNOWLEDGMENTS

It takes a whole team of people to publish a book and I'm so, so grateful for my amazing team!

To my sensitivity readers, thank you for helping me with Farrah's story and the emotions she went through to get to her happy ending.

To my critique partner/bestie, Katie Bailey, thank you for listening to my 342574895327059 voice memos about Bruce and Farrah. Are you tired of my voice yet? Please don't block me.

To my beta and alpha readers: Madi, Meredith, Hannah, Hannah L., Hannah M., Chelsea, and Grace… thank you for catching a million typos (sorry about the t-shit moment) and all those annoying little things that needed corrected. Readers can now enjoy this book without me knowing I misspelled S'mores a million times. Y'all are the true heroes.

To my assistants, Lindsey and Marilee, thank you for running things behind the scenes so I can write!

To all the readers and lovers of the D.C. Eagles, thank you for making my day, every day. Thank you for the posts, and photos, and videos and everything you do to shout out my books! I appreciate you all more than you will ever know.

To my family, who graciously and patiently lets me hide away sometimes so I can turn books in on time for their deadlines… I love you. Thank you for cheering me on while I do my author thing.

ABOUT THE AUTHOR

Leah Brunner is an Amazon top 25 best selling author who writes romance filled with explosive chemistry and relatable, flawed characters. She loves writing character driven stories that will tug at your heart strings and also make you smile.

When she's not writing, she can be found spoiling her Maine Coon cats, or watching The Office with her kids.

Although she's a Midwestern girl at heart, Leah is a proud Air Force spouse and has moved all over the United States with her husband and three children.

Learn more at leahbrunner.com

instagram.com/leah.brunner.writes
bookbub.com/profile/leah-brunner
tiktok.com/romcomsaremyjam

www.ingramcontent.com/pod-product-compliance
Lightning Source LLC
Chambersburg PA
CBHW030138310726
48970CB00005B/1481